Praise for *Head Grenade*

'This fascinating yet relatable novel is packed with colourful characters and a thrilling plot. Henderson's evocative, often satirical, writing style brings this coming-of-age tale to life with a thick coating of dark humour.' **Seanna Burnett - Editor & Writer**

'*Head Grenade* is a hilarious, relatable, intriguing jump into the mind of a young adult trying to just live a life in Brisbane. The narration takes everything on the chin, from increasingly niche restaurants to mysterious backstories to the general stresses of life, roommates and The Valley, all with a quirky deadpan, a host of interesting characters, and a growing thriller aspect that keeps an edge of tension.'
Nita Delgado, Editor & Reviewer

'Everyone could do with a near-death experience. From the corner of Edward and Adelaide Streets in Brisbane, Troy Henderson's debut novel, *Head Grenade,* is a genre-bending thriller peppered with comedy, street philosophy, science fiction, and romance right here on our own turf. Love in all its forms alights in darkness and memory – and not even the doomsday preppers are ready for this!'
L. E. Daniels, Author of *Serpent's Wake: A Tale for the Bitten*

'With a plot reminiscent of classic dystopian stories, *Head Grenade* is overflowing with relatable characters, well-placed quips and gritty depictions of Brisbane. The characters' pasts will draw you in, but you'll stay for their ever-more intriguing present.'
Meesha Whittam, Reviewer

'Manny's sense of humour runs through the whole book. *Head Grenade* is an authentically Australian book set in Brisbane. As a man in my twenties, I found it very relatable, especially the humour. I loved it.'
Rory Hawkins, Editor & Reviewer

HEAD GRENADE

Troy Henderson

HAWKEYE
PUBLISHING

First published in Australia in 2023 by Hawkeye Publishing.

Copyright © Troy Henderson

Cover Design by Alex Jay McDonald

A catalogue record of this book is available from the National Library of Australia.

ISBN 9780645714982

Proudly printed in Australia.

www.hawkeyepublishing.com.au
www.hawkeyebooks.com.au

For John AKA Hendo AKA Dad

(1955 - 2023)

For everything

ONE

WARD 4A smells like death. It should, it's the terminal cancer ward.

Worse than the smell of death is the sickly-sweet stench of hospital grade disinfectants attempting to neutralise the odour. This potpourri permeates the ward and makes me gag at first, but I get used to it.

The world is a lot calmer at night. It's 11:11PM, a typical time for hospital deaths. One of my jobs as an orderly is to collect cadavers and take them down to the morgue. There is no dignity in death. Bodies are swiftly shoved into a bag, placed on a metal slab, and wheeled into a large fridge before the rot sets in. The speedy nature of body removal is due to economics. It frees a bed for the next individual destined to live the last gasps of their life in this inhospitable place. Late night deaths are convenient because the hospital is crowded during the day.

The body transporter looks like an ordinary bed. The only difference is the internal lift system, which allows a body to drop into the bed's hollow interior. A lid goes on top once the body is inside, then a white sheet covers it, and presto, the incredible disappearing cadaver illusion is complete. We use this system so no one freaks at the sight of a dead human covered by a sheet with a toe tag poking out.

I wheel the lifeless body in its temporary coffin past the postnatal care unit brimming with sleeping newborns. Death and life pass like ships in the night.

I swipe my access card as the lift doors close and descend to the third basement level. B3 is unlisted on the lift's information panel. This avoids the possibility of curious individuals entering the morgue accidentally and seeing the last few days' dead people.

I roll the slab into the giant, silver fridge and touch the dead guy's chest. I don't see or feel anything. The cancer inside him, that I once would have been able to cure in moments, is invisible now. Another poor sucker I couldn't save.

This man would have loved and been loved.

Now, he's merely another unit of fertiliser.

If an afterlife exists, I hope he has already experienced reincarnation because it's cold, dark and lonely in the corpse fridge.

~

I arrive home covered in the stench of death and the smell lingers post-shower. It's an hour before closing time, so I walk to the pub. A fat moon sits in the sky, so large the transient silver-lined clouds fail to obscure it.

I buy a pint, sit out the back and tweeze clumps of dark tobacco from a new packet. I roll a smoke and listen to the drunks talking nonsense. There is a commonality in the way they talk, laugh and drag on their cigarettes. Only the faces change.

I go home with someone who could do better. But she's healthy, so I don't have to spend our time together feeling guilty that I can't fix what could soon become a chronic ailment or illness. I don't have to see her sickness every time I touch her. I don't have to feel anything.

She's gone before the sun hits my window.

I'm empty and hungover. A typical Thursday.

I dress for work, then pour myself into my car.

~

My day starts with a patient sprawled face down on the floor. It's an old man, with a transparent tube stuck deep in his rear end. His distraught wife kneels next to him, screaming. She's still holding the clear bottle and funnel she used to administer the whisky up her soon-to-be-deceased husband's butt.

'He was desperate. He begged me,' she pleads to me and another orderly.

A doctor swoops in and sees the two of us standing slack jawed. He orders the other guy to take the wife outside. 'Call a code blue,' the doctor says.

I press the code button on the wall. It won't make a lick of difference; the old man looks done for. I take a deep breath, trying to dislodge the heaviness in my chest.

The doctor presses his fingers against the man's neck. 'His pulse is weak, but he's alive.'

'What do we do?'

'Throw him on the bed.'

A nurse rushes into the room and helps lift him onto the bed.

The doctor pries open the old man's eyelids.

'Let's get him to ICU, stat.'

I always like when the doctors say 'stat', but there's rarely time to enjoy it.

'Administering adrenaline,' the nurse says to whoever's in earshot. She brings what looks like a pen from her front pocket and sticks it into the man's chest. He heaves and projectile vomits powdered eggs across the floor; my new Cons get splattered. The old man reaches behind himself to pull the tube out. I make a sound which could be translated as 'gross'.

The doctor's eyes widen. 'Probably should've pulled the tube out first.'

I open the room doors and the three of us race him along the corridor towards the intensive care unit. The old man claws wildly at the air. I hold his hand, squeezing it reassuringly.

Another nurse joins us. 'What happened?' he asks, his eyes about to pop out.

'He was on IV fluids,' the first nurse says. 'Looks like he couldn't do another day without booze, so wifey smuggled a bottle in, and next minute...'

I maintain my hold on the old man's hand and wipe some gunk from his eyes, which have flown open as wide as ping pong balls. 'I don't think this is the time for a lecture,' I say.

The nurse scowls.

Another doctor and several nurses greet us at the ICU room. The voices blend into white noise as they yell and crowd around the patient.

My radio squawks as I slip away from the crowd.

'Manny, go on break. Over.'

'Copy. Over.'

The rest of the shift is uneventful, but the terror in the drunk and dying man's eyes won't leave me.

~

A newly painted canvas sits on the easel in the lounge room – a field of flowers, grass covered with morning dew and fingers of sunshine stretching across the landscape. A few cows stare out at me.

'Pastoral landscape,' says my housemate, Elvis.

'You're getting better.'

'Cheers.'

Elvis and I met a few years ago when he was hospitalised in the aftermath of the tragic Santa Claus incident outside City Hall. I was there too, but lucky enough to escape unharmed. We formed a friendship while he was recovering, and we've been best buds ever since. While he was still bedridden, he fortuitously fixed the ward servers during a storm, so the nurse manager offered him a job in the IT department. He set up an innovative cataloguing system they adopted at all the Brisbane hospitals, and now he mostly works from home, lucky bastard.

He's in his usual spot on the couch. This week he's immersed in '80s action films. A never-ending cycle of Stallone, Schwarzenegger and Van Damme movies.

He was dubbed Elvis because his father, Rusty, won an Australian Elvis lookalike competition in the early '90s. After that accolade, Rusty toured local RSLs along the east coast. Met a nice lady one night down at the Tweed RSL. She was carrying the meat tray and he won the raffle. They slept together that night.

Nine months later he returned, touring the same circuit to dwindling audiences. This time, the woman was carrying more than the meat tray. Rusty met his newborn son, stayed around just long enough to name him Elvis before departing on a pilgrimage to Graceland.

Elvis spends most days watching films. Thanks to the internet, the possibilities are infinite. Before the '80s actions films this week, he watched anime, slasher horrors, film noirs, '60s sexploitations, post-apocalyptic dystopian dramas, coming of age independents, musical biopics, Disney cartoons, screwball comedies, necrorealism black and whites, neo-bizarros, sea-life sports pics and myriad others.

'Beer me,' he says.

I pull two Heinekens from the esky next to the couch and collapse on the lounge next to him. *Rocky III* is coming to an end; Rocky has rediscovered the eye of the tiger and knocked Clubber Lang clean out.

'*Rocky IV* next?' I ask.

Elvis's eyes remain glued to the screen. 'Nope. Watching Stallone's films in sequential order. *First Blood* is next.'

'Right.'

He swigs his beer. 'I still think they should have stayed true to the novel and have Rambo die in the end.'

'If they did, they wouldn't have been able to pump out the sequels of diminishing quality.'

He shifts in his seat, looking as serious as a myocardial infarction. '*Rambo: First Blood, Part II* is an iconic work in the '80s action canon.

7

He kills sixty-nine people, compared with only one dude in the first one.' Elvis is more animated now. 'But it's not all about the number of kills because the next three have way more. It's a balance of killing, cinematography, location and the overarching concept of one man versus many.'

I drain the rest of my beer, and we polish off the rest of a six pack.

'I'm going to the pub for a few more, you want in?' I say.

'Not today.'

I sweep the empty bottles off the table into a box for the recycling bin. Most of our rubbish comprises beer bottles and cardboard pizza boxes, so we don't have much use for the normal bin. I grab my wallet and leave Elvis to his '80s action marathon.

The corner pub is a few minutes walk away. It's another clear evening with stars dazzling the sky, so I take my time. The night air is so sweet and crisp I almost think twice about trading it for the dank surroundings of the dump I'm about to enter.

The key word being 'almost'.

Alcohol wins.

I'm greeted by the smell of stale beer, cheap cologne and failure. The bar floor is sticky as always. The soundtrack is Aussie pub rock, with the added noise of old drunks talking about glory days. It's like a depressing Bruce Springsteen song wheezing to life.

It's the kind of pub that serves alcohol in plastic cups after 6PM to curb glassings during bar fights. Despite the change, angry men still find ways to beat the tar out of each other on a weeknight. I ask the bartender for a pint of pale ale.

'We've only got Cobbler's Bay IPA. Delivery comes tomorrow.' She smiles through missing teeth. 'And how many times do I have to tell ya? We don't do pints, only schooners.'

She shuffles to grab a glass and pours what could be her millionth schooner of beer. The late nights and decades of cigarette smoke coupled with repetitive, drunken old man stories, would wear anyone down. She should be retired, playing in the park with her grandkids. I hand her a tenner, tell her to keep the change, then feel like a phony.

Thanks to the overpriced beer, I've tipped her fifty cents. I'll do better next time.

A raucous woman strides to the bar. The fluoro dress on her sizeable frame burns my retinas. I keep blinking to reduce the ultra-vibrancy. She's wearing matching green and pink earrings and lipstick. Save us, Batman.

This place has a rad jukebox, one of its few redeeming features and the second reason I come here. I take my overpriced, floral smelling beer to the jukebox and put a dollar in. I pick five AC/DC songs.

AC/DC is one of the few acceptable bands the regulars will allow you to play, and I normally wait until the regulars leave to play any deep cuts. A few weeks ago, some poor kid put on Sinatra's version of *Fly Me to the Moon*, and a toothless bear of a man pulled the plug and told the kid to get the hell out of here. He yelled obscenities and questioned the kid's sexuality for playing "crooning jazz garbage".

Personally, Ol' Blue Eyes is one of my favourite singers. I'm ashamed to admit I didn't stand up for the kid, though I did play it later as a tribute. I want to stand up for the little guy, but sometimes the big guys around here would make Goliath feel inadequate.

I sit with my beer at an old-fashioned tabletop arcade, the third reason I come here, and play *Space Invaders* and *Galaga* until my five songs are done. I leave a decent tip with the next beer, hoping the bartender will smile, that she'll approve of me.

Crickets.

I head to the pokie machine room to lose $100 at lightning speed. Hopeless hope. I grab one more schooner and move into the smoking area. There's only one person here who isn't old enough to have been considered for Vietnam conscription. I sit across from her.

We chat for a couple of beers and too many tequilas, which is precisely two tequilas. I excuse myself and make my way to the bathroom. The sign for the male toilet is a 1920s gentleman, the antithesis of my current self.

I take a slash in the sink; I don't know why.

The girl is still there when I return. A wave of drunken tiredness hits as the week collapses on top of me.

'I'm shattered. Gotta work early in the morning. Nice talking with you.'

We shake hands. I wince when I see, in my mind, she has tongue cancer. Every time I forget about my gift, the reminder is always painful and my heart cracks a little more.

The rain begins as I walk home. I throw my wet shirt and jeans into a clear section of the bathroom, put Otis Redding on the turntable, and collapse into a bean bag.

~

Head pounding. Eyes bleeding. The sun my enemy.

My mouth is so dry I can feel every nuance of my swollen tongue. My stomach burns and bile creeps into the back of my throat. I'm brimming with a combination of self-loathing and alcohol-induced nausea. A typical Friday morning.

I need fruit. I need water.

I need to vomit.

Staggering to the bathroom, I claw at the walls to propel myself towards the toilet. I close my eyes as I stand in front of the mirror and concentrate on removing the pain. Of course, I can't, not anymore.

Cold water washes over me, hopefully drawing the poisons from my body to the surface. My mind drifts to the water shortage and I turn the shower off. I have a ten-hour shift. I grab a shiny red apple from the kitchen, hoping it will offset some of the damage, and walk out to my car.

Rotten eggs and garbage assault my nostrils. Bottles and rubbish spill onto the ground as I open the car door. I drop my apple. 'Shit.'

Someone's egged the car's interior and thrown garbage onto the seats. For some reason, I left the windows open. It's a relatively safe neighbourhood, no murders or anything, but I forgot about idle teenage hands.

I remove as much of the rubbish as possible. Various mystery liquids and what I hope are condiments stick to the seats. Large eggs have soaked into the fabric. I hope they're organic free-range at least. I don't want to contribute to the battery hens situation in even the most peripheral way.

With a big black garbage bag over my car seat at least I won't have to spend the drive to work sitting in a puddle of rancid debris. The worst part is what a whole day of baking in the Brisbane summer sun will do, and it's looking like a scorcher.

I pull away, searching for a sliver of optimism, then stall the car in a narrow street. A morning commuter leans on the horn of their Pajero behind me. I'm cutting precious seconds from their day. I can see them tearing their hair out. In the moments before the engine turns over, it looks like the person could have a coronary. That's all I'd need.

I wave out the window apologetically as I weave the car through the rows of illegally parked cars.

Another day.

~

My radio beeps, signalling a job in pre-op. An old man ball shave, which the other orderlies call a 'cabbage shave' for reasons I've never bothered to find out.

A 50-something-year-old patient lies down on a bed in a hospital gown in a detached stupor. Every male coming in for prostate removal has the same expression, like Earth's gravity doubled but NASA forgot to let them know.

He says, 'This is not where I want to be.'

I'm hunched over him. He's on a bench, on his side, his legs spread wide. The electric razor meticulously removes his pubic hair to prep him for his prostate removal. He repeats himself in case I didn't hear the first time.

11

I force myself not to care. It's too painful otherwise. When you begin to lose your health, it's like waiting in a long line for a show you don't even want tickets for.

'It's not easy. I'm sorry,' I say. There's nothing I can do. Not anymore.

He mutters, 'I don't belong here.'

I assume he's referring to the hospital, but he may as well be referring to his life. Cancer and the flashing warning signs of mortality can make anyone question their life choices. I can echo his sentiments.

These points, with vulnerable people like this guy, are the times when the guilt hits hardest. I could have healed him and countless others like him, if only I hadn't lost my ability.

The accident took care of that. Took care of Mum too.

'I need to find a new motivation for living,' the patient murmurs.

Don't we all. While he talks, I listen and clip. He compensates for the imminent removal of his manhood by giving a last-blast testosterone-infused yarn about football, bar fights and sexual conquests. There's nothing I can do besides listen and act normally, to make him feel more at ease, like I'm not even here. Most men don't want another man seeing them spread-eagled naked. They certainly don't want the man holding his willy to the side and clipping away with a gloved hand to be too engaged in the process.

This guy's about to lose everything that makes him who he thinks he is.

I leave the room exhausted and needing more fruit. Half a Royal Gala isn't cutting it. Outside in the waiting room, old men discuss prostate sizes and cholesterol levels.

I spend the rest of my shift helping the ward nurses search for a missing high-risk patient. We eventually find him when he falls through the skylight into the day surgery unit. He breaks both arms in several places and breaks his jaw. There's blood, screaming and general unrest.

He was in the air ducts smoking meth, but he won't be smoking anything for a while. He'll be eating all his food through a straw for a few weeks.

~

I speed away from the hospital, immediately swallowed in the gridlock on Coronation Drive. One giant bottleneck. The council can't widen the lanes any further, or there'd be cars in the river. The frustration, the dissatisfaction, the lack of flow and movement. Gridlock is an impotent old man.

The car feels like a greenhouse on wheels in the oppressive heat. Drive-time, traffic morons drone over the radio waves.

My car reeks.

It's dusk by the time I pull up outside the house. I walk straight to the bottle shop. The attendant leans outside against the brick wall, smoking a cigarette. Sadly, I know her name. Heavy metal blasts from inside.

I join her for a smoke, standing next to her in silence, empathising with the mild irritations of her job. We watch scores of bats darken the afternoon sky, on the way to wherever bats go, from wherever bats come from. Seems like there are hundreds more of them every week, dispensing mountains of guano so acidic it corrodes the road signs along Shafston Avenue. Hearing the beating of their leathery wings above, I can only hope I'm not on the receiving end of acid rain.

I only have enough money for cheap wine. I grab a modest bottle of red with a blue squid on the label. The bottle smashes on the ground as I trip on the median strip while crossing the street. I lay still for a moment, like the dead body in a murder scene before the chalk outline person arrives but move to the side when I see oncoming headlights. It's only when brushing off small stones from my knees that I notice the blood leaking down my shin.

I close my eyes and breathe deeply.

When I open them, the cut is still there.

Of course, it is.

13

Every cut I can't heal reminds me of the "Goldfish Incident". Back then, it was like I could hold the sun, something so large and bright that it could touch anything, anyone and protect me, them.

Now it's a black hole.

The front door catches. The porch is swamped in leaves, and I almost miss the white corner of a note sticking out from under the welcome mat.

Remember the Goldfish Incident?
Where it all began.
Every beginning has an ending.
Yours is coming.

The synchronicity hits me in the chest, but it could be a wave of heartburn. I tuck the note into my pocket and walk inside. I pull open the fridge then stumble out the back, a cup of milk in one hand, a cigarette in the other. I stand there, staring at the cloud of bats.

My cigarette keeps going out and my cup smells of bourbon, but things could be worse. At least I'm not living in Ethiopia, or Haiti, or Bald Hills.

I sink into the couch next to Elvis and tell him about last night's pokie loss. He offers to pay my share of the rent, then pours crimson liquid from his cup into mine.

It's this simple gesture that convinces me to drop my guard and trust Elvis with the story about the most traumatic time of my life.

Another drop of wine hits my tongue. Another lick of smoke passes my lips.

'Check this,' I say, pulling the note from my pocket and handing it to Elvis.

'What's the "Goldfish Incident"?' he asks as he packs a bong and hands it to me.

I fire up the tiny blowtorch lighter and pull a deep hit into my lungs, then close my eyes and begin.

14

TWO

MY first brush with death was the day Raphael committed suicide.

I was eight. Raphael was my goldfish.

I was cleaning his bowl and repositioning some new accessories I'd bought with my meagre savings when he leapt from the temporary plastic container. My reflexes weren't quick enough, and I slipped on the waxed floor trying to catch him. Instead, he hit the floorboards and I accidently booted him into the chest of drawers as I crashed to the floor. We were eye-to-eye, mouths opening and closing in tandem. I tried to grasp him, but he was so slimy he kept slipping through my fingers.

I ran downstairs to the lounge room where Mum and Aunty Sue were sitting on the couch, watching supernatural cop shows and drinking red wine. Both were slack-jawed as they followed my flailing limbs upstairs to my room.

Our cat, Miss B, sat there booping Raphael's body with her paws. Mum shooed Miss B out of the way, but my fish had already stopped breathing. Sue picked him up, placed him in the bowl and pushed him around, but his lifeless body slowly floated upside down, straight to the top.

Mum rested her hand on my shoulder. 'Sorry, Manny. He's gone.'

I burst into tears.

'Are we going to flush him?' Sue asked.

'Sue!'

'Well, we're not going to bury it in the backyard, are we?'

I pulled my hands from my eyes. 'Why not?'

'It's a fish,' Sue said.

'He's my fish.'

Mum exchanged a look with Sue, then knelt and touched the sides of my head. 'We can bury Raphael in the backyard, and he can turn into a tree.'

I rubbed my eyes. 'Can I keep him next to me tonight?'

'Sure, hun. Sue, grab a shoebox or something from my cupboard.'

Sue looked ready to object, then sighed. 'Okay. Sorry about Raphael, Manny. He was a good goldfish.'

'Thanks,' I muttered. The fish was my only friend, and I'd lost him.

~

After dinner, I settled on my bed, staring at the glowing solar system stickers blanketing the ceiling, clutching the shoebox to my chest. The night-time was strange and unfamiliar. I recognised Mum's soft knock on my bedroom door.

'Manny?'

'Yeah?'

She was wearing a fluffy, jasmine-coloured robe and bunny slippers. She sat next to me on my bed, stroking my hair. That's one of the only memories of her I still have burned into my mind. 'You okay, love?'

I sniffed. 'Why did he have to die?'

She picked up the shoebox and placed it on my nightstand. 'Everything dies, honey. It's a part of life.'

'It's unfair.'

'Yeah, it is, but it's the way things are.' She hugged me. The scent of lemon shampoo and moisturiser still unlocks the memory if I'm in the right spot of a department store.

As most kids inevitably do, I asked the big one. 'What about you?'

'What about me?'

'You'll die too.'

She shut her eyes and smiled. 'Yes, but not for a very long time.'

She kissed me on my forehead, turned off the light and closed my bedroom door. I must have spent hours lying awake in the dark, staring at the green, glowing planets and stars on the ceiling, thinking about how everything dies. Those few hours were the darkest part before the dawn of my abilities. It was the first time the warmth and energy flowed through me. As though it were part of some hardwired instinct based on thousands of years of evolution, like survival or sex or religion. I didn't even think about it. I knew what to do. As with most behaviour outside of the ordinary, there was an element of fear.

I opened the shoebox and held Raphael in my hands. At first there was nothing, but then a mild current traversed my entire being and the room became brighter. Wonder replaced fear at a jolt, then I felt movement between my hands.

I threw the covers off and looked towards the still-full fishbowl on top of the desk. I crept over to the tank, my excitement growing and peaking as I dropped Raphael in. It took a few seconds for him to remember how to be a fish, but he was soon darting in-and-out between the seaweed and plastic scuba men.

Raphael the goldfish was back from the dead. I always figured there was a chance some of the miracles taught at Sunday school weren't real. But this one was. I'd freaking performed one.

Before I could enjoy Raphael's resurrection any further, the current inside me intensified. Time slipped, then a spike of lightning jammed itself into my brain. I doubled over as I stumbled through my bedroom door towards Mum's room, startling her awake. I can only imagine what was going on behind her wide-open eyes before I collapsed and pissed my pants.

~

An all-encompassing light eclipsed three dark shapes.

As my eyes refocused, two of the shapes took the form of Mum and Sue. They were standing next to an overweight, bushy-eyebrowed doctor with a stethoscope and white coat. My mind was cloudy, but I knew I was in a hospital. It looked like the ones on TV, with lime green walls, cream floors, off-white basins and strange smells. A nurse appeared from behind the doctor. Fatigue overcame me as I tried to sit up.

The nurse pushed me back. 'Rest now. Don't move.'

It felt like gremlins were attacking my eyeballs with ice-picks. I concentrated on melting the pain away. Slowly, it settled and various other sensations returned. I tried talking, but my mouth was dry, like it was stuffed with cotton wool. The nurse handed me some water, her large, soft breasts rubbing against my arm. I asked if I could have a strawberry thickshake.

It was the doctor's time to shine. 'Not yet.'

'Why, what's wrong with me?'

He turned to Mum and Sue.

'We'll need to run some tests, but my initial diagnosis is Emmanuel may have experienced an unusual type of epileptic seizure. We'll monitor him here for a little while, and he'll need to come back in four to six weeks for a check-up.'

'What caused it?' Sue asked.

The doctor answered between writing illegible squiggles in his folder. 'It's hard to say. It may have been triggered by an unknown source. Does Emmanuel have any flashing lights in his room?'

'No, just those glow-in-the-dark stars on the ceiling.'

'Has he been sleep deprived?'

Mum looked at me for a few moments. 'No. Well, I don't think so. Have you, Manny?'

'Sleep deprived?' I repeated.

'Have you been sleeping well?'

'I guess so, except for last night.'

The doctor looked to me. 'What happened last night?'

Sue answered for me. 'His goldfish died.'

18

The doctor put his pen in his mouth and chewed it for a few seconds. A blob of blue ink remained on his lips. 'Well, emotional trauma in combination with a lack of sleep *could* be reason enough to cause this. As I said, it's unusual, and slightly bizarre from what I can see on Emmanuel's initial scans.'

'What do you mean "bizarre"?' Mum asked.

'There are inconsistencies in his imaging, but it may be the machine,' he said unconvincingly. He paused, continuing to chew his pen and stare into the distance. More blue ink leaked, filling the cracks of his lips.

'Doctor?' Mum snapped. She looked like she was losing any sense of composure.

The doctor returned from his musings. He must have tasted the blue ink because he sputtered like he had a hair in his mouth, then rubbed his sleeve across his face, staining his white coat. 'Sorry. We'll send him to x-ray and get them to run a couple more tests to make sure. I don't mean to alarm you. Emmanuel is a healthy boy. In fact, his recovery is staggering compared with his initial presentations in the ambulance.'

My mind became a still lake, the memories of the incident appeared clear.

'It was Raphael,' I said.

The doctor's eyes darted between Mum and me. 'Who's Raphael?'

'His goldfish,' Sue piped in.

My voice grew stronger. 'I was holding him, then he was all warm and wiggly. Then I upchucked.' I looked at my hands, then towards the adults. They all snuck glances. They thought I was lying. 'I'll show you,' I shouted.

Mum wouldn't meet my eyes. 'Calm down, Manny.' Her gaze on the linoleum floor was steely. 'Raphael died, hun. You must have dreamed it.'

The inside of my head burned. 'I didn't dream it.'

'Manny, settle down, bud, you've had a big night,' Sue said.

They traded concerned looks. No one would admit I was telling the truth.

'No, he's alive. He's in my room, in his bowl! You'll see when we get home.'

I banged the overbed table, spilling orange juice across the tray. Mum tried to calm me.

I screamed.

'Okay, okay, quiet darl, there are lots of sick people here.'

After a full day of scans, poking, prodding, and a couple of terrible hospital meals, they released me. I puked through the wheelchair's spokes before getting into the car to leave, but was generally much better, aside from some residual brain heat. My scans were sent to the International Imaging Analysis Institute. It would take time.

I was happy to be back in my room with all my Ninja Turtles toys, Nintendo and LEGO. I was even more thrilled to have the confirmation I wasn't delusional. Raphael the goldfish was indeed alive and well, swimming in his bowl, all thoughts of suicide probably a distant memory. I'll never forget the looks on Mum and Sue's faces the first time they saw Raphael had returned, and realised I *was* telling the truth.

They referred to it forevermore as the "Goldfish Incident".

~

A couple of weeks later, Mum took me to the imaging clinic to pick up my results. I sat in the waiting room playing with a rip-off version of Jenga, methodically removing the small wooden blocks until boredom set in. Then it was smashing time.

When Mum returned from speaking with the doctor, her eyes were watery and bloodshot. She'd been crying again. 'Thanks, Doctor Stephens.'

'We'll talk soon,' he said. His head cocked to the side as he stared at me, the way a neanderthal would look at a dating app, or Beethoven would observe a synthesizer, seeing the potential but not how to operate it.

Mum must have noticed too because she ruffled my hair and pulled me closer. 'Let's go, Manny. We'll get lunch on the way home.'

'Can we get Maccas?'

Her eyes flashed to the smiling doctor. 'No, it's poison. We'll get something healthy.'

The dreaded H word. Kid kryptonite.

Mum thanked Doctor Stephens again. We walked from the air-conditioned banality of the clinic into the blazing hot car park.

She spent the trip home shifting her gaze from me in the back seat to a folder on the dashboard. The last few blocks before home she started smiling too hard, like a manic primary school jazz-tap teacher. For a moment, I felt like the results may not be so bad, but any sense of optimism was soon crushed by a feeling that choked the air as we sat in uncomfortable silence, parked in the driveway. That was a feeling I could easily conjure for years. It's weird how certain feelings stick. They're all in there somewhere, you just have to find the right drawer.

Sue visited later that night. I hid behind the kitchen door, peeking through the gap, and eavesdropped on the hushed conversation.

'The doctor said he's never seen one like it before, Sue.'

Sue stared out the window.

'Sue, are you listening? He's never seen one like *it* before.'

'It?'

'Yes, *it*. A clear ball inside someone's brain. Never. That's his job, that's all he does.'

Sue picked up a mandarin and peeled it. 'Think it's related to your project?'

Mum grabbed a glass off the sink and filled it with white wine. 'I thought it could be. By the way, it wasn't *my* project, it was my job. I had no choice.'

'Oh, right,' Sue said, and popped a mandarin crescent into her mouth. ''E was in charge, and poor little you went along with it.'

Mum sat on a barstool, head in her hands. 'You weren't there. E was - is, a brilliant man. We had the right intentions.'

Sue scoffed, then grabbed a glass off the kitchen counter. 'I'm sure all those test subjects would disagree, if they could,' she said, filling the glass with tap water. 'Have you told E about what happened to Manny? I'm sure he'd be very interested to know the experiments bore fruit after all.'

Mum stood, knocking the stool over. 'Get out, Sue.'

Sue raised her hands. 'Sarah, if you care about Manny, call E. At least talk it over with him,' she said as she walked out.

Mum sobbed. I held my breath, waiting for her to stop.

Eventually, she composed herself, dialled a number and left a voice message.

'E, it's me. Long time, I know. You wanted self-healing soldiers? Well, I've got something better. Call me when you get this.'

THREE

WHEN I was a kid, I used to think the square, red stop button on the bus was directly connected to the brakes, like an emergency measure. I never pressed it.

Even now, I hesitate the slightest bit, every time. As though I'm still unwinding a conditioned response or a milder version of the aversion therapy from *A Clockwork Orange*.

I get out at the corner of Edward and Adelaide Street, then stop to roll a cigarette. Thousands of businesspeople explode from the train station and scramble over the crossing. They expertly ignore the homeless people holding homemade signs littering the footpaths, no doubt grateful it's not them all dirty, dishevelled and struggling to survive.

Gold coins jingle in my pocket. I place a couple of them in a filthy, bandaged hand. She's pregnant, sitting next to a beautiful little girl with large eyes, knotted hair, and traffic soot smudged across her face. The little girl is probably four or five, already learning how unfair life can be. And soon, there will be another mouth to feed.

It tugs at my heart. I envy the others who can walk by. It's less painful to ignore. Brisbane isn't a dirty city, but today I can't help noticing its walkways are blemished by hundreds of black spots of old chewing gum.

A young, shoeless busker picks away at a Nick Drake song everyone's too busy to listen to. It's a soft melody that's barely audible over the traffic noise, interstate phone calls, and ravings of a street preacher outside the train station entrance. The busker looks up with grateful eyes as I toss a few coins into the open guitar case at his feet.

The CBD feels strange and unfamiliar. There never used to be so many homeless people here. I'm not sure whether society is devolving or whether I'm just noticing more of what's going on around me. Brisbane is meant to be booming – housing, infrastructure, Olympics.

Maybe that's the problem; maybe the progress was so accelerated that more people got left behind.

Further down, towards the tree-lined mall, I am accosted by one of the many charity muggers invading the city. I promise to donate $25 to a foundation so a cerebral palsy kid can have half of a supportive walking device. I'm not congratulating myself; I'm thinking about how that's going to hurt me until pay day. I'm walking around like a carefree philanthropist when I'm really one of the great unwashed. Only a week's pay from being displaced and experiencing nature's air conditioning like the others.

My thoughts of the gutter are interrupted. Prickling skin signals the sensation of being watched. A man is following me.

I catch his reflection in the Gucci store window. If he's trying to avoid acting suspicious, he's doing a bad job. He's wearing a bulky trench coat, making it hard to determine his body shape. It's not like anything's going to happen in a public place, but goosebumps cover my arms all the same.

I hook around into an alley and enter a soon-to-be-closed bookstore overrun with self-help literature and weight loss books. I peruse the shelves, looking out the corner of my eye for the man in the trench coat. I don't see him, nor any decent fiction.

Maybe I'm being paranoid. I'm feeling and acting like it. If it looks like a paranoid man, walks like a paranoid man, quacks like a paranoid man...

Shop after shop, I'm accosted by advertising and pushy salespeople. I become more disillusioned with society, until I find something I need.

Cologne.

I'd sprayed the rest of my old bottle attempting to cover the smell of car garbage. The scents wafting through the Myer perfumery trigger olfactory memories of Mum that hollow my chest.

I pay for the smallest, cheapest bottle I can find, which still feels wildly expensive. I grab an overpriced juice from a kiosk in the Queen Street Mall, people-watch for a while, then catch the train home.

A newly painted canvas sits on the easel in the lounge room.

A monochrome square. Pure.

Lazy.

Elvis is sprawled on the floor, watching *Jurassic Park*. The good one. I collapse on the couch.

'Do you do any actual work?' I ask.

'Mate, thirty minutes a week is all it takes. Got bots doing most of it for me. No worries.'

'Tell me something that is bothering you then, to make me feel better,' I say, rolling a cigarette.

'I'm finding it hard to decide what dinosaur's my favourite.'

It does make me feel better. 'T-Rex, no contest.'

'Velociraptor is not without its charm,' Elvis says, popping the top off the beer sitting on the table, 'but you're probably right.'

'What else did you do today?' I ask.

'Ordered one of those super realistic sex dolls. Warm-blooded and everything.'

Jeff Goldblum appears onscreen with impeccable timing, 'I'm simply saying that life, uh, finds a way.'

~

The morning sun is eclipsed by Elvis. He throws a couple hundred bucks on my bedside table and leaves.

My throat is a barren desert. I need cold juice.

25

I rip the fridge door open too fast and a plate of spaghetti falls out. I try to catch it with my foot. The plate shatters and spaghetti flies everywhere. The need to stick a foot out under a falling object is an evolutionary flaw as far as I'm concerned.

There's blood, there's swearing, there's frustration. I pull the dustpan from the corner cupboard and clear the mess. I shower, put on a clean, white t-shirt and a black pair of jeans, and limp to the bus stop.

There's nothing like Brisbane on a clear summer day. The sky is its usual brilliant shade of light blue; its beauty further accentuated by bulbous clouds floating along like colossal cotton balls. The bone-chilling misery of winter, both a distant memory and inevitability.

The bus arrives on time, a welcome anomaly. I join my fellow public transport commuters, all in this together, trying to survive another day. The bus snakes through the inner suburbs, over the hills lined with an array of trees and shrubbery. We pass cyclists, who pass runners, who pass dog walkers, who pass groups of carefree individuals sitting outside cafes, drinking coffee.

I grab a takeaway, long black from a pop-up coffee cart. Thin curls of steam escape my cup, adding to the smell of ground coffee beans and freshly baked bread wafting through the laneway. The sound of my boots on the cobblestones resonates against the walls. CBD workers and shoppers thread through construction projects. Delivery trucks jostle for carparks. The city has coughed itself awake.

The first coffee doesn't take; my moaning stomach requires food first. I walk into another cafe, chosen only for its bizarre name, Plantonymphomaniacs.

Optimism lasts until my bacon arrives.

'What's this?' I ask, gesturing to my plate.

The hairy-faced waiter, with large holes in his earlobes, twists his head like an uncomprehending puppy. 'Coconut bacon.'

I notice a tattoo of a whale on his forearm. It looks like the one from *Free Willy*.

'Where's the bacon?'

'Right there,' he points. 'Under the parsley.'

Morrissey plays in the background.

'Parsley is a breakfast gimmick. So much is wasted every day.'

'Pardon?'

'Nothing.'

I poke the weird pink flesh with my fork. 'So, coconut bacon isn't bacon covered in coconut or cooked in coconut oil. It's literally slivers of coconut?'

There's a tattoo of a chicken, a cow and a pig attached to a hot air balloon on the waiter's neck. The slow-falling penny drops, but he fills me in anyway.

'Dude, we're a vegan operation. I'm not sure you're in the right place.'

A "Cow Lives Matter" tattoo frowns from his other arm.

'It's too late now.'

'Can I get you anything else?'

'Coffee, please. You have coffee?'

'Yes, but no dairy. Nothing that comes from an animal.'

'I get it. Black is fine.'

I people-watch until I can't stand it any longer. My day is mostly wasted, like so much discarded parsley.

As I wait at the ferry terminal for the CityCat, thin waves of electricity run along my arms as if someone is watching me. I whip my head around to see nothing but trees and park runners. The sensation ceases when the CityCat leaves the dock. Is it still paranoia if someone *is* after me?

~

A newly painted canvas sits on the easel in the lounge room. A solitary figure stranded on a faraway planet. Spacescape.

Elvis, paintbrush still in hand, is watching the conclusion of one of the *Star Wars* movies that George Lucas insists on tampering with every few years for no one's benefit. Some creatives can never leave their creations alone or accept that they're perfectly good as they are. The artist's curse.

Elvis turns and throws a glossy leaflet at me.

'There's this new Italio-Morro-Cantonese fusion joint. You know it's good because all the real Italians, Moroccans and Cantonese eat there.'

Elvis orders. Twenty minutes later, the Italian-Moroccan-Cantonese fusion pack arrives courtesy of a German delivery boy.

I put the latest remastered version of *Sgt. Pepper's Lonely Hearts Club Band* on the turntable and turn the kid's channel on in the background. Coincidently, an episode of the Ringo-narrated *Thomas the Tank Engine* series is on.

'Reckon Madonna ever slept with one of the Beatles?' Elvis asks at the end of the episode.

'Timeline's possible, but I doubt it.'

'She was so big in the '80s.'

'Yeah, I don't get it.'

Elvis lights a cigarette with a Motörhead Zippo, then chucks the lighter on the table. 'For a while, Madonna always anticipated the next big trend in the mainstream musical zeitgeist. And she always changed it up.'

'Like some kind of precog chameleon.'

'Like a version.'

I put the bins out, then go to bed. Elvis slams the door when he leaves.

I wriggle around trying to find a comfortable position. The fusion food is refusing to cooperate and fuse in my stomach. There's a loud bang outside – another car accident. There's been a few of them lately. The tinkling of glass is incessant as parades of cars drive past my bedroom window. A poor man's wind chime, haunting and peaceful.

~

I'm startled awake by the "Garbage Truck Cacophony in A Minor". I pour tap water into the least dirty glass from the sink and swallow a couple of out-of-date multivitamins.

I stare at the knife block and briefly consider chopping off the end of my pinkie so I can take the day off. I'd end up at the hospital anyway, so I drive to work with all my digits intact.

The morning consists of wheeling people from day surgery admissions to the operating theatres, into recovery, then finally to their rooms. The best part of this process is using "the wombat" to drive people around the hallways. The wombat is a four-wheeled metallic contraption with a claw that grips onto the underside axle and lifts the bed. I do my best to avoid human obstacles while using the black joystick to navigate the beds through the serpentine hospital corridors. This morning's surgery list consists of lap bands, cataracts, a hernia repair, gallbladder removal, tonsillectomy, an endoscopy, wisdom teeth removal, thyroid surgery, endometrial ablation, carpel tunnel surgery, and an anterior cruciate ligament repair.

I spend the afternoon helping in the ER, where nothing too out of the ordinary happens. It's the usual array of broken bones, fishing injuries, home plastic surgery attempts gone wrong, a kid who ate a small LEGO house, a naked man with no physical maladies, and a lady who thought she'd been going through menopause but was pregnant.

Afterwards, I head straight to the Valley to eat Chinese. It's better than average. I wrap the leftovers and hand them to a homeless lady before walking towards the sound of blues music. It's a cocktail bar, but I'm not drinking tonight.

Hipster bartenders walk around pulling on their suspenders with their thumbs, complimenting each other's manicured, bespoke beards and moustaches. I am a sober ship in a sea of drunkards. A blues band butchers the works of Howlin' Wolf, assaults Lead Belly and kills Muddy Waters.

When I get home, Elvis is on the couch in the lounge room. He shuffles across and grabs a beer from the esky. It's some microbrewery monstrosity made from flowers or bananas or something.

'So,' he says, stroking his beard, 'you gonna tell me about E?'

FOUR

THE first time I met E, he burst through our front door carrying a silver briefcase. He had slicked back hair and the kind of hypnotic blue eyes Paul Newman or Sinatra were famed for. He wore a white lab coat over a blue button-up shirt and brown pants.

'Emmanuel, my boy. Pleased to meet you,' he said, extending his hand.

His fist enveloped mine. Before I could reply, he picked me up under my arms and spun me around. As he returned me to the ground, I felt a mixture of dizziness and elation.

'It's Manny.'

He clapped me on the back and bounced towards the kitchen. 'Manny it is. Come, come. We have plenty of work to do. I want to see this incredible ability of yours.'

I followed.

He placed the briefcase on the tiles, hugged Mum and pecked her on the cheek. Her arms stayed by her side.

E didn't appear to notice her frostiness. 'Do we have an area for us?'

Mum cleared her throat. 'I've set up the shed for you. When are you beginning?'

'No time like the present. If we're all ready, I'll take young Emmanuel – sorry, Manny, and begin.'

'Wait outside for a moment,' she said, coldly. 'I need to speak with Manny first.'

E nodded, wisely said nothing, and went out to the backyard.

Mum lowered herself and held my shoulders. 'Tell me once more, Manny.'

'Listen to what E says. Stop if I feel sick.'

'And?'

'Don't tell anyone.'

'Right.'

We'd been over that dozens of times. I had to learn how to control whatever happened in the "Goldfish Incident". Learn how to harness its power, to stop me from hurting anyone, especially myself.

Mum bit her lip, spun me around and ushered me to join E in the backyard.

We went straight to the shed. Whether it was his enthusiasm, or the attention I was receiving, I liked him immediately and couldn't understand why Mum didn't. The shed was musty and smelled exactly like old sheds normally do. He pulled a chain hanging from the ceiling to turn on the light and opened his suitcase on the metal bench. The velvet-lined case housed several small bottles and miniature terrariums containing various dead beetles: Elephant, Ground, Christmas, Dung, Scarab, Rose Chafer.

'Pick one,' E said.

A ladybird caught my eye. The least threatening.

'The ladybird it is. Or is that ladybeetle or ladybug for our American friends?' he laughed; it was contagious.

Like a switch, he flicked to being serious as he knelt to face me and placed both hands on my shoulders. 'Manny, the most important thing to remember here is to breathe and remain calm. Okay?'

'Yes.'

'Good boy. There's nothing to be afraid of. I'm here.' E pulled out two blue wires attached to some white pads. 'I'm going to attach these to you, okay?'

I scratched my arm with my fingernails. 'What are they?'

'They're to monitor your vital signs, so nothing bad happens.' He stuck the pads to either side of my neck, then withdrew a small black box and inserted the blue wires into a slot on its side. There was a series of beeps as the green and red lights lit up on the box. E clapped his hands. 'We're ready. I want to see what you can do, kiddo.'

I placed my hands on the cold bench. We commenced.

I picked up the dead ladybird and felt it immediately. The room became brighter, like it had with my fish. The same warmth flooded through me like a mild electric current. E's voice sounded distant but snapped into focus.

'Okay, Manny, put it down now.'

The room dimmed as I placed the ladybird back onto the table. Both of us stared at the dead bug for what seemed like minutes but was probably only a few seconds.

A twitch of its wings signalled its resurrection. The ladybird walked around a bit, opened its wings, then flew through the window into the big, wide world.

E smiled. 'Splendid. Let's move on.'

We spent the next few hours resurrecting dead bugs. Well, I resurrected dead bugs while E watched with a satisfied grin. I felt terrific until a wave of nausea kicked in and I puked a whole tin's worth of baked beans onto the floor.

E grabbed a small bottle filled with fluorescent red liquid. 'Never mind. Drink this. It'll sort you out. And don't tell your mother, she'll kill me.'

I nodded and swallowed the bitter tasting liquid without question. An explosion of multi-coloured lights danced in front of my eyes and the nausea receded.

E must have sensed I'd had enough. 'That'll do for today.' He packed the remaining bugs into the suitcase. 'You did well, Manny.'

When we went inside. Mum was holding a glass of wine, a vacant

33

look on her face. She put her glass on the table and came over to hug me.

'How are you, darl?'

'He's fine,' E said. 'He did a great job. He's something all right.'

'He's not just something, he's my son.'

'Relax, Sarah. He's a wonderful boy, and this ability of his is nothing short of astounding, more than we ever could have hoped for.'

Her eyes narrowed. 'You should know better than to tell a woman to relax.'

He held his hands up. 'My apologies.'

'You knew this could happen? These abilities?'

E shrugged. 'We didn't know what could happen exactly, but this is one of the better outcomes.'

'Better for whom?' Mum scoffed.

He nodded at her. 'Thank you for your hospitality, Sarah.'

Then to me. 'Wonderful to meet you, Manny. I'll see you next week, okay?'

~

Meeting with E every Saturday afternoon became a regular occurrence. Instead of playing with kids my age, it was the two of us. The red liquid helped, but I still experienced occasional nausea and migraines in line with the size of the animal I was treating.

But I was learning to control my response. I grew stronger, and it was addictive.

As the experiments wore on, E's mood fluctuated between excited and manic to cold and exasperated. He played the part of the weird uncle. One Saturday a few months in, E dumped a host of plastic-bagged, freshly anesthetised animals onto the bench. We'd knocked it up a notch.

'We've got a rat, a bat, a possum, a blue-tongue lizard and a bilby.'

I knew what was coming. I was more resilient but still wary, knowing the sickness could follow.

'I don't know,' I said.

'You like lizards?'

'They're okay, I guess.'

'Alright, pick one.'

The blue tongue's mouth was open; its weird tongue poking out the side. E opened the bag and dumped out the lizard. It stank.

Despite the repeated warnings not to do so, I shared my ability with the outside world with an impromptu dead guinea pig revival for Show and Tell. It was a success, depending on how one looked at it. The kids ran screaming from the classroom; my teacher said I was in big trouble for playing magic tricks. She placed me in detention until the other guinea pig appeared. Despite my protests there was only one, she lost her temper and called me a slimy liar. It was liberating to perform outside of the backyard shed, but it was the last time I performed "magic" in front of anyone.

E chastised me, but he didn't yell. 'Never, ever do that again, Manny. Or you'll spend the rest of your life getting prodded, poked and punctured by clueless doctors. No one can know. Only you, your mum and me.'

I nodded, glad I wasn't in more trouble.

Back to the shed, everything was as normal as could be, considering I was essentially playing God. As my mind sharpened, I could observe the afflictions plaguing the animals with more clarity: broken bones, torn ligaments, internal bleeding, explosive cysts, cancer.

The animals kept coming: a frog who'd cheated death by magpie, a roadkill Shih Tzu, a wild turkey with a broken leg, a poisoned ibis, a broken-backed green tree snake and a koala with chlamydia. It was a dangerous world out there.

One Saturday, E gave me a break from the animals. Instead, he ran me through a battery of tests. He attached more electrodes to my skull, scanned me with various handheld devices and took enough blood for me to faint in my chair. Apparently, a few sharp slaps to the face and a handful of smelling salts brought me back.

'Manny, are you okay?'

The world was fuzzy but soon regained clarity.

'I think so. Are we finished?'

'I've got all I need, but let's not tell your mother about this hey.'

I nodded eagerly.

'Good, now if I can isolate the alien proteins and combine them with the right catalyst, we're golden.'

'Alien?'

'Yes, alien, unfamiliar. Not the big-eyed, tall and skinny green creatures you're probably imagining.'

E wiped his brow and knelt, so we were eye to eye. 'Do you know what it means for something to be "unique," Manny?'

Images of *Antiques Roadshow* cycled through my mind. 'Like, special?'

'Close. It's so special it's the only one of its kind. Unlike anything *or* anyone else. You, Manny, are unique,' E said. He broke off his gaze to pack away his instruments. 'Let's continue this next week.'

The animals kept coming until we hit an unexpected roadblock in the form of an inconvenient seizure. I'd brought back a freshly squashed Siberian hamster when, suddenly, I was lock-jawed and pissing myself again. It had been an unusually long and gruelling session, and I was having more trouble focusing than usual. The hamster broke me.

The whole process was nearly vetoed by Mum when E brought me into the kitchen pale and covered in grazes. The wine glass exploded in her hand.

'Go to your room, Manny.'

E nodded. I walked upstairs, washed my face, then snuck to the top of the stairs. I gripped the banister and strained to hear their conversation.

'No. That's the last time, E. Get out of here.'

'Sarah, listen.'

'Don't you "listen" me. I've allowed this to go on long enough. You could've killed him. I'm putting a stop to this right now, like I should've done back then.'

E laughed. 'Honestly, I don't think I could kill him even if I wanted to. His immune system is incredible.'

'What?'

'Manny's abilities aren't merely a result of our experiments. There's something going on at a molecular level allowing him to control and accelerate the healing process. He's special. It's *why* he was the only survivor.'

Mum grabbed a dustpan and cleaned the broken glass off the floor. 'Don't remind me.'

'Sarah, can we cool off and discuss it?'

They spoke for a while longer and agreed on a two-week break. E promised Mum nothing bad would ever happen again. The first week back, E brought in a live pig on a red leash, and a large sledgehammer.

My eyes popped. 'What are you doing?'

I knew.

'It's okay. Manny. We're doing this final test. The last one.'

It wasn't.

I'd heard this several times before, witnessed him maim more animals than a child should. The animals were always anaesthetised, but it never made me feel any better about it. Even now I can still recall the crunch of broken bones and pops of punctured organs.

No, not the last time. The last time was the day E tugged on my shirt sleeve as I turned for the shed.

'Not today, boy. Today, we're going on a road trip.'

'Where?'

'I've got something special for you. What we've been working towards all this time.'

Aside from the percussive and confusing classical music bursting from the speakers, we spent the car trip in silence. E's hands gripped ten and two on the steering wheel. Though his gaze remained straight ahead on the road, he was in another world.

As we turned the corner, wondrous purples flooded the windscreen. Jacarandas in full bloom lined both sides of the street. Bloated mansions sat on immaculate lawns. Front yards were filled with manicured topiary, colourful gardens and long driveways. We turned into a driveway attached to the biggest home I'd ever seen. Moving towards the mansion was like sliding down a giant's tongue into its mouth. E drove to a shed at the side, bigger than our house. A roller door retracted.

An ominous feeling enveloped me. I didn't want to exit the car but there was a pull more powerful than ever before.

'What am I doing here?' I asked.

'This is part of what you've been training for, Manny. There's nothing to fear, I promise you. Now come.'

He rushed, tugging me by the arm, hurting my shoulder. E led me through the cavernous mansion. We stopped outside one room, its walls painted with cartoon princesses and butterflies.

Inside was a small, bald child swallowed up in a wheelchair. Beneath bruised, stretched skin and hollow cheekbones was a set of beautiful blue eyes.

It was a little girl. She smiled through bleeding gums. My heart swelled, and the white energy passed through me. My body buzzed – a soft electrical current travelled through me.

Fear emanated from her eyes and her trembling hands pulled at a thin fabric gown.

I wasn't fearful. I was hopeful, filled with elation.

This is what E had been training me for. Until then, I'd only been studying. This was the test: curing a person. Not a grazed knee or a broken leg. This was cancer, severe cancer. Even from a distance, I could feel her fading life force.

When E wheeled her closer, his eyes welled. She wasn't just any girl; she was *his* girl. E brought his daughter to a stop.

'This is Jam.'

She was fragile and beautiful.

'Hi, Jam. I'm Manny.' I reached my hands out to her.

She brought her delicately bruised and shaking hands toward mine. I knelt in front of her. The transference began immediately. Her fear extinguished.

Even with closed eyes I could feel her cells healing, her entire being regenerating. It took longer than any animal had previously. By the time I finished, there were tears on my cheeks, but they weren't mine, they were hers. I opened my eyes and stared into hers. They were magnificent, bright and filled with love. I felt what she felt: the happiness, the relief, the warmth of positivity bathing us.

I stood and stared at E, both of us smiling from ear to ear. He picked me up and wrapped me in a bear hug.

A tiny hand grabbed mine.

'Thank you, Manny,' Jam said.

E took a photo of the two of us with a polaroid camera. Then he picked Jam up and kissed her all over her face as she giggled for what was probably the first time in a long time. He lowered her and turned. 'Your mother will be thrilled when she watches the recording.'

'What recording?'

'I've recorded every one of our sessions. I didn't want you to become self-conscious and adversely affect your results.'

E drove me home, sans classical music, a relief. Instead, Jam sang Beatles songs the whole way. Once home, we walked through the doorway and I managed, 'I'm tired,' before collapsing to the floor.

~

I awoke to the sounds of Mum and E fighting. My eyes attempted to focus from my position on the couch to E and Mum in the hallway. Jam pressed herself into the corner of the room.

'Calm down, Sarah.'

'I will not calm down!'

They stopped when I walked in. Mum had been crying, but as usual pretended not to let on. She had a magic switch that allowed her to change moods in an instant depending on present company. 'What's happening?' I asked.

She hugged me. 'It's okay sweetie, don't worry.'

Whenever she said that, I worried more.

They returned to bickering like I wasn't there. Jam stood, shaky without her wheelchair, blinking and unsure.

E flailed his arms about. 'You can't take him, Sarah. There's more to do. This is world changing. Look at Jam, it's like she never had it!' he gestured, eyes bulging.

Mum turned and stared vacantly for a moment before her eyes fired up. She threw an empty vase at the wall. The vase shattered into hundreds of pieces that tinkled melodiously across the front entrance tiles. We were all so focused on her and the broken glass, we hadn't noticed Jam collapse to the floor, convulsing.

I'll never forget the look on Mum's face.

I thought her eyes were going to bug right out of her head.

She flew across the tiles and held Jam's head to stop it banging on the floor. Blood gushed from Jam's nose and her eyes were all whites, like an attacking shark.

'Shit.' E scooped her up in his arms. 'I'll fix it, I'll fix it. Her body's just been through a lot.' He left the wheelchair behind as he rushed outside and placed her in the car gently.

That was the last time I saw Jam.

After cleaning up the glass, Mum took me to my room and tucked me in. I was exhausted, but I couldn't sleep.

Mum would have gone to sleep that night not realising it would be her last.

~

At the conclusion of the story Elvis stares at me, then downs the rest of his beer.

'Heavy,' he says, lighting a cigarette.
I raise my eyebrows in agreement and spark my own.

FIVE

I'M sitting out the front in the morning sun, eating peanut butter and jam on toast, when a homeless person with a grey afro wheels a can-filled trolley across the road. I run inside and turn the couch cushions over to find a couple of gold and silver coins to give them. They thank me in garbled bursts before walking away.

It reminds me it's time to go see Aunty Sue.

I check the family tracking app; a bit redundant since she rarely leaves the house.

Sue started slipping about six months ago, but her paranoia has increased at an alarming rate. She and some friends from an avant-garde religion became convinced the end of the world was approaching in the form of a combined zombie alien apocalypse, and it was time to prepare.

She bought *Doomsday prepping for beginners: Budget Edition!* and began the checklist: shelter, food, water, light and heat. She moved through first aid, medication, hygiene and communication. Now she's deep in the midst of bunkers, tools and self-defence. The last two items were when I became concerned for her welfare. God help anyone who makes the misguided attempt of setting foot on her property.

Two months ago, she commenced work on "The Bunker."

I've just merged onto the highway when the car jerks and grinds to a halt. With a faulty petrol gauge, each drive is a game of Russian Roulette, and I've lost this round. The closest petrol station is a few kilometres back. I kick the tires and contemplate my options. There are two: walk or try to hitchhike. The type of person offering a ride could be the sort likely to have a cellar full of pickle jars filled with shrunken heads.

I don't feel like joining that club, so I walk.

The sky is blue and birdless. The sun bakes the whole landscape dry. The tar feels gummy beneath my shoes. Haze morphs the horizon.

The air conditioning in the service station is nothing short of stunning. I pay for a 5-litre jerry can filled with petrol and a fluorescent-blue, hybrid electrolyte drink for the trek back. I smash it in one go.

When I finally reach the car, I'm hot and sweaty but otherwise unscathed. I drop the jerry can, flip the fuel cap open and unscrew the lid. The funnel has fallen into the can.

The floor of the car is a dump. I search through the discarded bottles until I find a suitable receptacle. It's an energy drink bottle with a thin neck that might do the trick.

I fill the bottle with fuel as best I can, spilling most of it. I find a stick on the highway shoulder, use it to prop open the fuel flap and start pouring. I only deliver about half of the five litres into the actual car. There's a pool of petrol at my feet and it soaks my hands. I stomp the empty can, then hurl it over a fence. It looks and flies like a child's poorly designed, homemade rocket at a fun fair.

I hop into the car, which now smells of petrol-covered garbage, and turn the engine over. Tiny, red blisters cover my hands and begin mutating as I drive to the station on fumes to put more fuel in. My hands still stink of petrol, but things could always be worse. I could be living in North Korea, working in Japan, or sick in the U.S.A.

I can shower at Sue's.

Her house is at the end of a cul-de-sac, and only squatters occupy the other dilapidated properties. The bunker looms large as I roll up the street. Much larger than last time I visited. It doesn't look like it abides by council zoning permits. I was already concerned about the arsenal of weapons accumulating in her shed, but this is worse.

On the other hand, if the apocalypse turns out to be real and *does* involve brain-eating zombie aliens, I'm sure the elaborate weapons stockpile will be of great comfort.

The gate's latch catches and the hinges squeak. I forgot to spray it with WD-40 again. Sue's corgi, Scraps, barks himself into a happy stupor. He's dribbling and peeing himself while I stroke his head. He looks hungry. I leave Scraps to continue burrowing his many holes in the yard. Sue is digging next to a small mountain of white and brown dirt. She's dirty and focused, hunched over a shovel, removing earth from under the house. There are several unidentifiable machines and pumping devices making a cacophonous noise. Even neighbouring streets must be able to hear it.

'Sue!' I yell, waving like I'm drowning in a rip.

She looks up and presses a large yellow button on a remote, causing the noisy equipment to shut down. She removes her gloves, earplugs and protective glasses. The crazy glint in her eyes helps prove a long-held opinion that everyone looks better in sunglasses.

'Hi, darl. How are you?'

I fake a smile, avoid looking concerned and speak in a calm voice. 'Good. You?'

'I've taken the labels off the cans so when the time comes, every meal will be a surprise.'

'Well, that's something.'

Something mildly concerning.

I explain the petrol ordeal, then head inside and shower. Dozens of bottles of various body products clutter the bathroom sink. She's serious about this prepping business.

Feeling fresh and clean, I grab some spare clothes from the back room. Various apocalypse related junk fills the space.

I return to the front yard, traversing the many holes and potential death traps. There's an extra manic intensity in Sue's eyes. She looks as though she hasn't slept or bathed in days. This is more than mildly concerning.

'What are those bottles in your bathroom, Sue?'

She wipes sweat from her forehead. 'I found the recipes on the internet. I've made shampoo, conditioner and soaps. I've got scissors too so you can cut your hair. You don't want to waste too much shampoo.'

"Mildly concerning" be damned, she's bat-shit crazy.

'Do you think you can be here Wednesday?' she asks, 'I have an appointment at the rifle range, and I need someone to sign for my plutonium delivery.'

'Plutonium?' I repeat.

'They had a bulk buy special on piratesales.com.'

'What do you need plutonium for?'

She looks at me like I've asked why water is important for human survival.

'It's better to have plutonium and not need it, than need it and not have any.'

Touché.

I must choose my words carefully. Don't want to set her off.

'I was okay with the guns, grenades and even the home-made flamethrower, but plutonium? You must have more important things to spend your money on.'

Her eyes narrow. 'What are you trying to say?'

Stuff it. She needs a dose of reality.

'I'm saying, there is not going to be an apocalypse.'

The knife appears swiftly from behind her. Sun glistens off the sharp blade. Her hand trembles but her gaze remains steely. 'So, they've gotten to you, have they?' Sue nudges forward and spits on the ground. Scraps dodges in and out of my legs in a figure-eight.

'What the hell, Sue? Put that down! Jesus. I'm going home.'

'Language, young man.'

The madness recedes from her eyes. I turn and start walking. That's enough visiting for today. As I reach the gate, I hear her shriek. I turn around to Sue curled in the foetal position, clutching her head.

'It hurts!' she screams. Her eyes glaze over, staring right through me. 'Give me your hands and heal me.'

'I can't, you know I can't.'

'Please, just a little!'

My hands reach forward, not that it will help. I place them on her head, feel the black ball in her brain. Inoperable. Fatal.

She won't do anything about it, but I know she's faking this attack. I take my hands off her head. The screaming stops. Dirt and sweat covers Sue's body.

'Thank you. I don't know what happened.'

I want to tell her it's the placebo effect, but don't. 'You had another episode, is all. You need to go to the doctor.'

'Don't worry. God is working on it, but he's super busy dealing with adulterers and flat earthers right now.'

I sigh and run my hands through my hair, already crusted with dirt. 'Do you want me to stay?'

'No darl, you've helped enough.' She stares pointedly at the garage. 'Actually, you can stack those fallen cans in the garage. Leave me here to rest for a bit.'

I tread carefully to the garage, arrange the fallen cans, and place a green canvas tarp over the weapons stockpile. Several jars of glowing blue goo labelled "lysergic jams" are on the top shelf. Spread that on your toast in the morning and you *would* be toast.

Sue is still lying in the dirt like a corpse when I return. She opens her eyes and sits up. 'I'll be okay. Go home.'

'Okay, but take care of yourself. You need rest.'

'Cheerio, love. Thanks for visiting, take some of those jams home with you.' Her sunny disposition is even creepier after today's display. She shoves several crumpled $50 notes into my hand. She won't remember this in the morning, but I take them. I figure the less she has to spend on weapons, the better.

'See you,' I say.

'Yep. We must look over the Appocoplans and run the doomsday drill soon.'

I shut the gate and the machines start again. I sit in the car, my mind spins. WHAT. THE. HELL. She belongs in *One Flew over the Cuckoo's Nest.*

I reverse out of the driveway, not knowing what to do about her. Her strange behaviours from my last few visits compound. Last week she made me a cup of cheese. She boiled the kettle, put some grated cheese in a teacup and handed it to me to drink.

The time before, I was searching for a plate and found them all in the washing machine. Before that, she said she'd been taking photos on her iPhone of the aliens who are going to impregnate dead aliens and turn them into zombies who take over Earth. Before that, I found her stumbling around her garage with a torch, looking for Uncle Joe, who was twenty years gone. It's much more than worrying. And now she's got enough ammunition to arm the entire neighbourhood. Then again, zombie aliens probably take more bullets than humans.

~

I stop in the Valley on the way home. It's Furry Culture night at the Brightside. I'm not wearing a giant panda costume, so I'm not welcome. Instead, I go into Mojambo's, an African-themed bar, blasting loud, snazzy background music.

The bar's an abhorrent example of cultural appropriation, but the prices are alright.

Time slips. I've had a few Boilermakers and a couple of Electric Zombies, which seems fitting after the earlier zombie apocalypse talk. It's late and work is going to be bad tomorrow, but I wouldn't sleep if I went home. The home movie of my encounter with Sue plays in my head on repeat, and the little man operating it refuses to shut off the projector.

47

I move on to the next joint, a Rocky-themed dive bar called Clubber Lang's, a concept so niche it will probably be gone next week. The later it gets, the rowdier the Valley gets. It swells with the hedonists and party animals who never want tomorrow to come, because tomorrow is reality.

I stand at the bar while the girl next to me slags off her ex-boyfriend.

Dead eyes, bleached hair, paralysed smile, caked-on makeup. I can't stop staring at the small segment of her forehead where the fake tan missed, and the words "high maintenance" are all but plastered across her forehead in bold. She says every guy she's ever dated is a "scuzzbag."

'99% of guys are scuzzbags,' I say.

'I know right.'

She's a chatterbox, alright. I assume she's on amphetamines. I drink my blood-red cocktail and try to pay her attention but she's not making it easy. I give cursory nods while withdrawing deep into my subconscious. The conversation continues for another ten minutes but feels longer. I say nothing.

She is a sweet girl beneath the orange-pancaked facade. I have a microsecond to interject and make my excuse to leave.

I haven't eaten anything, so next stop is Trang's Good Time Chinese. Their special is Schezwan chicken and egg. It's delicious but eating chicken and eggs together kind of freaks me out. The possibility of eating a mother and her unborn daughter at the same time seems positively ghoulish.

The waiter serves sake, which is strange as it's not a Japanese joint. But I'm losing my buzz and not one to question a gift horse.

The Jiminy Cricket in my head says, "It's time to go home," but my body won't let me, not yet. I walk past a group of girls, vying for space and finding the perfect angle for a selfie. Their tongues protrude from swollen duck lips, their mouths looking like exotic, pink sea creatures. I walk straight to the bar at Knife Town and order a beer. I run into a drunk girl who has recently broken up with her boyfriend.

Her mascara has run, her perfume is pleasantly floral. She flings her arms around and points to an unseen person in the distance. I finish my beer; the drunk girl finishes hers and her story. I nod.

'Thanks, you're a good listener,' she says, 'I'm going to go dance with that Norwegian looking guy.' She hugs me and disappears onto the crowded dance floor.

My shirt is covered in fake tan.

The ambiguous signs on the bathroom doors are too confusing, so I turn and head into the night. I wander the street towards the strip clubs, carrying a nice buzz. 'One more hour,' I slur.

The streetwalkers are out in force, and the Valley ones are tougher than a $2 steak. I pay the $10 cover and wander into Glitters.

A messy drunk guy walks up to a young woman. 'How much for a lap dance?'

'I'm not a stripper.'

'Right, sorry.'

'Wanker.'

The guy looks over at me; I shrug. It's probably an honest mistake, but on the offensiveness scale, it's a social faux pas equivalent to asking a woman if she's pregnant when she's not.

I imagine my eyeballs are floating like the ice cubes in my vodka tonic. I linger on the gorgeous bartenders, until I realise there's only one. My left eye welds shut. My vision returns to normal.

I'm drunk.

I must be drunk because I'm trying hard to act sober and even I think I'm being smug and unlikeable. Maybe I'm just misunderstood. 'You've been through trauma,' I tell myself, without fully believing it. An overwhelming heaviness lodges in my chest.

I feel so unimportant I could disappear and it wouldn't matter one iota.

Transform from a happy idiot into a depressed mess today! Just add alcohol!

The next dancer on stage has a vestigial tail. She's gyrating in front of me and every time she bends over, her little tail pokes out. It lifts my mood, and I touch it with my pinkie finger. She rightfully warns me and my face burns.

The mood fluctuations are real.

They shouldn't be serving jugs of vodka tonic here. I make it to their well-signed bathroom stall before heaving my guts up. I buy a tin of mints from the bathroom dispenser and a glow-in-the-dark, ribbed condom for reasons unknown.

A fat, loud businessman type latches onto me when I get to the bar and buys me a beer. He grinds his teeth, which somehow don't turn to dust despite his best efforts. His eyes are lolling around like they want to burst free from their stalks and he's drenched in sweat like he's just exited the dunk tank at a carnival. He's telling some joke and laughing at himself while alternately elbowing me in the ribs and rubbing his nose with his shirt sleeve. I'm sure this guy is decent and sensible when he's sober, but he's not, so he isn't.

It's the epitome of everything wrong with drug users. That's cocaine though; a greedy drug turning ordinarily rational people into self-absorbed, bug-eyed, motor mouths. It's dull. I leave.

Across the street, the light of the 7-Eleven shines like a beacon. I am a moth.

A car speeds up as I cross the road. I squint and shield my eyes from the fast-approaching headlights. Inside 7-Eleven, an immense man with an impressive afro rocks the Slurpee machine back and forth, trying to get more blue to come out. I buy a Crunchie and walk to a nearby ally to smoke and rid myself of the paranoia that's rising and falling with each breath.

That sensation of being watched returns.

As I turn to walk up the street, I notice in my peripherals a dark figure wearing a trench coat. The figure disappears before my brain can process the image properly. Maybe I didn't see anything. I'm one-eyed and three sheets to the wind. Give me a parrot and a peg leg and send me out to sea.

It's later than I want it to be, but I'm not giving up yet. I stumble into Madam Bovary's, where there's no cover charge. Everyone is on their phones, looking like they want to be anywhere else but here.

There's plenty of bartenders but no one getting served. A twisty moustached, suspender-wearing gent finally serves me. He turns his nose up at beer instead of the featured cocktail. He places a woven mountain goat fur coaster on the bar before pouring the beer in a bulbous vase. He clasps his hands together in prayer pose, says 'namaste,' then slides the receipt in a silver ashtray across the stained hardwood bar. I'd say something, but I'm too scared to talk in case a stream of nonsense pours forth and I'm kicked out. I'm having enough trouble standing and seeing at the same time.

I leave the tip jar empty, save the coins for any rough sleepers I come across.

The bouncer wakes me in the chair. I wonder why there's a club in my living room before remembering where I am. He's cool about it, and I stagger to the exit without a fuss.

I tap my pockets. I'm fresh out of smokes, but the coat girls are usually good for it if you ask nicely. The coat girl's name is Mandy. She hands me a cigarette, lights a match, and holds it to the end while I inhale.

Though I'm grateful, it tastes like a G-string would if you could roll it up and smoke it. I cough and mumble a few words to Mandy about Barry Manilow sufficient to excuse myself from the situation.

UK backpackers pour from bars and into kebab joints like drunken lemmings. They collapse on benches, scoffing processed garbage.

I trip on the gutter into the street and coins fly everywhere.

I'm too drunk to walk, let alone drive. I stumble to the car, pour myself into the back seat, and pass out.

~

The phone alarm pierces my brain. I struggle into the front seat of my car. I have less than an hour to get home, shower, dress and get to work. Due to staff shortages, the hospital has been sending orderlies to assist the paramedic teams. Both sides aren't exactly happy about it, and I'm setting a terrible example of the benefits. Today's my shift. Outcalls always make for an interesting day, even if I'm essentially a glorified gopher.

As soon as I get home, I turn on the ice-cold water and sit in the corner of the shower for a few minutes.

Elvis isn't home.

If I think about the whole day I'll crumble, so I break it into steps. All I have to do next is get dressed, get to work, then tip myself into the back of the ambulance next to the crash trolley.

~

Both paramedics scrunch their faces as I sit behind them and tighten my seatbelt.

'You all good?' the driver asks.

My stomach churns but holds down its contents. 'Let's do it,' I say, pointing forward.

The driver shakes his head and pulls out from the ambulance bay. 'The smell is leaking from your pores. Where did you go last night?'

'The Valley.'

The other guy throws me a blister pack of Panadol from the dashboard and hands me a bottle of water as we drive alongside the river towards the city. Flocks of seabirds circle lazily around the motorised dinghies trailing the groups of boys' college rowing teams. The towing crews glide across the river, performing the catch and extraction in perfect unison to the barking strains of the coxswain at the bow. It's hypnotic.

'Where are we off to first?' I ask.

The driver signals ahead. 'Pancake House, we're starving, and it wouldn't hurt you to get some grub into ya. It might get rid of the smell.'

We sit in a yellow, plastic booth. I eat a fat, short stack with bacon and syrup, and wash it down with two cups of black coffee. We split the bill and hit the road. The first part of the day is uneventful. A stroke, a broken hip, an overdose, a car accident, and old people fainting from the heat. The paramedics save the people; I do the heavy lifting. We're mercifully finishing up when we receive an emergency call on the radio.

'Possible heart attack at Hibiscus Apartments in Toowong. Two units required. Male, age 35, MO.'

MO is the code for morbidly obese. Two units is unusual.

We arrive at the same time as the other paramedics. A woman is waving frantically, alternately gesturing inside and tugging her hair.

We discover she's the carer. The three of us prep the ambulance while the other paramedics grab their gear and run into the tiny unit to administer first aid. One of them comes back, his fringe plastered across his brow.

'Look, he's stable, but I don't know how the heck we're going to get him out of there. He's huge.'

'How huge?' I ask.

'Ever been on safari or a cattle ranch?' He grabs the radio from his belt and calls dispatch to find an answer.

The man is so obese we need builders to sledgehammer his front entry.

An hour later, we're leaning against a wall, smoking cigarettes while waiting for the builders to finish smashing open the front of the unit. The second team keeps the man stable. A small crane arrives in the back of a truck, hopefully big enough to winch him into the ambulance. The ambulance's suspension groans as we slot him into the rear cargo hold, and the crane does most of the heavy lifting. The stench emanating from the man is unbearable. His skin stretches to capacity over his gargantuan frame. Miscellaneous body fluids ooze from his legs; he's covered in painful-looking sores and rashes.

It's sundown when we arrive at the hospital, and even the wombat bed mover struggles as I steer the big guy straight to the ICU. He'll need to lose a couple of hundred kilograms for surgery to be a viable option. His carer says he has been bedridden for the last seven years. There must have been hundreds of wake-up calls before this incident. The first time he couldn't tie his shoes. The first time he couldn't see his penis. The first time he washed himself with a rag on a stick.

I'll be wheeling this astounding human around the hospital in a giant-sized bed for the next few months. Even if I still had my abilities, I'm not sure I could help the poor guy.

~

I kick open the door and make a beeline for the couch.

A newly painted canvas sits on the easel in the lounge room. A Fibonacci sequence of hundreds of interlinking circles spreading to the canvas edges. An angular wolf-like creature, with different coloured pupils, stares from the centre of the canvas.

Elvis is devouring a kebab with both hands.

I lift the greasy remote from the table, another kebab packet stuck to it.

He wipes chilli and yoghurt sauce from his cheek with a wad of napkins.

'Do you want to drop acid and watch the 4-hour extended version of *Woodstock*?'

A snappy bag appears in his hand. He removes one of the tiny acid-soaked squares for himself, then tosses me the bag. Each little cardboard square has a picture of Bart Simpson on it. I stare at Bart's face for a bit, then toss it back to him.

'Not tonight, man.'

He shoves the bag back in his pocket, finishes the last traces of the kebab, wipes his hands on the couch, grabs the remote and flicks to a documentary about crocodiles. We learn you're meant to zigzag when running away from a crocodile because they can't change direction as well as humans can, but I think doing a zigzag in front of a straight line may get you eaten faster.

I grab the communal tobacco pouch. 'Sue's getting worse. The bunker's growing and she's gathering weapons at a scary rate.'

'Anything good?' Elvis asks as he hunts through TV channels.

'Not fireworks, I'm talking serious explosives. She's even ordered plutonium.'

'We know where to go if there *is* an apocalypse.'

I walk to my room, through the clothes strewn across the floor. My bed has never felt so soft and comforting.

~

I stumble around to find one pair of clean underwear. Unfortunately, much of the material is worn away like an eclipse of hungry moths enjoyed an all-you-can-eat special. My stomach screams for nourishment and my mind conjures delicious possibilities on the way to the cafe. Thick cuts of juicy, crisp bacon sandwiched between freshly baked sourdough, slathered in butter. A cooked runny egg. Exotic yet dependable BBQ sauce. Freshly squeezed orange juice. I punch in my pin number at the ATM, salivating at the feast I'm about to consume.

My account balance is $1.28. Not even enough to buy a snag on bread from Bunnings. I drag my feet home and have Vegemite on the two end pieces of toast. It's the last of the food left in the house.

My phone dings. It's a bunch of photos from Sue. Selfies with her beloved bunker. Either guilt or concern drives me to her place.

We sit together at her kitchen table, the only clear space in the entire house. There's a glass of clear liquid in front of each of us. My glass is filled with reverse osmosis water; hers smells like gin. Dozens of empty pill bottles litter her kitchen counter.

Sue's eyes are wild, and she looks like she hasn't slept. If she has, it hasn't been in her bed, which is covered in boxes, quilts and clothing. She's ranting. I dip in and out of paying attention.

'Everyone thinks they're unique. That they don't have to work for it because the sun shines out their arse and everything will be given to them on a shiny, silver platter. This sense of entitlement is the biggest trap the younger generation find themselves snared in. The world isn't screwed up, you are. Happiness is a state of mind, and you need to accept your true self. The destruction of the earth is imminent. Anarchy and disorder rule. Chaos and the new order, all this will become a primitive wasteland.' She waves her arms manically. 'Then we'll see who's who and what's what.'

I sit still, taking occasional sips of water. Her ranting escalates.

'We're all connected, all knowing, all one. We are stardust.' She's shouting now.

'Everyone wants the panacea to well-adjustment. A quick fix of casually applied ideology. Dammit!' Sue's fist bangs on the table.

'They're bombarded with tidal waves of useless information.' She bangs again, spilling a stack of plates. They smash onto the ground and join their decimated counterparts.

She roars. 'Every single person has the same right to create their own way of dealing with modern stress. The insecurities and anxieties ubiquitously permeate the mass consciousness!'

My heart breaks for her. It's like I'm not even here. Her mind is on another plane.

'Humans are selfish. Intelligence makes us self-absorbed. The ultimate struggle. They'll never be satisfied until they join me.'

I sit and stare. She is looking way past me now. I push away from the table. I doubt she realises I'm leaving.

Her ramblings continue as I walk out into the yard with Scraps nipping at my ankles. I grab a bag of dried dog food and fill his bowl until it mimics the backyard dirt mound. I may have to find a place for him soon. Sue too.

I leave him with his face buried in the pile of biscuits and his tail whipping fast as hummingbird wings. The clack of the closing gate makes me wince. I feel like I'm abandoning them both.

'I don't know what to do. No, I don't know what to do about Sue.' I repeat the lines until they sound like a song.

The afternoon passes into the evening, and life begins to feel as hollow and pointless as a carob Easter bunny. On the plus side, my pay finally arrives, so I'll head out later.

~

It's a Sunday session at The Groove House and everyone's on drugs except me. No judgement, it's just I'm the only person who doesn't look like I'm having the best time ever.

I walk straight to the sensibly signed toilets and squeeze into the two-person urinal beside a tattooed steroid freak who makes me feel physically inadequate.

I grab a whisky and head to the smoking area where all the interesting people are meant to be, but everyone's zombified, staring at their phones while unconsciously bringing cigarettes back and forth to their lips with their free hands. All sitting together but with their minds separated. I return a few times over the course of the night and they're still staring bug-eyed at their flickering phone lights, living in the future while digital affirmations dictate their self-worth. But then again, I'm sitting here watching them, so I'm the real idiot.

I feel sorry for future generations, where no one will ever experience the liberation of being unattached to their phone.

The only tech-free individual is a grandma with saggy, faded tattoos and a witch face, chain-smoking through blackened teeth. Steroid boy from the toilet walks out and smokes his cigarette like he's doing bicep curls, then squeezes the butt between his sausage fingers and drives it into the metal tabletop.

My lungs tighten further as I have the last drag of my cigarette. I know I should quit smoking, know it's death, but don't care.

I scan the tobacco pouch. If the government wants to deter people from smoking, maybe they should try using reverse psychology slogans on the warning labels.

"Death is sexy!"

"Life is overrated!"

"Fast track an end to all your problems!"

"You may reek, but at least you look cool!"

"Keep going, our healthcare system needs you!"

I leave through the back door for another bar. One more. Either the streetlights are depressing or I'm projecting my own feelings onto inanimate objects again.

I walk into Ric's Bar, where the floor sucks, literally. Tonight, it's so sticky with Jack Daniels and Coke you could lose a shoe like you've trodden in quicksand. But the music's ace and the prices are right. $3 spirits, $10 jugs of beer, even the dealers posing as bartenders are pushing pills below the average price.

The bartender pouring my cocktail is dressed in a black and white, horizontal-lined top. She looks like a beautiful, geometric zebra.

Animals inevitably remind me of the experiments with E. When I had potential.

There's another note stuck under the mat when I get home. I take a deep breath and pick it up.

Remember the day she died?

I do, and I curse it.

I could have stopped it all.

Someone's lying to you...

Inside, Elvis is smoking a hookah and drinking a large, multicoloured Slurpee. I hold out the note.

'Another one?'

'Yep.' I hand it over.

He reads it and hands it back. 'Okay, story time.'

SIX

I flew down the stairs; my green Ninja Turtles suitcase sat alongside the rest of Mum's bags at the front door. Aunty Sue and Mum were standing red-faced and toe to toe. When I reached the bottom of the steps, Sue locked her hand around my wrist.

'Come on, Manny, please. He doesn't have much time.'

'Let him go, Sue,' Mum said.

Mum grabbed my other wrist; I was the middle piggy in a screaming banshee tug of war. A real-life Stretch Armstrong doll. They both let go at once and I fell into the staircase, banging my head and cutting my hand on a loose nail in the stair railing.

Sue grabbed Mum's arm, but Mum shook her loose to help me up. 'You okay, Manny?'

I nodded and shut my eyes, focused on the pain. When I opened my eyes a few seconds later, the wound on my hand was already healed. A single drop of blood on the white tiles the only evidence of an injury.

'Please, Sarah. Joe's dying, we need a miracle,' Sue pleaded.

'I know he is, but Manny is not Jesus, Sue, he's a nine-year-old boy.'

The sisters' eyes remained locked in a game of chicken until Sue looked away.

Mum sighed. 'We're leaving for a while.'

Sue softened for a moment. 'I'll never ask for another thing from you as long as I live.'

Mum looked like she was considering it, then looked at me and lowered her head.

'Please, Sue. Manny nearly died yesterday fixing that little girl. I only told you about it because, well,' she shrugged, 'there's no one else to tell, is there.'

Mum ran her fingers through her hair. 'Even if we knew Manny *could* fix Joe, it's not ethical.' Biting her lower lip, she looked to her sister. 'I'm sorry. I love you but I'm sorry. It's Joe's time.'

Now tears were leaking from Mum's eyes. 'Manny, go to your room please.'

I shuffled up the stairs and listened with my face pressed between the wooden balusters.

'Why are you wasting his ability?' Sue asked.

'Because it's dangerous. No one can know,' Mum said, flailing her arms in exasperation. 'Even if Manny healed Joe, what do you think the doctors would say about his miraculous recovery? Riddled with cancer yesterday, clean bill of health today. No. If word of his ability gets out, his life will be in danger.'

'What about family?'

'He *is* my family.'

Sue scoffed.

'He's only a boy,' Mum said. 'It's not his responsibility.'

Sue grabbed her keys and rushed to the front door. 'Don't leave,' she said. 'Joe was too sick to get into the car, but I'll carry him into it myself if I have to. I'll be back in an hour.'

Mum shook her head. 'Don't bother, Sue. We'll be gone.'

'Don't leave. Please.'

The sounds of Sue's fuel guzzling monster 4WD reverberated throughout the neighbourhood. I could understand her panic. She and Uncle Joe could never have any kids, and now Uncle Joe was about to die from liver cancer. Even for cancer, they say it's a bad one. She'd be all alone.

Mum locked me in a bear hug when I walked into the kitchen. After a minute or so, she finally released me, leaving salty tear stains on my right shoulder.

She composed herself; she was good at it.

I poured a bowl of Froot Loops. 'Why's my Turtles case at the door? We going to the beach?'

She couldn't meet my gaze. 'Something like that. We're going away for a while.'

'Why?' I asked.

She stared at me for a moment, then at the shed.

'Because we need a break from here. I need a break from here.'

'I don't wanna go before I watch Roadrunner.'

'Oh, fuck Roadrunner.'

My mouth hung open. Hot waves of shame covered my arms and face.

I tried to think of something to say to make her feel better. Nothing surfaced.

'Sorry, sweetie,' Mum said, and kissed me on the head. 'I'm tired. Go and watch Roadrunner. I hope the Coyote catches him one day.'

'He does, I saw it.' I moved towards the lounge room, stopping at the entryway. 'Are we leaving because of me, or because you and E are mad at each other, or because Uncle Joe's dying?'

Mum sighed. 'You're too smart for your own good.'

She walked over, knelt and locked eyes with me.

'It's not because of you, darling, but we do need to get away for a while. We're leaving soon, no arguments, no whining – I don't think I could stand it. Go watch TV, but when I tell you we're leaving, we're leaving.'

It took me a few seconds to unfreeze and walk into the living room, my bowl of Froot Loops forgotten.

After Roadrunner finished, I switched off the TV and walked back into the kitchen.

I ate the soggy cereal while Mum wrote some kind of letter.

'What's that?'

'None of your business. Not yet,' she said, smiled sadly and went back to it.

I dumped my empty bowl in the sink. It was my job to put Miss B into the cat carrier. The only thing Miss B hated more than the cat carrier was the bathtub, and we only made that mistake once. The faded claw mark scars were still visible on Mum's forearms a year later.

She snatched the car keys from the bench.

'Stay here, Manny.'

'Where are you going?'

'I need to talk some sense into your aunt before she does something stupid. Don't open the door to anyone. I won't be long.'

She left me to watch cartoons for a while: the one with the singing frog, the one where Bugs conducts the choir, the one where Daffy Duck is Robin Hood.

When Mum returned, she was sweaty, her eyes blotchy. There was a scratch on her arm, this one not from cat claws.

We left before lunch, to "beat the traffic." A few thousand other families had the same thought. Groupthink in the holidays is a tricky one.

Coronation Drive and the Riverside Expressway were choked up like a lifetime cheeseburger enthusiast's artery, so it probably didn't matter when we left. We made it out of the bottleneck and joined the rest of the city folk. For no discernible reason, the traffic started moving at normal speed once we passed Cornwall Street, as it does. I stared across the monotonous concrete landscape, punctuated by groups of trees and dumb billboards. I didn't know where we were going, but wherever it was, Mum seemed in a rush to get there. She wove through the traffic, taking any opportunity to advance, but eventually settled into a steady speed.

We were about an hour away from home. A solemn Miss B stared from her cat carrier.

Mum took her twisted seatbelt off and tried to fix it.

Bad timing. An understatement.

As she was about to click the seatbelt clasp in its holster, a large black 4WD careened in front of us. I managed, 'Mum, you'd better…' before the car in front hit the anchors.

Mum's last memory would have been a cloudy day, cars, trucks and *Brown Eyed Girl* playing on the radio. A steady pace on a highway that looked like a million other highways the world over. A perfectly ordinary memory, a perfectly dull memory.

My head smashed into the window as she swerved.

Red splatters exploded against the glass.

Our car left the road, hit the median barrier and flipped over towards a ditch. We were airborne, a poor man's zero-gravity experience. The seatbelt cut into my chest so hard it knocked the air out of me. With that, terror. Time slipped for a moment, then sped up like a loose treadmill band catching on itself.

Afterwards, I found out Mum received a punctured lung and a broken back in the accident, not that it mattered for long. Her poorly timed seatbelt removal resulted in her being flung against the car's side panel, through the windscreen and into a ditch. She would've drowned in the shallow, filthy ditch water a few agonising seconds later.

I'd broken a window with my face. Bolts of pain shot through me as I came to, and my skull felt like it was being ripped open. I screamed as waves of agony cascaded through my head and blood poured down my face. I unbuckled the seatbelt and tried to wipe the blood from my eyes. I shoved the door open, dragged out Miss B's carrier and stood on the hill.

Mum was face down in the ditch.

I raced over. Ringlets of blood ran along my arms as I reached to her, pain ripping through my shoulder as I tried to flip her over. I leant across and held her hand.

I could see her injuries in my mind's eye, but it was too late. She was too far gone.

A woman came down and helped me up the hill while speaking to emergency services. I sat on the ground, pulled Miss B from the cat carrier and held her against my chest. I closed my eyes, feeling both heavier and lighter at the same time.

Shards of broken glass had lacerated my face and arms, and I'd cracked my skull and snapped my collarbone, but I had healed all my torn flesh and broken bones before the paramedics arrived.

~

Life is a miracle.

You beat 300 million sperm to be where you are.

The odds are stacked against you from the get-go.

A single swimmer beating millions of other contenders to the egg to set up shop for nine months if you're lucky.

Then the hard part begins.

In the big scheme of things, I was born then almost died within the same breath.

My head was wrapped in swaths of bandages when E came to visit me in hospital.

'You look like the top of a cotton bud.'

His forehead scrunched as he looked me over properly.

'How are you feeling?'

As I tried to sit up, the blood rushed elsewhere so quickly I almost fainted. 'My head still hurts.'

'It will for a while,' he said.

'I healed most of it.'

E nodded, reached out and caressed my face.

'You did well, you don't want to push it.'

'Mum, she...' I got out before the tears burst. I bent forward, heaving into my sheets.

'I know, I'm sorry, Manny.' E patted my back in an approximation of a hug until I ran dry. When I lifted my face, there were two snail trails running from his eyes. Despite their arguments, he'd obviously cared about her.

A nurse flew in, scanned the machines and ticked off something on my chart.

I took a breath. 'How's Jam, is she okay?'

E waited until the nurse left. 'She's gone.'

My guts twisted like angry snakes. 'It's my fault.'

'No.' He grabbed my shoulders. 'It's not. You were doing what I asked you to. It's an incredible gift, Manny, albeit a dangerous one.'

'Am I in trouble?'

He inhaled and his face tightened. 'You're not in trouble, but you're not mature enough to control your ability yet. I pushed you.'

I grabbed his arm, a bolt of pain shooting through my head. 'I'll practise more.'

He shook me off. 'It's more than that. There are some bad people who will take you away if they find out what you can do. They'll lock you up.'

I'm surprised my eyes didn't explode out of their sockets. 'Don't let them find me, E.'

'That's the plan.'

E escorted me outside and wheeled me around the gardens in a wheelchair. Once we were alone, he paused and knelt to eye level.

'Do you trust me, Manny?'

I did.

'Yes.'

He pulled out a large silver cylinder. 'I need to do this to keep you safe, until I find another way. Okay?'

My imagination ran away as I thought about being thrown into a huge, tiled room, tied down to a table, being poked and prodded by faceless doctors.

'Okay.'

He pressed the end of the cylinder against my neck.

Click.

There was a prick, followed by a bristling sensation on my neck and across my scalp.

I rubbed my neck. 'It's burning.'

'It will for a short while. Let me know when it stops.'

I waited until the sensation passed and let him know. 'What was that?' I asked.

'Now, I'd like to do a little test.' E reached into his coat and withdrew a small white mouse by its tail. Its pink nose and twitching whiskers brought a smile to my face that soon evaporated when he squeezed the mouse so tight it let out a terrible squeak.

He looked around to make sure we were still alone. 'Hold out your hands.'

There was something cold in his eyes that sent a wave of fear through me.

'I don't want to,' I whispered.

He snapped his hand around my wrist. 'Hold out your hands, Manny. I won't ask again.'

Goosebumps raised across my flesh as E eyeballed me. I cupped my trembling hands.

'Good boy,' he said.

He swung the mouse around by its tail; it let out a tiny yelp when he slammed it onto the concrete and smashed its head open.

I flashed to Mum in the ditch. I shut my eyes tight, wishing to be anywhere else.

E dropped the warm, mangled body of the mouse into my hands. Nothing.

I could see its busted skull and mashed brains, but I couldn't heal it. E was rapid-fire tapping his shoe on the ground. He grabbed my chin between his thumb and finger.

'Anything, Manny? What do you see? What do you feel?'

There was no warmth, no light, no healing energy.

My skin prickled hot and a solitary tear ran down my cheek.

'Nothing.'

'You can't see anything like before?'

'I can see it, but I can't fix it,' I blubbered.

I think the slap to my face took us both by surprise, but it had the desired effect. I must have remained in a state of shock because E softened slightly and patted me on the back.

'Sorry Manny, but this is important. What I've injected you with suppresses your ability.'

'Like a special medicine?' I asked.

'Sure, call it that if you like, but this special medicine is experimental. If your healing ability comes back, don't try to heal anyone, or the bad people could come to snatch you. You're going to be staying with your aunt. I've told her to call me as soon as anything strange happens, so you must tell her if it returns, okay?'

I nodded. 'Okay.'

'This means you can no longer heal yourself if you get hurt, and you may get sick sometimes. I'm sorry.' His head snapped up; I followed his gaze. A man in a suit and sunglasses was standing at the other end of the gardens, arms folded.

'Who's that?' I asked.

'Don't worry about it.'

When E spun around and speedily wheeled me back into the hospital suggested it *was* something to worry about.

Back inside, he hugged me. 'I'll come to the funeral but won't be seeing you for a while after.'

E left me in the foyer for a nurse to take me back to my room, then rushed off.

As the nurse wheeled me down the corridor towards my room, I could see E arguing with the man from the garden. E was all flailing arms and pointing fingers before they both disappeared.

I went home to Aunty Sue's place. Miss B was already there. I didn't tell Sue about what E had done to me. She had enough to worry about.

In a double blow, Uncle Joe died while I was in the hospital. Sue was already a withdrawn, hollow shell, not ready to deliver any kind of comfort or love towards me. She remained this way most of the time I lived with her. Seemed as though the joint deaths had broken her spirit and brain. She became a drunken zombie Aunty Sue, straddling life and death, day in, day out.

Though we each grieved in our own way, we shared a common bond and realisation that burrowed deep beneath our skin.

Life is unfair. Deal with it.

SEVEN

I change into my royal blue work scrubs and trek towards the mental health ward in the east wing. The corridors of the hospital labyrinth smell of fresh paint and something acidic.

I give a small salute to a cleaner with ear buds fused to her ears, most likely to drown the sound of clueless visitors as well as her vacuum cleaner. I imagine the night-time cleaning requirements and maintenance of the hospital floors and walls is never-ending. Once the last square metre is cleaned, it's time to start over again, like painting the Sydney Harbour Bridge.

The mental health ward isn't as exciting as I'd first imagined, and twice as depressing. There are no happy stories to put a smile on your face or a kick in your step. Most patients are victims of drug or alcohol abuse, sexual or mental abuse, self-harm, suicides or dementia.

A young girl and I sit in rounded plastic chairs in the ward's lacklustre library.

It's a special shift.

My only job is to make sure she doesn't remove the bandages wrapped around her wrists and rip out the stitches.

'Suicide is an interesting concept,' she says, 'because you have to plan for it, you have to really want it. I guess I didn't *really* want it, and I'm not much of a planner.'

'I don't know what to say.'

She laughs. 'You don't need to be uncomfortable. It's just my experience.'

I shrug. 'Didn't want to say the wrong thing.'

She pats me on the knee, then pulls back like she's touched a hot stove. Physical contact is prohibited. The only hugs allowed in the mental health ward are those courtesy of the cold embrace of a large range of sedatives and anti-psychotic medications.

'Sorry,' she says.

'It's fine,' I smile reassuringly. I nod at her bandaged wrists. 'How did this start?'

She stares at the wall. Her jackhammering leg stops.

'You know what? That's the first time someone's asked me how it started, instead of what caused the latest "incident",' she air quotes. 'Shit, I hate it when people air quote.' She sighs. 'A million apologies good sir.'

I remove an invisible hat and bow my head. 'No apologies needed.'

She clicks her tongue. 'I think it started when I felt like oncoming cars sped up every time I crossed the road. At first, I thought it was confirmation bias or something, but it was real. You know the set of traffic lights at the end of the Story Bridge, where it splits either towards the city or straight ahead into the Valley?'

I nodded. 'Yeah.'

'I started experimenting. I'd cross over there as people reached the end of the bridge, and nine times out of ten, they'd speed up. Not enough where I was in danger of getting hit, but close enough to rattle me. It's like they enjoyed the rush of feeling close to killing someone, without actually going through with it.'

She breathes in and lets out a huge gush of air. 'It got me thinking. I don't think it matters what actions humanity takes, we're only speeding up or slowing down the cold, hard reality. We're all kaput. So, I began playing chicken on the highway.'

We both stare at the ceiling at a cockroach that shouldn't be there.

'It progressed?' I ask.

She fiddles with her bandage. 'I suppose it works both ways, being close to death. I began to enjoy the thought of being run over. I'd run across, leaving it as late as I could. Got winged once, but no real harm done. I stopped for a little while after, but then I spiralled and became obsessed with mortality and dying and society collapsing and all the bad things. I felt like I was taking up too much oxygen, and the nutrients of my remains would be more beneficial to sustaining the earth.'

She shudders. 'I'm being morbid, let's talk about something else. Pick a topic.'

My mind blanked. 'Uh, the guy at the front desk. His name's Nigel.'

'Is he a Nigel-no-friends?'

'Nah,' I say. 'He's happy as. Gets on well with everyone.'

She rubs her chin in classic thinker pose. 'Do you think it's authentic, or do you think he's had a lifetime of self-imposed pressure not to live up to society's expectation of Nigels?'

It takes a moment for me to process. 'I guess the first "Nigel-no-friends" forced all future Nigels to be extra gregarious.'

'Probably like being named Karen and not being able to be a bitch.'

'Yeah, rough.'

She yawns, it's contagious. 'I'm tired now, can you walk me back to my room?'

We leave the library and walk the corridors past zonked-out patients shuffling past.

'You know, despite all this,' she gestures around, 'all the support, infrastructure and programs, we're really all alone.'

'There's always hope,' I offer.

She laughs. 'I feel like trying to find hope in a crazy house is like looking for a needle in the ocean.'

~

It's curfew time in the mental health ward. Due to the collective consumption of depressants, the hollow-eyed, emaciated patients wander the halls to their rooms without fuss. They shuffle softly and talk quietly to themselves, grasping their IV poles for support as they return to their rooms. It reminds me of zombies returning to the grave before sunup.

Once it's lights out, I open the escape door and wedge it open with the wood block sitting against the wall.

He's waiting outside when I exit – the man in the trench coat. Goose bumps surface as he disappears around the corner. No, there's nothing. It must be the mental health ward making me paranoid.

I shake it off and walk towards the garden and a huge Moreton Bay Fig, bathed in moonlight. Near the base of the tree is the silhouette of a young woman. She's perched on one of the benches, the fluorescent purple tip of a vaping device floats around her head. She's wearing a white hospital gown.

She takes a drag and exhales a large cloud of blueberry-smelling steam.

As I approach, I make as much noise as possible, so I don't scare her, then gesture to the spot next to her.

'Hi, do you mind?' I ask.

Her gaze remains locked to the tree trunk. She tenses up. 'You here to drag me inside?'

I shake my head and pull out a packet of cigarettes. 'Nope.'

She relaxes. 'Then sure, knock yourself out.'

There's a slight breeze, the type people generally comment on how pleasant it is.

'I'm Manny,' I say.

'Hi, Manny.' She switches the vape and offers her hand. 'I'm Mila.'

My hand somehow feels rough and unsophisticated when combined with her soft skin and slender fingers. I pull out a tiny, pink lighter and spark it up. 'What are you doing out here?'

She raises the sleeve of her gown and shows me her bandaged wrist. Another one.

I try not to react, probably fail.

'It's not what you think,' she says. 'There was a 2AM fire alarm at my apartment complex last night, or this morning, I guess. I was racing around trying to put Poe in her box and collect her stuff.'

'Poe?'

'My cat.'

Mila takes a hit of the vape and blows another plume of blueberry into the night air.

'I was still half asleep when I grabbed her water bowl from the dishwasher. I must have left a knife standing sharp side up in the cutlery basket. It drove in far enough to touch bone. I only realised when I saw the blood dripping onto the tiles.'

I can't think of anything clever, so blurt out, 'You're meant to lay those sharp knives pointy end down.'

She laughs. 'Thanks, I'll remember next time there's a late-night fire alarm. Anyway, I lost a lot of blood.'

'You *do* look a little pale.'

The corners of her mouth raise. 'Nah, I'm always like this. Just my complexion.' She shrugs and takes another drag of her vape. 'I was sick a lot as a kid.'

I take a large drag of my cigarette. 'I didn't mean it in a bad way. It's like porcelain.'

I hope it doesn't sound creepy.

She holds her vape like a regular pen and draws in the air with invisible ink. 'Dear diary, today I was hit on by a cute orderly outside the nut house.'

'Mental health ward is the PC version,' I say.

'A funny farm by any other name...'

Two geckos race around the tree trunk. I take a final drag, then squash the cigarette under my heel, put it in the bin, and reverse the subject. 'That's a crazy story, no pun intended.'

73

'The paramedics didn't believe me either,' she shrugs. 'That's why I'm here.'

Mila stands and moves to the tree, placing her hand on its trunk. One of the geckos climbs onto her hand and runs up her arm, then back to the tree to join its friend.

It's like an animal magic trick, but she acts like it was nothing. She turns to me. 'Dad explained my condition, and they said I could leave tomorrow. So that's something.'

'What's your…'

'Hey!' a large, angry nurse bellows from the fire door. 'You're not allowed out here.'

The nurse stomps over to chastise me, escorts Mila inside by the elbow.

'See ya, Manny,' she says.

'Nice to meet you, Mila.'

The angry nurse gives me a final scowl before disappearing with Mila into the ward.

I kick the block aside and shut the door. Cicadas and crickets chirp the soundtrack as I walk through the hospital gardens towards the night bus.

EIGHT

IT'S immediately obvious the lady is a hoarder.

I'm back on gopher patrol with the paramedics. We're outside a mansion in Golden Lakes, a gated community with semi-resort type living for rich baby boomers. The enormous solid oak door is unlocked, and we follow the serpentine path through a valley of junk. The mountains on either side are made of luxury designer wear, shoes, jewellery boxes and, for some reason, stuffed animals.

It's worse than Sue's place, which seems almost minimalist compared with this.

The sound comes from a room down the hall; soft, like a small cat with a sore throat. We walk towards it. A chemical potpourri grows as we pass a pyramid of fragrance products and emerge into a room that could double as a rubbish tip. I scan the room and move towards a scraping sound, which is followed by small movements in the corner. A tiny voice is barely audible, muffled by hundreds of faded fashion magazines, stuffed bears, ornaments and clothes. It's like a giant has tripped and fallen inside a department store and knocked all the shelves over.

A small hand with long pink nails attached to a bone-thin arm flails about. We rush over. Her lips and face are filled with so much age-reversing poison it looks like she's been stung by a swarm of bees. It's all rejuvenating plastic surgery, gone too far. She's struggling to breathe under the weight of her gigantic breasts, and she's trapped under a huge shoe rack. The three of us sift through the junk to make a safe space, then strain as we pull the shoe rack off her.

Thankfully, she's okay, or at least she will be.

We move onto the next job and the next one and the next one.

Another day faced with so many sick people who I can't help.

It's like attending an orgy at the Playboy Mansion and discovering I'm impotent.

When I get to my car afterwards, there's another parking ticket on the windscreen. The whole day's work, a waste.

I sit on the couch and watch *Best of the 80s Video Jukebox*. Elvis eats crackers dumped in mustard pickles, alternately swigging his beer, and smoking a giant Buddha bong.

'The 80s was the time to be a saxophonist,' he says. 'They would've been knocking back tail 24/7.'

Cotton wool clouds my brain. Fearing I've had a stroke, I smile and touch the sides of my mouth. I'm fine, I think. I shuffle to my room, where sleep comes swift and deep.

~

I rub the sleep from my eyes as I drink the rest of the juice from the carton. Fridge magnets clatter to the floor when I slam the door too hard. As I stick them to the fridge, I read the general guide on house respect, seldom followed:

Avoid these common house issues which birth latent hostility:
Drinking all the milk or leaving less than a glass worth in the bottle.
Spooning peanut butter directly from the jar.
Leaving toast crumbs in Vegemite jar.
Leaving fans and lights on.
Half omelette left in cold, dirty water.
Finishing off the whisky.
Leaving clothes in the washing machine.
Not cleaning up spilt sugar, encouraging kamikaze ants to live in the coffee filter.

There's a separate note at the bottom:

HOUSE INSPECTION NEXT WEEK!!!

Next week is today. 'Elvis!'

'What?' he yells from the lounge room.

'House inspection today.'

'Again?'

'Yeah again.'

'Remember to cover up the bullet hole with one of your paintings.'

We make the house look respectable, and the agent clears us for a few months.

Elvis suggests we get a drink to celebrate our successful house inspection. He doesn't have to twist my arm.

Soon, we're in a dank hipster joint sitting on barstools, backs to the grimy window and reality. The pub's red lighting and hobo décor strive for shabby chic, but I can only confirm the shabby part.

An old John Lee Hooker song I've never heard plays over invisible speakers, or it could be phantom blues playing in my mind. We're on our second bowl of buffalo wings and fifth bourbon in tandem with a sizeable never-ending jug of beer. Time slips.

Elvis goes to light a cigarette, with another reminder from the moustached, suspender-wearing bartender we're sitting in a smoke-free zone. The tension between him and Elvis increases with every drink.

I give the bartender a reassuring wink, though he may think I'm coming on to him. He takes a tray of glasses into the kitchen. Elvis places the half-empty jug of beer under the Dark Moon beer tap in front of us and flicks it on, filling it to the top. He drinks it to its previous level, spilling half of it down his front. He wipes the foam off his face with his shirt sleeve right before the bartender re-enters the scene.

I sit and stare at my reflection in the bar mirror between the bottles of whisky. I can only focus with one eye open. Elvis eats peanuts. I forget what I've been talking to him about, something reassuring, I think. I shake my head. My memory spins into gear. I was talking about the bartender.

'Maybe he's had a bad day, or he doesn't like his job.'

'He's a bartender,' Elvis says. 'It's pretty simple. Don't be a prick if you want to work in the customer service industry. If you don't like it, get another one. There's a jobs crisis, and a thousand slick haired, tight jeaned, bearded knobs who'd cut off a heavily tattooed finger to work in this dump.'

I finish my bourbon. Elvis slaps a $100 bill on the bar and signals for two more. The bartender looks unsure, glancing from the note to Elvis and back, eventually shrugging, and free pouring a couple of bourbons, expertly bouncing the ice off his bicep and directly into the glasses.

I nod approvingly towards Elvis. 'Pretty impressive, right?'

'Big deal,' he mutters.

Elvis checks his phone and springs from his chair, which clatters to the floor.

'I've gotta go to work.'

'Now?' I ask.

'Admissions system emergency.'

Sounds like bullshit. It's late, maybe a few ICU cases, but nothing that couldn't wait until tomorrow. I shrug it off. He grabs a cab; I walk home. The air is cool, the sky is clear.

One of those nights I feel everything might be alright.

~

My first thought upon waking is Aunty Sue and her apocalypse bunker. I call to no answer, text to no response. I drive, not sure whether it's guilt or genuine concern that finds me winding down the roads towards her house. I see the mountain of dirt before I've even reached her gate. She's been busy, and now there's a giant satellite dish, made of what looks like aluminium foil, perched on the roof. It looks more like an outsider art installation than an interstellar communication device, but I guess if she isn't hurting anyone, then it's alright.

Scraps barks with joy and rushes over as soon as I enter the yard and rolls over so I can scratch his tummy. His ribs are poking through. Sue is focused and dirty.

'Hey, Sue.'

She takes a few moments to recognise me before stumbling over.

'Hey, how are you?' she asks, like she's still not certain who I am.

'Fine,' I say. 'Seems like you've been busy around here.'

A light goes on in her eyes. 'I've been working at a cracking pace, love.'

'Scraps is looking a little lean, you been feeding him enough?'

She waves her hands dismissively. 'So, he's skipped a few meals. Like you said, we've been busy. And it's good for him to practise intermittent fasting. You can feed him if you want.'

My eyes move towards the shed. 'What are all those?'

'Milk bottles,' she slurs. She's drunk, or high, maybe both.

'I know what they are, but there must be hundreds of them.

'842 to be exact, so far. Enough water to last four people for 280 days. By that time, the battle will be over, and God will have intervened and smote the invaders.'

I scan the yard. 'The dirt mountain is getting out of control. What's going on?'

'I'm extending the bunker. I have no power right now. I had to reroute the lines, but we can cook some canned braised steak and rehydrate some vegetables on the portable gas stove.'

'Is that safe?'

'They're not market fresh,' she says, 'but they're palatable.'

'I meant the power. Is that safe?'

Her hands move manically, scratching her arms and head. 'Oh yes, fine. I didn't do it all myself. A man from our group is an electrician and he's taking care of it. He's coming tomorrow to finish it off. Want dinner?' she asks.

'It's morning.'

'Breakfast then?'

Every fibre of my being wants to leave immediately.

'Sure,' I nod, 'for a bit, but I can't stay for long.'

The longer I'm there, the less manic she appears, and the canned steak doesn't taste too bad, sort of like good plane food. Maybe I should put her in a home, though I doubt she'd let me.

'Have I shown you the booby traps yet?' Sue asks.

I swallow another mouthful of canned steak and preserved yams. Breakfast of champions, prepper edition. 'Booby traps?'

She uses the kitchen table to stand, then staggers off. I follow her outside, leaving the rest of my breakfast yams behind. She waves her open palm across the yard, showcasing the booby traps like a proud mother.

'This one is the Impaler, this is the Crusher.'

I sigh. 'Just be careful, okay.'

'You're the one who should be careful,' Sue says. 'You nearly walked into the Mangler. It's the silver one next to the front gate. That will show the debt collectors too.'

I hope she's joking.

'Debt collectors, what do they want?'

'Everything, but I won't let them dear, don't worry, I've still got 60 days to pay them.'

'How much?' I ask.

'Nothing significant, forty grand or so.'

'Forty grand? Where are you getting that kind of money?'

'Don't worry, I have a plan, but I can't tell you yet. I'm hiring a storage locker. Now finish your yams.'

I need to leave. I wrap her in a hug. She's all bones and loose skin.

'I'll come and visit again tomorrow, okay?'

'Okay darl, drive safe.'

I call Damascus Health Services from the car and book her in for rehab.

They have no spaces until Wednesday. I hope she makes it until then.

I spend the day at home watching movies; it's all I can afford to do.

There's no sign of Elvis, and he's still not back by the time I go to bed.

~

The sun-drenched dirt pile dwarfing Sue's house is so captivating, at first I don't notice the shiny black sedan parked out the front. I can't imagine a scenario where a visitor to Sue's place isn't bad news. I turn my car around and park out of sight, approaching on foot. I peek over the gate. Scraps isn't barking and licking me to death, which means he's inside with Sue and her visitor.

I quietly open the gate, navigate the dirt mounds, equipment and booby traps, and sneak around to the laundry at the side of the house. Sue and her guest are in the kitchen, and I have a good view from the laundry's casement window.

It's an old guy. White hair, sensible clothes, looks about eighty or so.

Sue is sifting through the boxes lining the benches and finds two clean mugs, then drops a tea bag in each one. She stares at the old man sitting at her kitchen table, then opens several cupboards until she finds a box of pills and dry swallows a handful of them.

The kettle clicks. She pours the tea and places one of them in front of the old man, indicates for him to continue.

'We lost all our research in the fire,' he says, 'and I've been working for twenty years trying to replicate the formula. I'm so close.'

The realisation hits. The math doesn't work, but I know the old man in the kitchen.

It's E.

'Why Manny?' Sue asks.

'Manny is the key.'

Sue rolls her eyes. 'Super healing.'

E nods. 'The concept is that it significantly boosts the immune system, rendering many elements of traditional medicine obsolete.'

Sue's face scrunches tight. 'I know what you did, experimenting on all those babies. You're worse than the Nazis.'

'It was worth it,' E says. 'Manny was the end-product, the great hope for us all. Imagine, no more sickness, no more death.'

Sue shakes her head. 'So, what happened?'

'The formula we developed caused a mass to form in the middle of the subjects' brains. It was unstable. We called it a head grenade, because it ruptured and exploded in every single patient bar one. We dubbed them Kid A.'

'Manny,' Sue says.

I hear the words, but they don't sink in.

'I tested him the other day, like you asked me,' Sue says, 'but he still can't heal.'

'Yes, but only because it's dormant. The accident may have affected the mass in his brain, but beside the point.'

He's lying. I only lost my healing ability because he injected me after the accident, like I told Elvis. E continues. 'When it ruptured in our test subjects…'

Sue and E both turn towards the sound of Scraps barking, but I duck before I'm seen.

'Shut up,' I whisper as I pat Scraps, attempting to calm him. I pick him up and rub his head, so I don't miss anything.

'What happened to these other test subjects?' Sue asks.

E sips his tea. 'They perished. Every single one.'

Sue rests the cup on the table, her hands shaking. It looks like it takes every bit of her strength not to throw the scalding water into his face. 'So why didn't Manny die in the accident then?'

'Because he could also heal himself as well as others. The kid's a freak.'

'You're a monster.'

'No, I'm a scientist.'

'But you're not God, and you've got no right,' she says, rising to pour the remains of a bottle of liquor into another dirty glass.

'No right?' E says. 'He wouldn't be here without me. They would've taken him.'

Sue uses the table to get to her feet to go through her cutlery drawers, plucks out a soft pack of Peter Stuyvesants hidden for an emergency. She flicks the bottom of the pack until a lone, bent cigarette pops up and lights it with trembling fingers, takes a long drag.

'Isn't this nice?' E says. 'Tea and me. Like an old married couple.'

'You're despicable.'

'You didn't think so, once upon a time.'

Sue reaches over to slap him, but he ducks it. She takes a hard drag and blows out an angry cloud of smoke. 'I've got work to do. Goodbye E.'

'Don't we all?' says E. 'Thanks for the tea.' He begins to walk away before spinning back. 'If you'd like to see the progress, come by anytime.' He takes a purple key out of his pocket and leaves it on the dining room table.

Sue picks it up and tosses it at him. It clatters on the floor. She claws her fingers through her hair as she watches E leave. I stand on the spot until she comes in and searches through the cupboards. I consider going to talk with her, until I see her talons clasp a bottle of vodka and pour half of it into a pint glass. Though I feel like a coward and shame floods me, I navigate the booby traps and walk off.

~

A family of ducks delays the ferry to work, but I arrive on time. The orderlies are lazing around the office. I draw the short straw and get the job to restock all the linen in the wards and find all the missing wheelchairs. It takes all morning.

Afterwards, I limp out of the hospital towards the ferry terminal.

83

I've barely conjured up my soft bed when a voice breaks me from my daydream.

'Manny! Wait up!'

Running down the hill, the man reminds me of those super slow-motion videos of the fat guy getting shot in the stomach with a cannonball. He's one of the nurses from emergency. He's beetroot-red and breathless.

'Glad I found you.' He takes a few moments to catch his wind. 'The boys. In the office. Said you'd left.'

'What's up?'

'It's your aunt.'

My stomach lurches. 'What about her?'

He bends forward and rests his hands on his knees, then goes into a coughing fit. I pound him on the back. He takes a huge gulp of air and rubs his face. 'She's here. She's in here, I mean. They found her passed out in her driveway. She's in ICU. Had this note in her hand. It's for you.'

I grab the note. The guilt rocks me. I should've helped earlier.

'I'll come back up and see her,' I say. 'Thanks for chasing me.'

I walk back to the hospital to find Sue's attending doctor.

Another year, another cry for help. It's the anniversary that always gets her. I totally forgot about it.

The doctor tells me a passing cyclist called an ambulance after finding Sue sprawled unconscious on the road next to a half-full vodka bottle. She'd walked up to the letterbox to leave me a note and managed to vomit, pass out and roll down her driveway. The paramedics found her, clutching a floral overnight bag with Scraps passed out next to her. He'd lapped up a tiny amount of whatever cocktail she'd consumed and couldn't handle his drugs or booze either. Fortunately, one of the paramedics took Scraps to the vet.

I'll have to remember to write them a thank you note.

I wander up to ICU and find Sue's bed. She's next to the obese patient from last week, who's in a reinforced bed, snoring into his oxygen mask like a drunk buffalo. I try to decipher her unsent suicide letter. It's an incoherent warble, but the words 'ALIENS' and 'RAPTURE' are underlined in bold red.

They've already pumped Sue's stomach. She's semi-responsive, but she won't wake up for a few hours or maybe even until tomorrow.

I take her hand in mine and look inside. She'll be okay, though the black ball in her brain isn't going away anytime soon. If only I could fix her.

The receptionist gives me the room number Sue will be staying in once the ICU clears her. I pick up her overnight bag from next to her bed and take it to her room on level three: the rehab clinic. They know her well.

I drop off her bag, roll a cigarette and head to the ferry again. I just miss one, but I'm in no rush.

My heart rate slows, I stare out across the water. The sunset burns the sky, sending it a brilliant pink. The scattered clouds look like fairy floss.

The ringing phone jolts me from the clouds. Unknown number.

'Hi, Manny, this is Doctor Barnes. We spoke earlier.'

'Is she okay?' I ask. 'It's not the first time she's done this.'

'She's as well as she can be, considering. Quite dopey still.' He clears his throat. 'There's been a somewhat troubling development. She told me she'd only had a few glasses of vodka, but I'm looking at her tox screen here and it shows considerable levels of propofol in her system.'

'The stuff that killed Michael Jackson?'

'Well, yes if you know that, you're probably also aware its primary function is for general anaesthesia. In fact, we use it here.'

My stomach drops. I don't like where this is going.

'Manny, I've got a representative from HR here to observe the call, is that okay?'

I nod.

'Manny, are you there?'

My brain feels like it's been dipped in molasses.

'Yeah, I'm here, sorry.'

He clears his throat. 'I'm being careful with my words here, and I'm not accusing you of anything, but have you had any shifts in the operating theatre over the past six months?'

I shut my eyes and think. 'Not specifically OT, just pre-op drop-offs from day surgery and post-op pickups for the wards.'

'One second.'

There's silence on the other line. My mind is scattershot. His voice returns.

'So, you potentially had access to the theatre drug cupboard.'

It's not a question.

This is bullshit.

'No. I wheeled patients around, dropped them off and picked them up, that's it. You're falsely accusing me and I'm not liking it.'

Another voice comes on the line, a woman's voice.

'Manny, we're not accusing you, but we need to rule out all scenarios. Your aunty has been given a powerful anaesthetic that shouldn't be used outside of an operating theatre. We need to crosscheck the theatre stock with the records, and we're sure it'll all check out. You can have some time off while we sort this out, and we'll get back to you as soon as we can. In the meantime, we'll have to request you stay off hospital grounds. Once your aunt comes around, she can hopefully shed some light on the situation, because we do need to find out how this happened. Sorry about all this.'

I hang up, skip the next few CityCats while I sit and process and smoke.

Hours later, the moon shimmers on the water, forming its own cliché, diamonds or busted glass or whatever. I draw the smoke deep into my lungs and release a cloud of grey smoke with silver-lined edges.

My mind's reeling, but the trip home is uneventful and familiar, as is the sight of Elvis on the couch when I walk in the door.

A newly painted canvas sits on the easel in the lounge room. Like Picasso double dropped, candy flipped and painted a masterpiece. This is a work of art. This is worth something. It deserves to be displayed in one of the world's premier galleries.

Instead, it's next to a pile of pizza boxes, beer bottles and a bucket bong. It's position amongst the junk only makes its appearance more surreal. An incredible work, though I do not vocalise this to Elvis. Instead, I tell him about the vodka and propofol and banishment.

'Where's the vodka now?' he asks.

'What do you mean?'

'I mean, maybe your aunt was telling the truth. Maybe she thought she *was* only drinking vodka, but someone had laced it or something. The bottle's probably still at her place.'

His words hit me so hard I jolt. I pull out my phone and call Sue. It goes to message bank, so I try again. This time she answers, still dopey.

'Is someone dead?' she drawls.

I switch on the speakerphone. 'Sue, it's important.'

'Hold on,' she says, 'let me turn on the light, I hear better when it's light.'

Elvis rolls his eyes.

'Okay,' she says, 'what's so important?'

'How did you get the propofol?'

'I don't know what you just said. I don't even know why I'm here.'

She's either lost her short-term memory or she's telling the truth.

'It's the Michael Jackson drug,' I say. 'That's why you're there. It's for surgery; only doctors can prescribe it.'

'I don't know any doctors,' she says. 'The only one who even comes close is...' Sue pauses.

Elvis and I look at each other and say in tandem, 'E.'

Silence on the other end.

'Sue, I know he visited you this morning.'

Her voice breaks. 'No, no I don't think so. I don't remember.'

'I was there, Sue.'

'Don't remember that either.'

'That's because I saw you drinking booze at nine in the morning.'

'Manny, there's something…'

'Hang on a second,' I say. 'This is important. Did you have anything else besides vodka, any pills, food, anything at all?'

There's nothing for a few seconds.

'A can of beans. That's all.'

Elvis whispers. 'In the vodka for sure.'

I nod. 'Rest up and take it easy, Sue,' I say, then hang up, snatch my keys from the table. 'Let's go.' We jump in the car. Elvis's face scrunches up.

'Still can't get the stank out, hey?' He winds down his window; I do the same.

'Man, I've emptied so much Febreze in here, it's part of the car now.'

I knock the wheely bin over as I'm reversing out the driveway – lucky it's empty. I put it right ways, get back in and drive to Sue's. A random burst of fireworks lights the sky over the parklands as we drive along the Inner City Bypass.

We pull into Sue's driveway, the mountain of dirt like a great sleeping giant.

Resting against the fence, in front of the headlights like an escaping criminal in the searchlights, is the vodka bottle.

Elvis jumps out and picks up the bottle, unscrews the lid as he's walking back, sticks his nose in the opening. 'Smells like plain old vodka to me.'

'It would. Propofol is odourless; I checked. It's a different vodka brand to the one I saw her drinking this morning too. She'd already downed a bottle before any of this.'

Elvis holds the bottle up like he's trying to catch the moonlight. 'Doesn't look any different either. Only one way to find out,' he says, bringing the bottle to his lips before I knock it away, spilling some on our arms.

'You're bloody joking, right? You could kill yourself. I'm going to bring this back to the hospital for testing.'

Elvis screws the cap back on. 'I thought you weren't allowed on campus. I'll drop it off for you. No worries, man.'

When I shoulder check before leaving, there's a white transit van with blacked out windows parked up the street. 'Was that van there when we got here?'

'Dunno,' Elvis says. 'I was focused on dirt mountain here.'

'Seems strange is all. That tinting is intense.'

'Probably just a couple of kids smoking up a Dutch oven.'

I reverse out of the driveway and nail it for the hospital. Elvis plays around on his phone. I pull into a primo spot at the hospital entrance, then scrounge around in the backseat.

'What are you doing?' Elvis asks.

'You can't walk in the front doors with a half full bottle of vodka.' I grab a scrunched-up shopping bag from under the passenger seat, 'Chuck it in there.'

I switch to Triple M on the radio. Surprise, they're playing Cold Chisel. Halfway through *Breakfast at Sweethearts,* a white van with blacked out windows catches my eye. It's parked on the street. It could be confirmation bias, and I can't swear it's the same one I saw at Sue's earlier, but goosebumps traverse my arms just the same.

Cold Chisel gives way to The Angels gives way to Aerosmith gives way to Red Hot Chili Peppers gives way to Men at Work. Pretty sure I could program their playlist no sweat.

Elvis finally returns, rips open the door and chucks the empty plastic bag in the back.

'Dropped it off, all gee. Told them to give it to Doctor Barnes, and they seemed confused at first, but I explained how you've been accused of stealing from the drug cupboard so it's important.'

'Geez, tell everyone why don't you.'

Elvis shrugs.

'What took you so long?' I ask.

He cocks his head to the van. 'I was watching that suspicious van, waiting for a couple of government heavies to jump out and abduct you. If they wanted to, they would've taken you by now. Don't worry, I snuck around the side and took down the license plate.'

I'm unsure whether he's joking or not. When he doesn't smile or snigger, I assume he's being serious.

'If it *is* the government,' he says, 'who you gonna call?'

Then he does smile. 'Probably a coincidence, man. You keep being this paranoid you'll end up in Bat Wing,' he says, using the politically incorrect moniker for the mental health ward. Bats in the belfry, batty, batshit crazy. Choose your bat-phrase.

Elvis opens the glovebox and pulls out the pack of rollies. 'What's the bet they'll follow?' he asks, deftly rolling me a cigarette before rolling one for himself. 'If they do,' he says, 'you're staying up with me to take acid and watch *The Dark Side of the Rainbow,* the version combining *Dark Side of the Moon* and *The Wizard of Oz* where they sync up.

'What if they don't?'

'Don't sync up? They will. Combining any two unrelated movie and musical works is bound to create a matching audio-visual amalgam.'

'No,' I say, 'what if they don't follow us? The van guys.'

'You can go to bed early.'

'Deal.'

We peal out of the park and sit idling at the exit, the van directly across the road.

'Flash your high beams,' Elvis says.

I do, but I can't see anything through those windows. 'Now they know we're onto them,' he says.

We pull out of the carpark and down the hill, both sneaking glances in the rear-view mirror. Still in the habit of not lighting up on hospital grounds, I forget about the cigarette dangling from my lips until Elvis reaches across and sparks it up.

When we reach the traffic lights at the bottom of the hill, the van isn't behind us. I turn right onto Coronation Drive towards Toowong instead of left towards home, curious whether the van will follow. Nothing so far as we pass the Regatta AKA the Great Gatsby AKA the F. Scott Fitzgerald. At the next set of lights on the left, there's a huge building that used to be student accommodation, now a hotel for drug addicts and homeless people. And on the right is the Royal Exchange, the RE, the heritage listed home of dirt-cheap alcohol student nights, one-night stands and cover bands.

I pull an illegal U-bolt at the lights back towards the city, and there it is in the opposite lane, the white van.

'Shit man, what do we do?' I say, tossing the cigarette out the window, watching it in the side mirror as it flickers and sparks in our wake. We round the bend and I floor it, racing along the Brisbane River, now a black, sparkling snake.

We don't get lucky. A speedy getaway is redundant with so many sets of traffic lights. The van stops two cars behind us, blacked out windscreen making it look like a dangerous, one-eyed insect.

Elvis takes a drag of his cigarette, blows a huge cloud from the corner of his mouth. 'We could try a little off-roading through the park at the back of the Piney, then rally around the backstreets.'

It's a bad idea, but I can't think of a better one.

I jam down the accelerator as the light goes green, speeding along the Inner City Bypass towards Kangaroo Point.

We take the exit. The lights of the Gabba, a beacon for sports tragics, pulls us closer.

Approaching the traffic lights at the corner of the stadium, I pray they stay green.

'If I time this right, I'll be able to floor it up Main Street, then we'll cut across the park behind the Pineapple.'

'I've never seen a kangaroo in Kangaroo Point,' Elvis says.

'Are you even listening?'

'Yeah, yeah, just trying to ease the tension.'

I slow right down before the traffic lights. The person in the car behind leans into their horn.

Elvis yells out the window. 'Sorry mate, gumment's on our tail.'

Green to amber. My signal.

I slam the accelerator and the car shoots forward, tires screeching as we hook around to the left and up Main Street.

Elvis looks back towards the traffic lights. 'They're stuck there! Nice one.'

I confirm in the rearview mirror.

'If we can get the next set and swing into the park, we're golden.'

We fly up Main Street, green lights all the way.

I charge into the right lane, adrenaline everywhere. 'I bet there used to be heaps here, but they probably cleared them out to build houses.'

'What?'

'Kangaroos.'

The park is a huge rectangle. The Pineapple Hotel at one end, our street is connected to the street leading out on one side. Unfortunately, it's on the other side.

'Dammit, those bloody wooden post things.'

'Probably to help stop fugitives evading capture,' Elvis says.

'Not funny. Hold on.' I reverse, then drive the car up and onto the footpath. The car fits through the narrow gap into the park.

Elvis spins around in his seat. 'They're behind us, man.'

The rear of the car slides out as the wheels spin in the dewy grass, but finally catch, and we race across the park.

'They'll never fit through that gap in that big arse van,' Elvis says.

I nod, focus on the other side of the park and the huge chain blocking the exit.

Elvis must see it too, because he says, 'Ram it.'

Mud and grass spray like dirty confetti behind us.

The chain looks big enough to tie down King Kong, but my foot stays down as we narrow the gap. The front of the car crumples as it contacts the chain, but we've got enough velocity to rip the chain's attached metal posts out of the ground as we burst into the street.

There's a cacophonous noise as the posts slide along the street, sparks flying in our wake, and we run into a street sign. The car stalls and there is almost total silence aside from the hissing of the radiator.

'You okay?' I ask.

Elvis pats himself. 'Yup.'

Steam pours from the bent bonnet as I crank the ignition. It splutters to life for a moment. I park the best I can before it conks out.

'Abandon vehicle,' Elvis coughs.

We're on the corner. To the right, three streets down, our place. Headlights round the corner at the end of the other street: the van.

We bolt down towards home. As we turn into our street, the van rounds the corner where the smashed-up car sits. We leap the fence of the closest house and hide behind the bushes right before the van comes around the corner and slowly prowls the street. We wait in silence for a few minutes, only broken by the sound of Elvis sparking another cigarette.

The garden lights up and we stand up from the bushes as a little old lady bursts out her front door with a rolling pin.

'What are you two hooligans doing in my yard?'

'Hiding from the government,' Elvis says.

'Well hide somewhere else from the bastards.'

'Sorry,' we both say, and leap the fence towards home.

'Well, that's about enough excitement for tonight,' I say. 'I'm going to shower, then bed.'

Elvis stops and grabs my arm. 'Sure, you can have a shower. Cleanliness next to godliness or whatever. But we had a deal, remember?'

~

We chew on tabs of Bart Simpson acid, before watching *Dark Side of the Rainbow*. Some sections work, but I'm not convinced of any synchromysticism. It works the same for Radiohead and Charlie Brown, or Fantômas and SpongeBob SquarePants.

Hours later, still wide awake and buzzing like a hummingbird, my mind zips down the yellow brick road. I consider a walk along the potholed tar one. Elvis declines an invitation and instead goes to bed, or at least pretends to. He makes a phone call on my way out.

Once I reach the park – the one we haven't recently disfigured – I wander aimlessly, eventually arriving at the swing set. Swings aren't as much fun in your late twenties when you're by yourself, so I sit at a bench by the river.

The world is a lot calmer at night.

A delicate breeze brushes across the water. My nostrils fill with the rich scent of salt and muddy mangroves, my ears with the sound of water softly lapping against the rocks.

I sit entirely still while my body performs the most basic task of breathing. I close my eyes. Only darkness, with occasional flickers of colour, pulsing with intensity. The flicks become kaleidoscopic realms of surrealistic fireworks, then suck into nothingness. How long this continues I'm not sure, for a few seconds or an eternity. I hold the palms of my hands over my temples to prevent my thoughts from spilling onto the grass.

Time slips.

When I lift my head from my hands, she's walking towards me.

An angel with a broken wing, except she's walking a black cat. She smiles as she approaches. It's her, the girl from the psych ward.

I must look like a bug-eyed mess. I sure feel like one. My tongue and lips stumble to form words, but I must say something before it's too late.

'Hey,' I say. Pure genius. At least, the word comes out.

She laughs. It's melodious, the kind of laugh that could cure cancer.

94

'Hi, Manny.'

For some reason I pretend to search my brain's short-term memory drawer for female names starting with M. Truthfully, her name hasn't moved far from the forefront of my mind.

'Mila.'

'That's right.'

'How's the wrist?'

'All good. Will have a gnarly scar though,' she says, showing me the large pink snake with black stitching coiled on her wrist.

I attempt to focus. My vision bursts into kaleidoscopic rainbows.

Her eyes are big, blue and beautiful.

I turn to the purring fuzz ball in front of me. 'So, this is the infamous Poe.'

'She wanted a walk.'

'I didn't know cats went for walks.'

'Poe does.'

I need to fidget, reach for the tobacco pouch in my pocket. I roll a cigarette to calm my nerves, but my fingers fumble and the paper refuses to cooperate.

'Do you come here often?'

The cliché escapes my mouth before I can stop it. I tighten my lips; my teeth are turning into fangs. Mila smiles, no fangs. Good. My jaw and shoulders loosen.

'Yeah, but normally not this late. Couldn't sleep,' she says checking her watch. 'You realise it's 2:37AM?'

My legs turn into rubber and slither over to the river. 'No, I didn't.'

A shooting star streaks across the sky. It's either a sign, or nothing, but we both smile. Mila sits next to me. Her energy fills me with optimism. She looks at the heavens.

'Did you know the atoms in your left hand could be from one exploding star in a faraway galaxy, and the atoms in your right from another?'

95

I hold out my hands, stare at them too long.

'Pretty cool, huh?' she adds.

A spider descends on a glistening thread from the tree above and rests on the bench. I'm hallucinating. Poe leaps onto the bench and nuzzles her head under my hand, purring as I stroke her soft fur.

'Have you read *Charlotte's Web*?' Mila asks.

She must have seen the spider. It's real. Calm floods me.

'In primary school,' I say. 'The cartoon was cool too.'

'It really should have been Charlotte who received accolades for being terrific and radiant, not Wilbur the pig.'

'And humble,' I add.

'Yes, and humble.'

My mouth blurts, 'Can I grab your mobile number?'

She hesitates. 'I've got issues.'

'Don't we all?' I say, finally managing to roll my cigarette.

She traces the scar on her arm. 'I mean, I don't have a phone right now. I use pay phones, so give me yours.'

'Brisbane still has pay phones?'

'A couple, yeah. Universal Service Obligation. They're free.'

'Got a pen?'

'I've got a memory.'

I rattle off my number.

'Bye, Manny,' she says, leaning down to peck me on my forehead, leaving me unsure of how to respond. She disappears along the path with Poe in tow. I stare at the sky, watching the stars explode and dance around. 2:37AM or something, she said. I should go home soon.

Time is elastic.

Brain on fire, I could cook an egg on it if I were hungry.

Mouth an arid cave, I'd love to drink a post-mix anything right now. My feet thankfully return from the river and become normal sized again.

I roll and light another cigarette, forgetting I already have one on the go. I throw the other one into the grass. Sparks fly around like little ant-sized fireworks. I pick it up and extinguish it in the bin.

I glimpse her in the distance one more time, a silhouette in the streetlights.

She disappears and I finish my cigarette.

'Poe. Good name for a black cat.'

Something twigs in my brain, but I can't unravel the thread. I smoke one more cigarette. The world softly brightens and seems like a slightly better place. The walk from the park takes longer than it usually does. Space and time askew. It's not long until the sun will show its bad self, but it's not the end of the world.

I collapse into my bed.

~

I'm sluggish but chipper by the afternoon. Elvis is passed out on the couch, but towards the end of *Back 2 the Future*, he opens one eye when I mention food. I make breakfast fried rice and sautéed Asian green beans. I scoop half the rice from the wok and pack it into two small bowls and turn them upside down onto large white plates. The plates are the last two clean ones in the house, despite the recent house inspection. I arrange the green beans alongside the tiny rice mountains. Then a pinch of sesame seeds and a zigzag drizzle of hoisin sauce across the lot. A meal fit for an emperor.

Elvis grabs the bowl without looking at me and devours it with gusto. 'This is bloody delicious.'

We sit in silence and clean the plates.

'Did you go out last night?' I ask.

'No, why?'

'I heard you on the phone when I left.'

He pauses for a moment. 'Work related.'

'At midnight or whatever?'

'Yep,' he says. 'Good rice. There more?'

I nod. He moves to the kitchen, no doubt hoping I didn't notice the change of subject. I consider prying more but think better of it.

He comes back with more rice. 'Where did you end up last night?'

'The park. Sat by the river and tripped balls for a while, then saw the girl from the hospital, walking a cat.'

'What was she doing walking around at that time of night?'

'Don't know.'

Back to the Future finishes up, so we watch *The Jetsons* while scooping mounds of fried rice into our mouths.

Elvis points at the TV with his chopsticks.

'I wish we had this kind of setup. Poured straight from bed, into a shower and an automatic dressing machine. A robot delivering you breakfast.'

'I delivered your breakfast like a robot.'

'True, thanks. Reminds me, I need a shower, it's been a while.'

I notice the faded red blotches on his left hand. He catches me looking.

'Painting,' he says, peeling himself off the couch and into the bathroom. I keep watching, something niggling at the corners of my mind. The painting easel is in my peripherals. I focus on the current canvas. It's filled with cool colours, not a lick of red. He exits the bathroom, brushing his teeth, a towel wrapped around his head.

'Do you always brush your teeth the same way?' he asks.

We go back to the busted-up car. No police note on it or anything, so we push it back to the front of the house, where it will stay unless I find a couple of grand to fix it.

~

Two bits of good news. Nothing's missing from the drug cupboard at work, so I still have my job. They even apologised for the mix-up. There's still the troubling question of where the propofol originated, but I can't do much about that.

Secondly, Sue lends me her car, so I have wheels now. The traffic lights take forever, as they do in a rush. As I inspect myself in the rear-view mirror, a white, nose hair stares back.

I didn't even know white nose hairs were a thing.

The light turns green. I shake off this disturbing occurrence and accelerate, threading the traffic, ducking and weaving like a prize fighter.

The clouds become static through the windscreen as the city moves into the foreground.

I'm running late, forced to park in the exorbitantly priced visitors' carpark. The hospital may heal the sick and dying but isn't above taking advantage of the bereaved or tardy.

There's a commotion outside the front of the hospital. Several police officers are trying to disperse a large crowd watching what is most likely their first hostage situation.

A stick insect junkie type has a doctor captive. One hand grips her shoulder, the other holds a hypodermic needle to her neck. His thumb rests on the plunger and he's screaming.

The doctor, ever the professional, remains calm, though everyone knows one can only stay cool in a junkie-run hostage situation for so long. The police have their guns raised and are shouting over each other, which only causes the man to become more bug-eyed and nervous. The doctor tells the police officers to drop their guns.

They hesitate for a moment but comply.

She whispers something into the man's ear. He shuts his eyes tight and shakes his head side to side, then softens and releases his grip, bringing the syringe away from her neck. The doctor takes the plunger from his hand, drops it to the ground and kicks it away, then envelopes the man. He bursts into tears and wraps her in a colossal bear hug.

The crowd erupts in applause.

The man is smiling as they cuff him and shove him into the police cruiser. I walk past when one of the officers comes up to the doctor and asks what she said to him.

'I told him I loved him, that everyone here did.'

A feeling of calm seems to permeate the building, and for the rest of the day, the hospital is a tranquil ocean compared with the hostage incident.

When I get home another note is stuck under the mat. I take a deep breath, exhale, and pick it up.

You were meant to be looking after her.
All those secrets hidden under all the garbage.
All she did for you after the accident.
From the past, come the storms.

Elvis is eating pizza and watching *Point Break*, the good one. He shuts it off when he sees the note in my hand.

'What's this one about?'

'Sue. After the accident.'

I begin.

NINE

THERE were two funerals that week. Mum's funeral was a Tuesday, Uncle Joe's a Thursday.

If the number of people at your funeral defines what type of person you were, you'd think my mum was the most gregarious person in the world. Her funeral was attended by hundreds of military personnel I'd never even met.

As we lined up outside the church, dozens of people with short haircuts came up to me and told me how sorry they were, how driven, smart and lovely she was.

E came up and gave me a hug at the end of the funeral and said his goodbyes.

'You will be alright with your aunt for now, Manny.'

'What about you?' I asked. 'What about our experiments?'

He shook his head and looked away.

'We're done, kid, and I've got to stay away for a while. Do you understand?'

I dragged my foot across the concrete.

'Yeah, I understand.'

I didn't.

~

Uncle Joe's was a bit different. If the number of people at your funeral defines what type of person you were, you'd think Uncle Joe was a real arsehole. A grand total of four people attended his service.

It was Sue, me and two fat, tattooed, bearded biker types who must have worked with Uncle Joe. Both drank from hip flasks they kept hidden under their denim vests. I don't know why they bothered hiding it when the preacher seemed uninterested in the whole ordeal. After the service, they drank at the pub across the road, then back at Sue's after she'd driven us all home, drunk.

I watched TV with Miss B snuggled in my lap, while Sue and Uncle Joe's two friends drank his whisky and listened to his Credence Clearwater Revival records on a portable stereo system in the kitchen. I hadn't eaten since breakfast, so I walked into the kitchen to ask if I could eat something for dinner.

Drunk Sue was getting double-teamed over the kitchen bench.

I went to bed hungry. It wasn't the last time.

~

A significant life insurance policy came through after the accident, as did a large Army superannuation pension. Sue, Miss B and I moved into a cavernous mansion along Manly Esplanade.

With the money, came a penchant for gambling. Post financial windfall, she must have blown through a million bucks, and in a couple of years, she had to sell the mansion. A textbook case of easy come, easy go.

Coupled with Sue's gambling was a keen interest in alcohol. Uncle Joe had drunk his whole life, while Sue barely touched the stuff, but his death seemed to be the catalyst for her increased consumption. It was kind of ironic, in the non-ironic Alanis Morissette way.

Sue split from her old aimless self to embrace her new life's purpose as a drinker. The funeral set a dangerous precedent. The day Joe died she must have decided to carry the torch like some surrogate spirit-swilling spirit.

I get it. She probably thought she had nothing left aside from the burden of an orphaned child, so she grabbed a bottle-shaped life preserver.

There may be a less than rose-coloured filter over this time. I'm sure for the most part she looked after me as well as a drunk with severe mental problems and communication issues could. I know on some level it wasn't her fault. The alcohol was poisoning and destroying her body and brain. Sometimes she'd become blackout drunk and not remember anything she'd done or said the next day. I dreaded those nights.

A rasping voice would crackle from the kitchen. 'Come here, Manny.'

I'd drag my feet; it was like being pulled in by a tractor beam.

Not going in would be worse.

The cooktop light was the only source of illumination. It found the cragginess in Sue's face, psychosis pulsating from her. An overflowing ashtray, empty wine bottles and beer cans strewn across the table and floor. One night, she got so one-eyed drunk she didn't realise I was right next to her.

'Manny, get in here!'

A wine bottle smashed on the ground as she slipped off her chair and hit her head on the corner of the kitchen table. Blood poured from a gash in her leg. I grabbed a tea towel and held the cloth to her leg for a second before Sue slapped me so hard that I slammed into the fridge and saw stars. She raised her head, hair matted with blood and perspiration.

'This is your fault.'

Struggling to stand, she fell into broken glass. She cut her legs further and ripped open her dress.

'He was an arsehole, but he was *my* arsehole. He was all I had. But you couldn't save him. It's all your fault.'

A bloody, claw-like hand reached out and grabbed the bottom of my t-shirt.

'WHY. DIDN'T. YOU. SAVE. HIM?'

She didn't get it. Saving him could have killed me. Or maybe she did get it.

And now, my ability was non-existent. I was a reverse superhero. Everything to nothing.

I was no use to anyone, destined to live my life as an ordinary chump with nothing to contribute. Sue didn't understand. She tried forcing me to heal small animals she'd caught and maimed herself. Of course, I never could.

It was horrible, but she wouldn't let up. Then, in one lesson of persistence, Sue was vindicated by a possum she'd snatched from the backyard.

The possum was panting and shivering on a bunch of newspaper strewn across the kitchen table. Sue had smashed it with a shovel. I could see its insides through the gouges in its fur. It didn't have long. Despite knowing I couldn't heal it, I reached out and touched the possum anyway. Then it happened.

I could sense its broken bones and battered organs.

Warmth and light flooded me, as familiar as riding a bike, as easy as breathing, healing.

In seconds, the possum had sprung to its feet, jumped off the table, and dashed straight out the open back door to the nearest tree.

Sue's eyes blazed. 'I knew you were holding out on me, Manny.'

'But I couldn't,' I protested.

'You just fucking did. You should be happy.'

But I wasn't. It wasn't elation flooding me, it was fear.

My ability was back, and if it could find me, so could the bad people.

~

It was the summer holidays after that when I had to use my ability again.

I could count the number of friends I had at school on one finger. Ben was it.

We met during an arcade super session in the city when we were eleven, instantly bonding over *Time Crisis*, *Street Fighter*, and air hockey. By the time we were twelve, we'd upgraded from arcades to skateboards and pre-teen activities like hanging out, throwing rocks and swimming in the quarry. We spent a lot of time there.

Though we never saw other kids at the quarry, coke cans, cigarette butts and old *Playboy* and *Picture* magazines littered the ground, signs others congregated there too.

One day we rode our BMXs to the quarry to engage in a dirt rock war. Dressed in combat gear, we had battle plans drawn up, food and supplies, the works.

We pretended we were the last two troops from opposing armies, launching grenades at each other's skulls. It was dangerous but we were twelve and bulletproof.

At one stage we broke for a ceasefire, rebuilt our forts, chased a rogue snake, ate sandwiches and snorted some Wizz Fizz.

Post-ceasefire, we gathered another stockpile of rocks and the ferocious battle recommenced. Wave after wave of earthly projectiles flew as we narrowly avoided significant injury. I was so caught up in the fantasy it took me a minute to notice the lack of incoming fire from the opposite trench.

I peered over the top of my barricade, expecting an ambush. Nothing.

I ran over into Ben's trench with a rock in each hand but dropped them when I saw him. He was standing, staring vacantly at some unseen spectre, deathly pale and covered in sweat. Then he folded and clutched his knees as he power-vomited over his shoes and the metre radius around him.

He grunted once, collapsed to the ground and started convulsing. His skin was way too white, his eyes bloodshot and rolling back into his head. He was dying; I needed an adult.

I jumped on my BMX and rode home faster than any kid had ridden before. I burst through the door, crying and screaming for Aunty Sue's help. She called an ambulance and then drove us both back to the quarry. Time slipped.

We were almost too late.

I froze on the spot, watching my dying friend.

Sue pushed me towards him. 'Do it, Manny. Help him.'

I protested, 'I can't. I'll get in trouble.'

'Who cares?' she said. 'Use it. He'll die if you don't.'

She was right. Even when the ambulance got there, they wouldn't be able to drive into the quarry.

'Do it, Manny,' Sue said, a manic look in her eyes.

I knelt and took Ben's hand. I felt an instant flash between us. I could see several twisted ropes of ugly, black masses pulsing in his disfigured insides. It was hard to hold on.

Focus.

Inky blackness leaked through his insides.

Focus.

Ben groaned. 'It hurts, Manny, my tummy hurts.'

I tried to draw it out but could barely move the twisted black ropes inside him. I held on, only letting go when I couldn't bear it anymore.

Ben's eyes fluttered open. 'You helped me, I felt it.'

A siren blared in the distance. Sue ran towards the quarry's entrance.

I stayed. 'Shhh. Close your eyes. They're coming.'

He closed his eyes. A few minutes later, Sue led over a couple of paramedics holding a stretcher.

Ben's eyes fluttered. 'You helped me.'

That's all I remember before I blacked out.

~

I usually wake up screaming as soon as I smash through the windscreen. This time, I sat bolt upright, silent and sweating.

Ugly walls, metal beds, floor cleaner, beeping machines.

Ben and I were in the same hospital room, me closer to the door, him next to the window. His parents were there. Sue sat next to me, reeking of gin.

The doctor told Ben's parents an aggressive stomach tumour had manifested in his stomach. A black ball of death, big as a Valencia orange. And it had burst, spread.

I'd seen it when I'd touched him at the quarry. Inky black tentacles snaking through his body, destroying everything in their path. His chance of long-term survival was zip, short-term not much better. He needed surgery. The plan was to keep him comfortable.

I was free to go home, but they said I could sit at his bedside that night. He was due to have surgery to remove the abomination pulsating inside him the next day.

A few hours later, Sue was gone, Ben's father had gone home to take care of his sister, and his mum had gotten up to go to the bathroom.

It was my chance.

I took his hand in mine. I could save him – sure of it.

His skin was translucent. That grotesque ball pulsating in his gut had radiated its poison throughout his body. The ball glowed as my body warmed, but then a darkness enveloped me. There was too much sickness in him, he was more cancer than boy. He wouldn't last a week. The angry black ball and its tendrils pulsed, hummed and a sharp, cacophonous swarm buzzed through my head.

I lost concept of time; his life force was leaving his body.

My head throbbed. Every cell in my body cried out.

No.

I collapsed to the floor and busted my head open on the bed's foot brake. The last thing I remember was convulsing, blood running over my face, so nice and warm against the cold linoleum floor.

~

When I woke, I'd never been so thirsty. I had to peek through bandages just to see. I was groggy, and my head weighed a tonne.

Sue was holding my hand. She no longer stunk of gin, must've switched to vodka. Standing behind her was E, bloodshot eyes, unshaven, fidgety.

I looked across the room. The bed next to the window was empty.

'Where's Ben? What happened?' I mouthed.

Sue patted my hand, telling me to rest.

I was going to be sick.

'What happened?' I repeated.

Sue shuffled in her chair. She didn't need to tell me.

Ben was dead.

Instant, overwhelming guilt. The dam burst and the tears didn't stop.

I couldn't save my mother. Couldn't save Jam. Couldn't save my only friend.

E moved in front of Sue. 'Manny, did you try to fix him?'

I couldn't look him in the eye. 'I had to, he was dying.'

E shut his eyes tight and rubbed the bridge of his nose. 'You never should have done anything without me. And you,' he turned and snarled at Sue, 'I told you to tell me as soon as it came back.'

Sue looked like she'd been slapped. 'I… I did.'

'No, you bloody well didn't. I spoke to the dead kid's poor mother. I asked her if anything unusual had happened and she said Ben told her Manny helped him in the quarry. Luckily, I assured her it was most likely the incoherent ravings of a dying child. Jesus, Sue, don't you get what's at stake? They could come and take him away.'

Sue stood her ground and stuck her finger in his face. 'They, they, who's they? You don't care about, Manny, you only care about your damned experiments. He's nothing but a guinea pig to you.'

E laughed. 'You know who "they" are. You led them to him, and now his mum's dead.'

The slap looked like it surprised Sue as much as it did E and me. Her hand went to the big "O" of her mouth. E rubbed his left cheek.

I pushed myself up. 'What are you talking about?'

'Nothing, Manny,' Sue said. 'Adult stuff.' She turned to E. 'Let's get this over with.'

E nodded. Sue moved out of the way and E sat in the chair.

'Remember last time, I gave you something to protect you?'

'Special medicine,' I said.

'That's right,' he said, withdrawing a silver syringe from a small black case. 'I've improved it. It'll last longer this time, until you're big, until you want it back.'

I took a few breaths and stared at the syringe.

'I never want it back.'

E nodded, cleaned my arm with a cotton ball dabbed in alcohol, and stuck the needle in.

~

I withdrew over the following months.

My physical recovery was swift. My mental recovery, less so.

They gave me a week off school, forced me to visit a counsellor and keep a feelings journal. I told the counsellor what she wanted to hear, wrote down what she wanted to read.

I spent a lot of that time reading or watching cartoons in my room. A schism between childhood and adulthood. Childhood was misery, too much death; I wanted to leave it behind.

In the months after Ben died, several other kids who had frequented the quarries got sick.

An independent investigation launched after several of them died. It didn't take long for the investigators to discover a now-defunct hazard removal company had been dumping toxic waste there for years but neglected to inform anyone.

Within a year of Ben's death, a total of 18 kids had died because of this gross negligence, except for one. Me.

All the parents filed a class action against the company responsible. They won. A small consolation, their kids were still gone.

Meanwhile, I'd never even had the sniffles. I was in what the medical experts deemed perfect health.

Regular brain scans at the institute persisted, but the results perplexed various doctors. The only common thread was the clear ball in my brain they maintained was unlike any growth or tumour they'd seen before. They weren't sure how I was alive. It was inaccessible, inoperable, buried between the hemispheres.

A grenade waiting to explode.

~

Shin kicks, ankle taps, kidney punches, corked legs, sack whacks, wet willies, Chinese burns, hair pulls, head butts, noogies, horse bites, crow pecks, knuckles, slaps, smell the cheese, wet towel whips.

Apart from navigating those standard hurdles, school was ordinary.

Like the average modern teenager, I withdrew. Though my reclusion wasn't due to shin splints, acne or the incredible discovery of masturbation, it was because isolation was all I felt I deserved. In retrospect, it was some sort of depression, but that was rarely recognised as a real condition at the time. With Sue caught up in her own story, I lacked any support that could've led from the darkness and steered me towards sunnier pastures.

High school was lonely – I kept to myself and mostly avoided others. I did well in most subjects and passed without any problems, but mainly because I wanted to leave as quickly as possible. Isolation and loneliness are harder to bear when you're surrounded by hordes of people.

Sue descended further into a vortex of alcohol blackouts and psychotic behaviour. She still firmly believed it was my fault she had no husband or sister; that I could've saved them both.

Those experiences should've been enough to warn me off drinking for life.

They didn't.

I moved out of Sue's place as soon as I graduated high school, barely seventeen. I spent a few weeks applying unsuccessfully for various bar jobs, my lack of experience offering the narrow scope between glassy and dish pig.

I'd had enough rejections for terrible jobs I didn't want, then fate intervened.

One day, as I passed the Wesley hospital, I saw a huge Red Cross van painted with a sign asking for blood donations. I'd never given blood before, and due to watching too many American shows, thought I'd get paid for it. And you do, but in cookies and juice, which any cookie aficionado knows is a mismatched combo.

The hospital's nurse manager was donating in the chair next to me and we got to talking. She said they needed orderlies. I started my first and only proper job that week. It was the same hospital I was born in, reborn in after the accident, and watched my best friend die in.

It's not a small world, it's just a small town.

The job wasn't everything I hoped it could be, but it was something. We all want something. Even that homeless pregnant junky bumming cigarettes outside the 7-Eleven wants something. From deadheads to hedge fund managers, we're all equal in that respect.

On my first shift, the memory of my suicidal goldfish Raphael returned clear as a freshly washed windscreen at a set of traffic lights. The hospital had maintained the same look and feel and smell. Stuck in a perpetual time warp.

Another decade passed, and still, little changed.

TEN

THERE'S no place sadder than Bluebell Ward, AKA the children's cancer ward.

If you still believe in a loving god with influence over the day-to-day outcomes and actions of humanity, try visiting Bluebell one day. If there *is* a god, but they don't have control over what's going on, I feel sorry for them, forced to watch the horror show unfolding below on planet earth.

The beds of Bluebell are filled with dark, sunken eyes, bones swimming in skin. The kids, endlessly poked and prodded, are like extras from a concentration camp film.

Bright happy murals cover the ward, but it's more like a sad joke. Bone cancer in a four-year-old never retreated due to a painting of a unicorn standing under a smiling rainbow.

It's late, and the ward's quiet. As I round the corner, I almost run into her.

A little girl clutching the front of her gown with one hand, a portable IV pole with the other. Her tiny body is filled with tubes, and there's an ugly map of bruising across her almost translucent skin.

I crouch to eye level. 'Are you lost?'

'I had an accident,' she says in a soft voice, the front of her gown all wet. She raises her head; her sunken eyes are like two beautiful blue marbles with galaxies in them.

I kneel. 'Oh darling, it's okay, we'll get you cleaned up. The bathroom's over here. I'll find you a fresh gown and find a nurse to help you out. I'm Manny.'

'Hi, Manny,' she smiles. There's blood in her teeth. It dribbles from her lip.

My heart cracks a little. It's not fair.

I grab a tissue from one of the carts and wipe the trickle of blood from the corner of her mouth. As my hand touches hers, I can see inside she's riddled with ugly, black, twisted ropes. Something else in her blood too, like poison, infiltrating everything. She's getting worse.

I usher her towards the bathroom and as I remove my hand a clump of her hair sticks to my hand. She collapses. I scream down the corridor, then drop to the ground to hold her. She weighs as much as a small dog. There's no code button near me.

'Help!'

The hospital has never felt so empty.

Where's the night shift?

'Anybody!'

The little girl coughs up blood onto my arm. 'I'm scared, Manny.'

'Help me, please!'

My radio.

I rip it from my belt.

'Base. I need a code blue outside Bluebell.'

A code blue bell outside Bluebell. They should rename this place.

She burrows into me, trembling. She says something I miss, so I lean down.

'What was that?'

'Please stop yelling,' she says.

'Okay,' I say, bringing her close.

'Thanks for holding me.'

'It's alright, I've got you, it's going to be alright.'

She snuggles into my chest. My heart blooms and breaks.

The crash cart team seems impossibly far away as they round the corner at the other end of the hallway. I hold her against my chest and use the wall to stand. She starts to seize. Oh no, please. I move as fast as I can without jolting her tiny body and hand her over to the approaching crash team. She's gone floppy like a rag doll cat and slick with sweat.

They work on her. Chest compressions and rescue breaths.

Her chest isn't rising. They tilt her head, try again.

No.

Her little feet jolt with every compression. Her face goes blue.

No.

The nurse aspirates the needle, which looks thicker than the little girl's arm, and injects her. She twitches, convulses. More compressions.

My gut twists as the medic presses down on her tiny chest.

The sound she lets out when they accidently break her ribs will never leave me.

The team stops. It's useless.

We all step back, the fluorescent lights bathing this little human who deserved better.

She's still, beautiful, pain free.

When the tears come, I realise I've never cried since I was a kid. I make up for it.

~

Everyone is sick. If I touch them, I can see it all. My mind reels. The cashier at the IGA has herpes and early-stage dementia. The old lady across the street has breast cancer, and she probably won't know until it's too late. The mailman has haemorrhoids and a swollen prostate. The teller at the Commonwealth Bank managing my meagre savings, lung cancer. The guy at the bottle shop has a kidney stone. Even here in the hospital, a doctor in the orthopaedics unit will need his spleen removed soon, a bunch of other doctors are in various early stages of organ failure. The nurses have endometriosis, the orderlies have liver issues. Everyone is broken and sick on some level.

I can't heal any of them or even tell them because they'll think I'm crazy. Maybe I am. Before tonight, it never bothered me enough.

But this little girl, who never did anything wrong, who probably experienced nothing but sickness over the term of her short life, that bothers me. Dying in a cold hospital corridor scared to death, in the arms of a stranger. That's it. Whether it's the last straw or straw that broke the camel's back, pick your straw cliché, it's that one. I need the healing ability back.

I head home and unload to Elvis, who sits there steepling his fingers as I tell him it's Jam all over again, it's Ben all over again, and I need to find E and the truth.

Once I'm finished, he tosses me a pre-rolled rollie and a lighter.

'Maybe she's still alive,' he says.

I drop my cigarette. 'The little girl? No, she was blue, I saw her.'

'Not the one tonight,' he says, 'the first one. Jam.'

I feel like I've been dunked in an ice bath. 'What?'

'Well, did anyone tell you she died?'

'E said, 'She's gone.''

He shrugged. 'Semantics, man. She could still be alive. If you want to find E, find her first, then work your way to him and get your healing thing back.'

I pick up my cigarette off the carpet and lean back in my chair.

'Damn. I didn't really, uh, I don't know what I thought.'

'If she was that sick, she would've spent a bunch of time in hospital, so it depends on what hospital she went to. If she spent time in ours, I could find it right now from my work laptop, but to access the records of the other Brissie hospitals I'll need to head into work. Can't access the database remotely.'

Elvis pulls out his laptop and logs into the hospital server. 'Let's go for the low hanging fruit. We might get lucky. These reports pull best for exact matches. What's their surname?'

I stare at the ceiling. 'Dunno.'

'That's nearly a non-starter then. Also, how far back we talking?'

'At least twenty years,' I say.

'Another issue if she's not in our system. Any files over ten years old may not have been kept. I've ensured lifetime backups for our joint, but who knows about the government hospitals.'

I grab us a couple of beers and crack the tops with my lighter.

'Wouldn't the government hospitals have digital backups of all the patient info?'

Elvis laughs. 'It would take the government ten years to eat a bowl of cereal. First, they'd be paralysed with choice of which cereal to purchase, then several emails on which milk would be suitable, then it would take a few committee meetings to decide which bowl and spoon to use. Then a whole specialist department would be created to take charge of renaming breakfast to something more politically correct and voter friendly.'

'How would the word breakfast be politically incorrect?'

He takes a swig of beer. 'The word 'break' is insensitive to recent relationship split ups or couples on a break, to people with broken bones, or temporary reprieves from work.'

'Jesus.' He's thought this through.

'The word 'fast' is offensive to the dim-witted, the slow walking, a range of intellectual disability rights organisations, intermittent fasters, the breatharians. Pretty much offensive to the meals of lunch and dinner, not to mention morning tea, afternoon tea, little lunch, the list goes on. Equal rights for all meals. I can see the slogan already, 'Food can't speak up, so we have to!''

Elvis picks up a Rubik's cube off the table and performs a series of lightning-quick, dexterous moves to solve it within seconds.

'Maybe Sue knows their last name,' he says.

My eyes break from the colourful cube. 'Genius.'

I pull out my phone and call Sue. Nothing. I dial hospital switch, ask them to patch me to Sue's room, then flick on the speakerphone.

The hold music is a distorted acoustic guitar melody, though it's not meant to be. They always crank the gain too high on hold music, like they're trying to infuriate you even more while you're waiting, for no real reason.

She eventually picks up. 'I was in the bathroom.'

'That's great. Sue, what's E's last name?'

'Why?'

'As in the letter Y? His name is E Y?'

'No,' she says. 'Why, as in why?'

'I don't have time for an Abbott and Costello thing. What's his last name, Sue?'

'It's Bowler,' she says.

I spin the lighter on the table.

'Very funny. I get it.'

'What?' she asks.

'Ebola. Hilarious.'

'I'm serious, Manny. His last name's Bowler, B-O-W-L-E-R. I'd say that's why his nickname was E.'

'That's weird.'

'Scientists have a weird sense of humour, and he was one of the weirdest.'

Elvis hits me on the knee and whispers, 'Ask about Jam.'

I wave him away. 'Sue, remember E's daughter?'

'Never met her, but the girl in the wheelchair you fixed up, yeah. Marmalade or Marmite, wasn't it?'

'Jam,' I say.

'That's it. What about her?'

'Did she die? E said she's gone.'

Sue explodes into a coughing fit. 'That doesn't mean she's dead, you dingbat,' Sue says. 'They left town is all.'

I hang up the phone.

Elvis snaps his fingers in front of my face.

'Okay,' he says. 'We're good to go. But we can't just stroll through the front entrance, into the office and browse the state medical records. Normally, these searches go through official channels and every step needs to be documented meticulously.'

Perhaps noticing my disappointment, he pulls two more beers from the esky and pops the tops.

'Man, we're doing it, but we need to be stealthy. Oh,' he adds, 'There's every chance this search will trigger a flag, which will be picked up by whichever government organisation takes care of this sort of thing.'

'How are we going to do this then?' I ask.

We scratch our noggins like a couple of monkeys.

Elvis sits up and slams his beer onto the table.

'6E,' he says. 'It's being painted, and it's right next to the office.'

'So?'

'So, at the end of your shift tomorrow, go to 6E and down through the emergency stairwell. Pop a chock in the exit door, you can get changed out of your scrubs and then we can come back through undetected.'

'Perfect.'

~

The receptionists in the hospital lobby are already wearing elf ears and Santa hats. Sad fragments of tinsel are taped to the walls next to plastic reindeer faces and candy canes. A tiny Christmas tree with faded baubles and seizure-inducing lights sits on the desk.

One of the receptionists holds out a box filled with Santa hats as I walk past.

'Tis the season,' he says, smiling, with too many teeth.

'Can't. Health and safety,' I say, without breaking stride.

'Some of the other orderlies are wearing them,' he says to my back.

The older I get, the more I understand the Grinch's point of view.

Most of the day is wheeling patients to X-ray, neurology and cardiology.

A broken leg here, a stroke there, heart attacks everywhere.

Fifteen minutes before the end of my shift, I accept a final job on my radio.

The 3B nurse hands me a urine sample jar, and I head to room seventeen. The door's closed. I press my ear to the wooden door. Someone's yelling. No, it's singing, something familiar, but it's too muffled to make out. I open the door a crack and poke my head through to check if the patient's okay. Not only is he okay, he's jumping on his bed, nude, singing *Waltzing Matilda*.

I walk in, shut the door and throw him a hospital gown, which he proceeds to wrap around his head for the grand finale. Once he's done, he buttons the gown and takes a sip from the teacup on the tray next to his bed and calmly sits down like the most batshit crazy thing in the world hasn't just happened.

'What's all this then?' he asks.

'Here, for your urine,' I say, handing the urine sample container to him. 'There's a bathroom over there.'

He salutes. 'You've got it boss.'

After a few minutes, he emerges from the bathroom with a huge grin.

'Thanks!' he says, handing back the empty container. 'Didn't need that cup after all, there's a toilet in there, so I used it instead.'

I must've disappeared into thought, because next thing the guy's yelling at me through a rolled-up newspaper, 'Earth to wardsman, Earth to wardsman. Come in, wardsman.'

I slowly reach out and grab the empty container, unsure what to do next. They don't teach you what to do if a patient is too stupid to pee into a container.

'Wardsman's outdated,' I say. 'I'm an orderly.'

'Disorderly more like it.'

As I walk out, the guy starts playing the piccolo trumpet solo from *Penny Lane* through the rolled-up newspaper.

When I return the empty sample container and explain what happened, the nurse laughs too hard to write in the chart. I leave the ward, laughing nurses echo in my wake.

Ward 6E stinks of chemicals and looks like a horror movie set, with its empty rooms, half-painted walls and splattered plastic sheeting covering most surfaces. I find a suitable door chock, a wooden stirrer left next to some paint cans, then head to the exit door. The stairwell smells of concrete and mould. My shoes leave solid prints in the thick dust. Looks like no one's been down these in decades. I leave the wooden chock in the door. It's thin enough to hold the door ajar but make it look like it's closed.

~

Hours later, Elvis and I are back there. I grab the paint stick and leave it where I found it.

Elvis checks his phone. 'Good, there's only one dude at base in the office. Someone must be sick. I'm going to trigger a job at ICU, that should give us about fifteen minutes by the time he walks there, finds out nothing's going on and gets back.'

He confirms the job on his phone through the hospital's booking system.

'Okay,' he says, 'now we just need to wait for him to accept.'

We move as soon as the guy accepts the job and leaves the IT office. Elvis punches the keycode to enter, ducks his head in to confirm it's empty. He pulls up a chair in front of a computer. I pace the room, biting my nails.

'I can't use my own login details,' he says, 'so gimme a tick to circumnavigate the system.'

I laugh. 'Proper hacker stuff. Is it easy enough to do on this system?'

'Should be, I built it.' His fingers work dextrously and random code flies across the screen. A bank of servers hums next to me, generating enough heat to melt an icy pole. It's either the servers or breaking into a state government database that's causing me to sweat through my shirt.

While Elvis punches away at the computer, I stare at a laminated Garfield poster stuck to the wall. 'Why does Garfield hate Mondays when he doesn't even have a job?'

Over the clack of keyboard keys Elvis says, 'I think it's to do with eating leftovers. Okay, I'm in the state server. We're going back twenty years, right?'

'Yup. A five-year window either side should do it.'

He types Jam Bowler in the search bar and hits enter. An old school hourglass spins around on the screen. Elvis spins in his chair to face me.

'And Jon probably goes to work on Mondays.'

'Doesn't Garfield hate Jon?' I ask.

'That's all an act. Garfield bloody loves him; he just doesn't want to show it.'

'But he's a cat. And isn't lasagne better the next day?'

Elvis shrugs, 'Maybe Garfield doesn't think so. Or maybe it's from Saturday.'

The computer dings, he spins back. 'Shit. Nothing.' He wipes the sweat from his forehead. 'I'm going to try just the last name.'

Hundreds of results with the name Bowler appear, no Jam or J. Bowler hits.

Elvis grabs a container of Redskins and we each take one and shove it in our gobs.

'Haven't had a Redskin in ages,' I say, through the pink wad gluing my jaw shut.

'They're not called Redskins anymore,' Elvis says. 'They're Red Rippers now, because of racial overtones or undertones. Racial tones. But I don't get why they thought it was better to name them after a Russian serial killer instead.'

I stare at the wrapper. It *does* say Red Rippers. Lightbulb.

'A different name,' I say.

Elvis's face twitches. 'What?'

'Maybe E changed Jam's last name when they disappeared or something.'

'But her hospital records would still be under the original name.'

He bops the head of a stormtrooper bobble head on the desk. 'Let's get out of here, we're getting nowhere fast.' He stands.

'Wait,' I say, 'what if you leave the surname field blank and only type in her first name?'

Elvis sighs and falls into his chair. 'If I type in Jam, you're going to get millions of hits for variations like Jamie, Jamon, Jamieson, I mean, there will be thousands of James in there too in the initial search.' He checks the clock. 'We should get out of here soon.'

My leg is jackhammering. 'Do it anyway.'

I grab another Red Ripper and my jaw goes to work.

Elvis types in 'Jam,' hits enter and crosses his arms.

The name James dominates, as do the variations of Jamie, Jamie-Lee and the rest. Jamal, Jamison, Jamila, Jamon, Jamieka, Jamieson, Jamir, Jamiyah. No Jam.

When the phone rings, I bang my head on the shelf next to me. Sue.

'Hey, what's up?'

'I was thinking about the names thing before. His daughter's name would be different.'

My eyes flicker to the Red Ripper wrapper. I switch to speaker phone.

'Say again.'

'The mother died in childbirth, real sad situation. I remember your mum telling me that E thought it would be nice for his daughter to keep her mother's last name.'

If I gripped the phone any tighter, it would shoot out like a wet bar of soap.

'You remember it?'

122

'Easy-peasy, my favourite whiskey.'

'Jamieson.'

'You got it.'

'Thanks, Sue,' I say, and end the call.

'You heard, Jam Jamieson.'

Elvis sighs, hits enter.

One result, and it's for Mater Children's Hospital. J. Jamieson.

'Click on it,' I say.

'Alright, alright,' Elvis says impatiently and goes into the file.

The file is only open for a few seconds before a pop-up warning box appears.

Restricted access

'We've gotta split,' Elvis says.

The screen flashes the warning.

But I'd seen enough. An address. One I know well.

It's Sue's place.

Tomorrow's going to be an interesting day.

ELEVEN

I head into the hospital an hour before my shift starts. Sue's room is empty.

There's no one manning the nurses' station either, so I ring the black-handled, brass bell. A thin, male nurse appears from the stockroom. 'How's it going, Emmanuel?'

'Not bad. Hey, my aunt's missing. Sue – she was in room nine. Have you seen her?'

'This is the first hour of my first shift on this ward. They pushed me up from ICU. What does she look like?'

'About this high,' I say, hand level with my shoulder. 'Long, silverish hair down to here, and the room right there.' I point.

He rubs his thin beard between his thumb and forefinger, bearded man sign language for "I'm thinking". 'Oh yeah. She did have a visitor about half an hour ago, an old guy. They went for a walk. Have you checked the gardens?'

'She shouldn't be leaving unless she's accompanied by a family member. Who was this man?' I ask.

'It should be here in the visitor log.' He spins the logbook around.

I already know.

'Yep, her brother, Emmanuel. You named after him then?'

My brain struggles to compute. 'She doesn't have a brother. There's only me.'

'Well, under relationship it says brother. Look, I'm sure she'll be back.'

He looks at me for a few beats before I rush off.

I check my phone, redial Sue. It rings several times before going to voicemail. I leave a message, then head to the security office, ask them to keep an eye out for her on the cameras. Back in the main foyer, I see the man in the trench coat out the front of the hospital. He raises his arm and hails a taxi. I run towards him, but my world spins as the car connects. I'm face-to-face with the bonnet of a green Hillman Super Minx, driven by an old guy departing the drop-off zone.

By the time I get up off the ground, the trench coat guy is well gone. The only identifying factor I have is the bloody trench coat. He may as well be the Invisible Man.

The old guy checks on me, chuffed I'm okay. He makes a joke about my face imprint on the bonnet, says he'll give it a cut and polish when he gets home. We shake hands, he hops in, cranks the Ramones on a little black boombox and drives off.

I eventually find Aunty Sue back in her room.

She's sitting on the edge of her bed, staring at the floor.

Her face is ashen and her skin looks like it's about to fall off her bones.

A doctor writes in her chart. He pulls me aside and tells me her blood toxicity levels show evidence of radiation exposure. He asks me if I know anything. I look to Sue, who shakes her head, then I turn to the doctor and do the same. He exits the room, whistling the Harlem Globetrotters' theme tune.

I open the windows so Sue can get some light and see more than the inside of a psych ward bedroom. The garden space is an oasis of greenery and colourful flowers, meant to promote a sense of calm.

'So, you found E's daughter, then?' she asks.

'Hit a roadblock. Know where she lived though. Your place.'

She fidgets like she's holding invisible rosary beads. 'He used to use it for experiments, made me promise not to tell. Didn't want you to know anything until it was the right time. When they left, he gave me the place. It's mine.'

'That's why he made you promise?'

Her face darkens. 'Blackmailed more like it. Said if I told, he'd tell too.'

'Tell who?'

Sue stares out the window. 'Can you grab me a few things from home?' she asks, then hands me a handwritten list of items: bunny slippers, blue dressing gown with the flowers, homemade shampoo and soap, digital radio, two packets of Jolly Ranchers.

'I'll have to go after my shift. Okay?' I ask.

She mumbles okay back.

I try again. 'Sue. Tell who?'

She stares through me. 'You,' she says. Then she's back to the window.

My radio beeps. The small orange screen of my radio lights up. *ICU transfer.*

'I'll be back.'

'Sure, Arnie.'

~

The bed supports groan in tandem with the man mountain on top of it. I'm puffing, out of shape, but compared with this guy I'm a Hawaiian Ironman. *The Little Engine That Could* comes to mind as I heave the bed up the incline and through the hospital corridors.

I think I can, I think I can.

It's little wonder this guy's knees gave out. Joints and ligaments aren't meant to support a human this size. The aroma of baby powder and stagnant sweat fills my nostrils.

'Boy, it's a real rabbit warren in here,' he says.

126

I hear variations of this statement hundreds of times a week. If I took a nip of vodka every time a patient uttered 'rabbit warren,' I'd be dead from alcohol poisoning by lunch.

My large compadré and I finally reach his ward.

I knew I could, I knew I could.

I open the doors to his new room, line the bed up, press the footbrake, plug everything in and head to the next job.

The afternoon shift is outcalls with the paramedics. Nothing out of the ordinary until the fourth one. A sixty-nine-year-old male unconscious in his bed, stuck to his girlfriend. The paramedics and I arrive to the screams emanating from one of the bedrooms. It's a young woman, either late teens or early twenties. She convinced her new/old boyfriend to pop a couple of Viagra pills. He took five. They were midway through when he started convulsing. The convulsions were probably caused by an aneurysm. The paramedics work furiously, but he's still unconscious. I grab some ice and a bucket of water to rid him of his erection the old-fashioned way. It works, but not without a nasty fallout. As we unstick them, unidentifiable matter explodes everywhere.

The guy drops in and out of consciousness as we lift him onto the stretcher and load him into the ambulance. Poor dude, an almighty brain explosion from trying to please a girl. It could have been any of us.

I wrap up the inconsolable girl in a soft, blue blanket. She's suffering from shock and trauma. We load her in too, side by side. She's still crying and babbling. Her life and her colon will never be the same.

An unknown number buzzes on my phone.

'Hello, Manny speaking.'

'You want to meet up?'

'Mila?'

'Got it in one. I was calling pre-emptively for a date. I'm free this weekend.'

127

'What do you want to do?' I ask.

'Eat something, then do something fun.'

'Sounds good.'

I leave straight from the hospital to Sue's to grab her requested items. Visiting hours are over by the time I get back to the hospital but I'm still in work scrubs so slip through. Sue is sitting statuesque on her bed.

I place the items next to her and pull up a chair. Some of the colour has returned to her face, but her head is still lowered, and she won't look me in the eye. Two perfect trails of tears trace the creases of her face and spill, forming a puddle on her dress. She continues to stare at her clasped, trembling hands. It's like she's connected to a mild electric current.

'It was an accident,' she sobs.

I tilt her chin up so she can see me, but she still won't look at me.

'What was? What are you talking about?'

'E blackmailing me. Why I didn't tell you about him giving me the house, and why I couldn't help you find him.'

'But you did. You told me about Jam.'

'You deserved to know.' She shuts her eyes and takes a huge breath.

I move in front of her. 'Tell me, Sue, how bad could it be?'

She meets my gaze for a second before her eyes shift to the corner of the room.

'Remember, I was desperate, Joe was dying. You were the only one who could help.'

I grab some tissues from the box next to her bed. She absentmindedly takes them.

'Your mum said you were going away, didn't say how long. I pleaded with her to let you fix Joe first, but she refused.'

'I remember, yeah.' My face burns, blood rushes. 'Tell me.'

Sue stares at the ceiling, silent.

I repeat, 'Tell me.'

She sniffs and wipes her nose with her gown's sleeve, bides her time.

A deep, shaking breath. 'They came around and picked me up; said I had to help find you. It was never meant to end that way.'

The blood rushes through my temples. 'Who's they?'

She shuts her eyes, painfully drawing out the moment before continuing.

'They were in suits, serious looking, but not government, I don't think. Could've been Russian or German or one of the other European ones.'

'That narrows it down.'

'I knew you were heading towards the coast – said I'd identify the car if I could come along. Thought I could last-ditch convince your mum to bring you back and help Joe.'

I rub my eyes. 'I remember the fight you had before we left.'

Sue shrinks into herself, a trembling hand loosely clasping mine. 'She came to visit me before you left that morning. I'd been drinking, and worked myself into such a state, I wasn't thinking clearly, but she wasn't listening. I wanted to stop Joe screaming, I wanted to stop him dying. It wasn't fair. So, I convinced them to bring me along to find you. And we did.'

The strength leaves my muscles, and I let go of her hand and lie on the floor. The cold vinyl feels comforting.

The accident. There it is again.

From the past come the storms. And the blood, I remember the blood. I recall the snapshot of the scene, the numbness leaves, and my mind achieves clarity. Maintaining calm is challenging. I talk, but it comes out in a whisper, like a sad, deflated balloon.

'You left her to die.'

'I screamed at them to turn back, but they wouldn't. Next thing, I was waking up in bed. They'd drugged me.'

I find my voice. 'You left her to die.'

She bursts into tears and reaches to my withdrawing limb like our hands are in a consolation dance. The crying morphs into a coughing fit into one of the tissues, bright specks of red left behind. She wipes the blood from her lips, her teeth stained like a wino.

'You don't know how much I wish I could take it back,' she says, 'but I couldn't check if she was okay.'

I hand her more tissues. 'You left me to die too.'

Sue composes herself. 'I knew you'd be alright. Your ability would keep you safe. All I could think of was my dying husband.'

I'm not sure how much time passes.

'I hope you'll forgive me, Manny. But I understand if you can't.'

It takes all my energy to rise from the floor. The room spins as the bile rises in my throat.

'I've gotta get out of here.'

I throw the box of tissues on the bed and bolt.

'Manny,' Sue yells after me.

I refrain from telling her how much I wish it had been her that died.

She keeps calling as I move down the hall, but I can't make out what she says.

So elated before about my date with Mila, I'm reminded every silver lining has a cloud.

This calls for all the drinks. I drive straight home and have a shot of whiskey to calm my nerves and slow the frenetic, swirling thoughts. It does nothing. More.

I text Elvis, nothing. He's gone.

I drink for both of us.

Breathe. Drink. Think. Breathe. Drink. Think. Breathe. Drink. Think. Drink. Drink.

The walls are oppressive. My nails bitten to the nub, hands clammy, mouth salty, the lounge room spins as I run towards the backdoor and puke on the carpet on the way. I fall into the garden and hurl twenty years of pain and anguish and alcohol.

I spend the rest of the night smoking cigarettes in the kitchen, waiting for Elvis. He never shows.

I collapse into bed, and my heart threatens to beat out of my chest. Jaw clenched, swallowing acidic saliva, microwaved brain, cold limbs, until I pass out into dreamless sleep.

TWELVE

A newly painted canvas sits on the easel in the lounge room. Frenetic and frantic, visceral movement wrestled onto linen. Earthy musculature, pulsating veins, throbbing organs. Action and attention; deficit malfunction rolled into a tightly wound kinetic ball.

Elvis is getting good at this art thing but if it's any reflection of his psyche, it's pointing towards a demented one.

Scratching around for a tobacco pouch, I notice a purple key on the floor next to the lounge room table. I pocket the key without thinking. It could be a coincidence that it's the same looking purple key as the one E left with Sue. I mean, maybe there's a shortage of other coloured keys. Maybe purple is the new silver, or maybe it's a *Purple Rain* anniversary thing for Prince fans. But I doubt it.

The next ferry arrives at Mowbray Park in ten minutes, so I grab my stuff and walk to the terminal. I spend the trip scanning the homes lining the river with a mixture of envy and wonder. Who are these people, and how can they live like this when most people can't? What occupation allows them to be so grossly overpaid they can afford a mansion and private dock with an unused yacht? How do they sleep?

It probably seems perfectly just and fair to them, but those living a few streets back in cockroach-infested council flats would have a different opinion.

I disembark at Eagle Street and head straight to the key cutting place next to Central Station. It only takes a few minutes, and I choose purple too. I pocket the keys and walk aimlessly around the city for a while. My mind flicks back to Sue.

Forgiveness and understanding can be hard with someone who is essentially a mental patient, more so when it's family. But sometimes all it takes is a new day. She wanted to save her husband. She thought I could. She's right, I probably could have saved him, and she didn't know she'd be partly responsible for my mum's death.

Still, hard pill.

I stumble across City Hall, the first time I've returned since "The Santa Claus Incident". Some sort of performance is happening in the main square, featuring a bunch of awkward Navy marching band nerds in Santa hats. They're holding assorted instruments, performing their regimented robot walk.

I round the corner towards the bus stop, trip over a homeless guy holding a white sign with 'Rotating Golden Laser Beam: Ask me How' scrawled in thick black pen. I flick him a few gold coins. Our eyes meet, locking like opposing magnets.

'What is actually going on in the world?' he asks. 'What is everyone doing?'

'I don't know,' I say, rolling a cigarette.

'Exactly. No one knows what they're doing, but we all keep doing it. It's crazy, goddamned crazy,' he rants. 'Why doesn't everyone stop faking it? Why is everyone smiling when they're depressed as hell? Divorces are up and suicides are up.'

'I know,' I say. 'And I don't know.'

'Everyone's chasing cash and becoming sterile.'

He continues talking while I remain silent, standing, staring, smoking.

'The ego is terrified of the truth. And the truth is it doesn't exist. What was Jesus doing for the eighteen years between being a kid and being a minister? He could have been doing anything.'

More staring.

'Everyone's energetic immune systems are compromised.'

I shrug and walk towards the Adelaide Street 23 bus stop.

'How many ice cream men have committed suicide because they're tired of listening to *Greensleeves*?' he shouts after me.

I turn, lift my arms and shout, 'Who knows? Good luck.'

But he's no longer sitting there. In his place is a charity mugger asking for donations for an organisation specialising in Monkey Helpers, called Monkey See, Monkey Do. I rub my eyes, cartoon style.

I know I'm not crazy, the homeless dude was there a few seconds ago.

But that's exactly what a crazy person *would* say.

I get off the bus close to The Brass Fiddle. It's filled with business phonies and high calibre escort looking types. The guy in front of me takes way too long choosing from the drinks menu, trying to impress the blonde bartender who's way out of his league. No dude ever laid a bartender by winking and asking her for a wet pussy from the shots section. That move probably has the same success rate as wolf whistling from a construction site.

Time passes, as do the drinks.

An eccentric-looking, robed guy appears next to my booth. The crazies are out in force today across Brisbane. Must be some kind of lunar thing.

'You mind if I sit?' he asks.

I shrug. 'I'm about to head out for a smoke.'

He looks out of place here, but so do I. Maybe why he sought me.

'Okay, I'll come with,' he says, following me.

We snake through the gauntlet of businessmen towards the back and somehow move swiftly from small talk into discussing interdimensional beings. Well, he talks, I listen.

'The only reason we haven't been contacted by life on other planets is because it's a vibrational thing, man. We can't see them because they're in another dimension. We're not attuned yet.' He shifts in his seat and withdraws a plastic baggie filled with a multitude of different branded cigarette dogends.

'You know about The Age of Aquarius?'

I nod. 'From that hippie musical right? *Hair*.'

He sips his Coke. 'Yeah man, that's what's happening. And everything happens for a reason. Intuition versus instinct, moving to your middle chakra, bro. Look at this.'

He disrobes and shows off the impressive and intricate tattoos covering his entire back.

I nod, then excuse myself to get another beer. He keeps talking. Judging from his rapid-fire stream of conscious ramblings, it's apparent he's been a voice with no ear for some time. His voice disappears as I reach the bar, drowned out by red-faced, sweating suits shouting over each other. I point to the beer tap. The Irish, backpacking bartender nods and grabs a pint glass from the wire tray.

While the Guinness settles, the bartender pulls me in close and moans about his friends drinking at the pub while he works. I give him a "what can ya do?" eyebrow raise, then shuffle through the crowd back to the bamboo-lined smoking area, where the strange guy is still talking, uninterrupted. He pulls up the sleeve to show his other foreman.

'Fibonacci, the golden ratio man. See?'

I roll a smoke and take a large, satisfying gulp of black liquid. Too polite to leave, I'm stuck.

'Dogs with souls, man. You ever talk to an amethyst crystal?' he asks.

'Nope.'

'Oh dude, they're sentient beings, you've gotta be careful what you say to them.'

The tentacles of my mind reach towards the past.

The accident replays, a broken projector on loop.

'The roads are veins man, and the brain is the city,' he says.

'Uh-huh.'

'It's like that guy says. "The universe inside us all, a drop in the ocean, the ocean in a drop." Ya dig?'

135

'Yeah.'

'The duality of the universe. The Earth is a person. Major extinction events are around the corner.'

'Yeah.'

'I mean, education, man, get the kids and ask them "Who wants to run around and hit things? Who wants to sit quietly and read?" Get it?'

'Yeah.'

He only pauses for a second when the last drinks bell rings.

'DMT man, you see that documentary?'

'Nah.'

'I was going to say you've got to do it, but you do what feels right. Don't watch a doco about it, do it for reals. I did it, said goodbye to my family and friends and everything, man. My whole life was a construct, created by my mind. Legal drugs and medication, that's a problem, man. Epigenetics, it's a thing, look it up. The men who stare at goats. Fear and loathing. Yeah.'

I stare at his Coke glass. 'How come you're not drinking?' I ask, trying to move the conversation back to some semblance of reality.

'I've reached my limit man. Done. Total alcohol saturation. Can't live without the liver.'

'What happened?'

'I was on three bottles of wine a day, man. PTSD from drone operating. They thought drones would make it easier. Let me tell you, it doesn't.'

He thrusts his palms in my face like he's showing stigmata wounds.

'I have the blood of a thousand souls on these hands, even if I only pushed the button. I killed 'em all. I know how those poor fellas on the Enola Gay must have felt after they dropped that sucker on Hiroshima. Fat Man, Little Boy, the beginning of the end of it all. The start of fear and the end of innocence. Fuckin' Einstein and

136

Oppenheimer. And man, it was okay until the end of the '60s, the last gasp. Hells Angels at the Altamont. It's all downhill from there.'

My brain feels ready to explode. I down the rest of my Guinness. 'Anyway, I've gotta head now. Thanks for the chat though.' I offer my hand.

'All good my brother. Take care. And hey, remember, if you can't roll, you can't rock. If you can't rock, you can't roll. And if you don't have rock and roll, you've got fuck all.'

'I'll remember.'

I remembered too much once I arrived home. After replacing Elvis's purple key on the floor where I found it, my head hits the pillow and the words of the eccentric dude dance and twirl in my brain like one of those rhythmic gymnasts with a colourful ribbon trailing them.

Sleep comes reluctantly, and when it does, it's in jagged blocks.

~

Coffee. Now.

I prepare a cup of brown swill AKA Nescafe Blend 43. If they settled on forty-three as the best version, I can only imagine the horrendous taste of the first forty-two incarnations.

I fish a bent Marlboro Red from my backpack and search for a lighter to no avail. It must've disappeared to the same place old socks and Tupperware lids go. The toaster pulls double duty and I burn half the cigarette, but at least it works.

My coffee is tepid and useless. I need a redo. Breakfast too.

I arrive at the local coffee shop to the discouraging sight of a considerable snaking line. The guy in front of me spends ten minutes yelling into his phone and when it's his turn to order, he orders a decaf latte. It confirms my suspicions that people who drink decaf are insufferable. Or pregnant. Possibly pregnant and insufferable.

I order a takeaway, long black, a ham and cheese croissant, and walk to the park with a newspaper tucked under my arm. I don't know why I bother paying for the paper when I mostly end up only reading the comics and the front page. The other sections hold zero appeal.

The front page is plastered with a fear-mongering campaign about another shark attack at Diamond Beach. Humans forget the ocean is the shark's domain; they aren't easily domesticated. Sharks spit out humans because we're bony but the obesity epidemic and hole in the ozone layer hand delivers fat and juicy morsels. I wouldn't blame them. The article says more people die getting crushed by vending machines while trying to rock out the last chocolate bar than by sharks.

Today's lesson: "Sharks don't kill people. Vending machines kill people."

I read *Calvin and Hobbes*, finish the croissant, then give the newspaper to a little old lady outside the front of her house, watering her petunias. We chat for a moment; she asks if I can remove some leaves clogging her gutter. My good deed for the day done, I walk home a little lighter. As all things are, it's temporary. Another note stuck under the welcome mat. Another haiku-like broken poem.

> *You're the key to salvation.*
> *The tonic for a sick world.*
> *It's all inside you.*
> *Cancer's a bitch.*

'Yeah right,' I scrunch up the note and throw it to the ground. Littering guilt kicks in, so I stuff it into the toaster, sending tendrils of smoke and wisps of ash into the air. Carbon footprint guilt kicks in. Guilt about feeling so much unnecessary guilt kicks in. And so it goes.

~

A private number on my phone screen. I answer. 'Mila?'

'I'm doing a short shift this arvo,' she says. 'I finish at six.'

'Cool, so what do you want to do tonight?'

'Classic night-time date stuff.'

'Like bowling, drive-in, '50s diner?' I ask.

'I guess we could start with a bar. There's a new American rockabilly place called Wolfie's. We could meet around seven o'clock.'

'Sounds like a plan.'

I neaten my beard with a cheap electric razor, pluck the white nose hair and tweeze a few rogue eyebrow hairs refusing to conform. My face looks kind of blotchy despite using various C-grade celebrity endorsed moisturising creams. I exit the shower, towel off and book a cab.

Elvis is watching *National Lampoon's Vacation* for the umpteenth time. Luckily, the prodigious amount of weed he's smoking probably disables his short-term memory. He reaches into the esky and grabs a big silver bullet Sapporo beer.

'What are you doing tonight?' I ask.

'I'm doing it. Working tonight. Might watch *The Room*, the worst film ever, worse than *Plan 9 from Outer Space*.'

'Tall order.'

'You've got the psych ward, cat girl date, right?'

I laugh at the crude description. 'Yeah. Drinks at Wolfie's, then I don't know.'

'Wolfie's? Hipster douchebag central.'

'Hipster is an outdated term.'

He opens another can. 'Oh yeah, changing trends so no one can pigeonhole them. Gimme a break.'

'I'm not going to hang out with them though, am I?'

White light bathes the lounge room, and the taxi driver lets out a long, obnoxious beep.

I jump up and stuff my belongings in my pockets. 'That's me.'

I tell the cab driver to drop me off at Wolfie's, receiving only a blank stare. He has no idea where he's going and is deep in conversation on his phone with a fellow driver when he runs up the back of a canary-yellow Nissan Pulsar. I walk the rest of the way, thinking about the thousands of other people I'll see once in my life and never again.

With time to kill, I head to a nameless bar with no signage except for a single red globe attached to metal spider legs. Ultra-hip.

Inside, it has pictures instead of table numbers, beers from microbreweries at the far reaches of the globe, and music that didn't exist last week. I check out the defaced versions of classic paintings and a nude portrait of sexy Queen Victoria. Spray-painted designer skateboards with no wheels hang on the walls with vegan-friendly twine. Weirdest of all, a resident mime.

I finish my White Russian, roll a cigarette and escape through the back door.

The walls of Wolfie's showcase an array of large taxidermy animals. Dozens of discarded bras hang from their horns. The animals' obsidian eyes glare down at the hoard of sweaty drug fiends gyrating on the dance floor. A three-piece rockabilly band in cowgirl outfits play on the same catwalk the go-go dancers will be strutting down once the band finishes their set.

Whisky traverses my bloodstream and my heartbeat regulates. Hopefully the sweats and fidgeting will abate soon. Mila's running half an hour late; I'm on my third whisky. I push through the crowd to the smokers on the street. I've never been stood up before, and I don't have her number.

Maybe work went late.

Maybe she got hit by a car.

Maybe she got abducted by aliens.

Maybe she can't stand me already.

A Rolling Stones song I've never heard before slinks from the speakers. Outside, the smokers stand in circles, zombified, staring at their glowing smartphones. Inside, the toilet symbols confuse me and I have no choice but to go to the disabled one.

I take a slash in the sink; I don't know why.

Mila is two hours late. It's confirmed, I've been stood up.

I lurch to the casino, drunkenly confident my luck will turn around.

Gambling is my destination. Alcohol is my gateway.

It's not like vices become a huge gorilla on your back right away. They're stealthy, silent. A reflected portrait of a damaged soul who is not in control. But then it starts to mutate and fester unabated until it becomes full-blown addiction.

I'm in the fluorescent hell of the casino bar. I grab a pint, play the pokie machines, watch people. Time slips, the nips get bigger, the blackout segments longer.

I hit a feature with my last spin. A single gold coin becomes hundreds. My spirits are temporarily lifted, though I know I'll still burn through it all.

I move on to an unintentionally bogan themed sports bar, park myself next to two drunken ladies bobbing their massive blonde perms to cheesy '80s rock blasting at ear-splitting volume. I alternately smoke cigarettes and drink tequila shooters with beer chasers. True to form, I lose all my winnings. I'm left with $2.30. All silvers.

When I wake, it's next to a dumpster.

The sun is peaking over the horizon. I check my phone for missed calls. Nothing.

I walk in the direction of home, make friends with a group of shoeless, mascara-smeared, transgender quiz hosts making their way home after a big night on the tiles. The first droplets of rain hit as I turn into my street. I trudge up to my front door, lean on it for a spell to gather my brain, then attempt to insert the key, only pausing to read the note attached to the door. It's from Mila.

Hey Manny

So sorry I missed you tonight. I had to bring Poe into the clinic to sort out her incessant meowing and I couldn't get to a phone.

Want to hit the links tonight? (Tonight, as in Sunday night, as I can only assume you've been out. Yes?)

Happy Dragon Putt-Putt 7PM.

I'm going to whoop your butt!   *xxxooo Mila*

I smile, tuck the note into my pocket and collapse on my bed. The ceiling fan spins so frantically I can't ignore the possibility of it detaching and mutilating me. How can I sleep when there's a chance I'll become a hideous sideshow freak?

The Astounding Human Ground Beef Burger, that's what they'll call me.

Somehow, I sleep.

~

Rain belts the house, shakes the windows. Elvis is on the floor, intensely concentrating on some sort of yoga, pilates or yogalates manoeuvre when I walk into the lounge room. He opens a single eye as I enter.

'How was the date?' he asks.

I make a miniscule gap between my thumb and pointer. 'I was this close to calling in a missing person's report.'

Elvis shifts into lotus position, giving me a once over. 'That bad hey?' Then into downward facing dog.

'She was a no show,' I say. 'But we're on tonight.'

I swivel to the TV, which is playing the wizard fight sequence between Merlin and Madam Mim from *The Sword and the Stone*.

Elvis alternates between cat and cow pose. 'Your clothes are still on the line.'

'Shit.' I bring my saturated clothes in and string them around the kitchen on the chairs, doors and whatever else I can find.

'What are you up to tonight then?' Elvis asks.

'Putt-putt. Mila left a note. You didn't hear her or anything?'

'Nope,' he says, changing position. 'Is putt-putt a euphemism for some kind of kinky sex thing? Like a Cleveland Steamer or an Alaskan Snow Dragon?'

'No, literally little golf putt-putt, though it *is* at the Happy Dragon.'

Elvis reclines into savasana. 'Can you grab me a beer? One for yourself too.'

The esky's empty, so the fridge it is. He's already watching *Terminator 2* when I return with the beers, and offers to drop me off if he can borrow the car.

We roll up to the putt-putt place. There's a giant, smiling red dragon watching over it, belching huge fog clouds. The scent takes me back to the blue light discos from high school; fog machines and strobe lights unsuccessfully masking the bad dancing and unbridled lust bursting from awkward teenagers. I open the car door.

'Shit,' Elvis yells, clutching his head. He moans and bends forward, smacking his head into the steering wheel. He pulls back, blood trickling down his nose.

'My head,' he groans. 'A skull-splitter. But it's okay.'

'What do you mean "it's okay"? That's not normal.'

'It's happened a few times now, but it doesn't last long. Don't worry.'

I rip open the glovebox and grab a couple of travel pack tissues.

'Thanks,' he says, and clamps down either side of his nose.

'How long have you been having these?'

'A gubble of muns.'

'A couple of months? You've gotta go to the hospital, see a doctor or something.'

Elvis shakes his head. 'No way, man, not happening.' He nods towards the entrance of the Happy Dragon. 'Go, I'll be fine.'

I hesitate. 'You sure?'

He smiles in a way he probably hopes is reassuring, but I'm distracted by his bloodied teeth and sunken eyes.

'Okay, but take it easy.'

'Yes, Mum,' he says, waving me off. 'Get a hole in one.'

Mila is already at the neon front counter. We hug; she smells incredible.

We grab a couple of beers in a bucket and head to the first hole: a giant crocodile. There's a healthy mix of young families, stoned teenagers and dating couples here. Mila effortlessly sinks putt after putt while spouting random facts and wiggling seductively to distract me. It works, even if the facts are spurious and her wiggling is exaggerated.

'Octopuses could be from space.'

Tink.

'Did you know Elvis Presley practised the sleeping beauty diet? Slept most of the day and only ate a single meal when he awoke.'

Tink.

'Bees die when they sting you. Imagine how furious you'd have to be to sacrifice your life for revenge.'

Tink.

'Not that I'd feel a bee sting. I can't feel anything – that's why it's so easy to cut myself up. Spent my whole life wrapped in figurative cotton wool.'

Tink.

We work our way halfway through the course to the dreaded "super windmill", the hardest shot on the course, except for maybe meerkat madness.

Mila pinches off a chunk of fairy floss and jams it into my mouth.

'Fairy floss and beer isn't a good combo,' I mumble through the sugary wad.

'Let me concentrate,' she says and lines up her shot, sending the ball straight through the spinning blades into the hole. Mila curtseys and throws her club into the air, singing *We Are The Champions*. Then she grabs the club from the bushes and sits next to me at the ninth hole rest stop. 'Would you rather drown or be burned to death?'

'Neither.'

'What about if you had a gun to your head and had to choose?'

'I would pick the gun.'

She jumps to her feet, waving the club around like she's conducting nature. 'Alright, bad example. If your family were all kneeling, blindfolded in front of a firing squad, what then?'

I bounce the golf ball off my bicep into my hand.

144

'My mum's dead, and my aunty is in hospital, but I get the hypothetical. I'd pick drowning. Who the hell would choose burning alive?'

'I don't know,' Mila says, balancing the putter vertically on her outstretched hand.

'Your first date yardstick?'

'One of them.'

We play on. She does most of the talking, and I'm happy to listen. We're stuck behind a group of bratty, teenage girls making noise and taking selfies. I'm about to suggest we play through before Mila cuts me off.

'If we're not careful, the next stage in human evolution will involve babies springing from the womb, posing with pouty duck lips and tilted, upward-looking heads.'

She pulls me through the group of girls, who fail to notice we've overtaken them. Mila grips the putter and stares into the distance. 'Right now, someone is getting shot or raped or beaten. Someone is departing the world, someone is entering it, someone is the most important thing in the world to someone else, someone isn't.'

I shrug. 'And here we are playing mini golf.'

'Right, and here we are playing mini golf.'

'I'd rather do this than work.'

She points the end of the putter between my eyes. 'You should start watching beheadings online before work.'

'Why?'

Tink.

'Because no matter what happens to you that day, at least you'll still have your head.'

I can't argue with that.

We drop our putters back at the mini pro shop and walk to a nightclub down the road. Swag is spelled in pink, neon lights across its façade. That, and the bass-heavy noise from the club, is a sure sign I will not like this place but it's the closest joint and we need to escape the rain. A promo guy in too-tight short shorts, a bright lycra singlet, and ridiculously white teeth bursts out in front of us, clutching a couple of unidentifiable cans. 'Want a free Organic Blue Panda?'

'What is it?'

'It's an energy drink. A mixture of ancient herbs, taurine, caffeine.'

Mila gets up in his grill. 'Energy drinks are poison and everyone's going to get sick and die from them.'

A cloud across his face, the guy retreats.

We pay a cover charge but get two free drinks. A terrible dance version of *Smells Like Teen Spirit* blasts through the PA. It's distorted, but not in a good way. I'm pretty sure all Kurt Cobain stood for is being obliterated in this one moment.

Two steroid freaks move in to take up half the dance floor. Built like brick houses, they flail about stiffly. They're like two awkward Godzillas towering over the fleeing, yet still inexplicably dancing, civilians of downtown Tokyo.

We sit on pleather couches and drink apple whiskeys. I scan the patrons. 'Everyone looks depressed and anxious.'

Mila leans close and yells into my ear. 'Next time you turn on the faucet to brush your teeth, think about the little African kid emerging from squalor and walking ten kilometres to collect a bucket of water so contaminated it could kill him. I don't think that kid has depression or anxiety. He doesn't know any different. Anxiety and depression are modern-day, first-world luxuries.'

I shrug.

Mila stares at a girl dancing with one of the steroid dudes. 'She looks like a ballerina, with her beautiful dress and painful shoes.'

The song skips to another unnecessarily butchered rock classic mixed with another monstrosity. 'I don't want to sound like an old man,' I say, 'but why can't the DJ play a complete song?'

Mila takes a sip and smooths her dress, then motions outside. We walk out to the deserted smoking area. The outside world is much better.

146

'It's simple,' she says, pulling out her vape. 'It's because people's attention spans are shot and it is kind of what DJs do, in case you haven't noticed.'

'I've noticed.'

'The real travesty is they get paid more than real musicians who actually play their instruments.'

We finish smoking and she points inside.

'Let's try again, shall we?'

We head to similar lounges, but further away from the speakers.

Our eyes return to the hulking giants still gyrating on the dance floor. They're like two gorillas who've learned to dance by watching groups of kids tease them at the zoo. They're captivating – I have to give them that – and Mila looks equally enthralled.

'It reminds me of a bull in a China shop,' she says.

'I'd like to know the series of events resulting in a bull entering a China shop.'

'Same, but I don't think you can use that saying anymore. China shop is probably offensive to Chinese people, and a bull is probably offensive to vegans.'

'What about the word 'in'?' I ask.

'Oh no, in is definitely out.'

She springs from her chair. 'Let's go eat. All this bull talk and I'm starving.'

We end up at a vegetarian restaurant trying too hard to have its own identity, like it's pilfering the décor from places the owners visited on their last South American Contiki Tour. It's filled with bohemian types, dressed in comfortable, sensible, cool pastel colours and sustainable fabrics, appropriated dreadlocks, cheap rings and left-leaning ideologies. The food's adequate.

We catch an Uber home; the driver talks about how tonight hasn't been busy. We ask him what it's like being an Uber driver. The usual.

Thankfully my room is in relative order. I grab a couple of Coronas from the fridge, pop the tops, insert the lime wedges, then fall into a beanbag while Mila scans the records on the rack. 'How about Hendrix?' she asks.

I swear my heart beats a little faster. 'Whatever you like, as long as you put the records back in their sleeves.'

'Record Nazi hey?' She spins *Axis: Bold as Love* on the turntable.

We spend the night sitting around listening to records, drinking Coronas.

It's perfect.

~

My arm's around Mila. Her head's on my chest. Her long hair cascades down her back. She feels warm and comforting and I tell her so. If I could bottle this feeling, I would, and then sell it for a hundred bucks a pop. But we both have work. Temporary bliss interrupted.

I flick the kettle on and prep two bowls of Corn Flakes with honey and almond milk. After washing the dishes, Mila stares at the polaroid photo stuck to the fridge. It's of Elvis and me smiling from his hospital bed. She plucks it off and reads the caption.

'What's "The Santa Claus Incident"?'

My brow furrows. 'You don't remember that thing like five years ago? The drunken Santa?'

'I don't watch TV.'

'It was national news.'

Mila shrugs.

'I'll show you where it happened sometime,' I say.

She kisses me goodbye.

When I stick the polaroid on the fridge, I notice a note written in Elvis's scrawl next to it.

We need to talk. 7PM at Gimme Shelter.

I make a mental note. I'll have to head there straight from work.

148

THIRTEEN

I spend the morning in the respiratory ward, arguably the next most depressing ward after Bluebell. A dispirited parade of lifetime smokers slowly passes by, hunched over, downcast, dragging oxygen tanks behind them like boulders. They make lines for the outdoor gardens. Red-faced, they've barely enough energy in their trembling hands to withdraw a pack of their favourite brand of smokes from their dressing gowns. It's too late to give up now. The damage is done, the horse has bolted for the glue factory.

The hospital doesn't allow flowers in the respiratory ward, it's the pollen. It's a pure and simple pleasure withdrawn. You're in big trouble when a flower could potentially kill you.

I head to the gas cage and bring back a trolley of oxygen bottles. While depressing, the respiratory ward is better than the pre-op area for the sole reason I don't have to shave old men's balls. I've clipped enough old men to last a lifetime.

The second half of the shift is in the intensive care unit. Everyone in the ICU is hooked up to wires. I hope if I ever end up in this state, someone will pull the plug.

I finish my shift and make it to Gimme Shelter before 7PM. Elvis is already perched on a barstool, drinking beer. I pull up a seat next to him and the bartender gives me the same brand.

'What's up?' I ask, taking a huge gulp of beer.

'Let's have some beers and I'll work into it.'

'You can't do that.'

'Trust me,' he says.

We sit in silence until a thought hits me. 'Why here?'

'The house may be bugged.' Elvis pauses, looks around.

'You're kidding, right?'

I wait for a non-existent punchline.

'Wish I was. Want to shoot some pool? Tonight's on me.'

We drink high-quality, microbrewery, pale ale and eat low-quality chipotle wings between games of pool. We both suck but achieve near Minnesota Fats levels of greatness in the magical period between beers four and six. Elvis sinks the eight ball and racks them for the two guys who've left their buck on the table. He picks up the small cube of blue chalk, then turns to me and looks me in the eyes. 'Manny, I'm in deep.'

'How deep?'

He rubs the blue dust onto his shirt, we walk to the barstools. 'Mariana Trench deep.'

The flat edge in his voice – it's serious. I've never seen Elvis proper serious.

'Okay. This has something to do with your job, I assume?'

'You assume correctly. But not the hospital job.'

'You've got another job?' I ask.

'I guess you could say that I'm freelancing.'

'What's the deal?'

He drains half his beer in one gulp. 'I'll get to that. It's more about who I'm working for. Aoki.'

My face remains blank, it means nothing. 'Sounds like a manga character.'

'So innocent, Manny.' He shakes his head before continuing. 'Aoki's a famous Brisbane criminal. An institution, like Riverfire or the Ekka or XXXX off the wood at the Brekky Creek. Except he's Japanese, or rather, he's Chinese and wants people to think he's Japanese.' Elvis leans over and grabs a knife off a small, wooden, cutting board and waves it in front of me. 'His name means "Big

150

Serpent," but he's also known as "The Whittler," and he's not into wood carving.'

I snatch the knife and look around the room. Thankfully no one sees, and the bartender was changing a keg. I put the knife back next to the uncut limes. 'How the hell did you end up working for him?'

Elvis drains the second half of his beer. His head drops. 'I was drunk.'

I scoff. 'No shit.'

For the first time, I really notice how tired and exhausted Elvis looks, like it's happening in front of me. He brings his head from his hands and stares at them. I watch him zone out, shake him gently by the shoulder. 'What's this job?' I ask.

He bites his lip, leans over, grabs the knife and, before I can react, slices it across my palm.

'Shit!' I knock my beer onto the tiles.

The bartender rushes over with a green, dish rag at the sound of the breaking glass.

Elvis and I stare at each other, wait until the guy stops muttering and returns to his position behind the bar.

I stare at the lines of blood leaking through my closed fist.

Elvis clutches my wrist. I pull away but his grip is iron.

'Open your hand,' he says.

I look down and slowly open my hand, a tiny pool of blood in my upturned palm.

Elvis grabs a couple of serviettes to soak up the blood, then puts his hand on mine.

I feel the energy and warmth instantly. Time slips and I'm back in the shed, fixing hundreds of injured animals. A white light explodes in my vision and I'm back in the bar.

I open and close my hand; the gash is closing. Soon there's only a few red stains on my palm. It's hard to compute but there's no denying it. He's healing. Behind my back.

'What's going on?' I ask.

Elvis takes a huge breath. 'A few months ago, some old guy came up to me and offered me a deal. Said he'd pay me five grand to test some formula, like a drug trial. I said it sounded too good to be true. He pulled out an envelope filled with cash and said it's mine if I do what he says.'

My skin prickles like I've been covered in tapdancing ants in stilettos.

'E?' I ask.

Elvis nods.

'What's he up to?'

He signals for two more beers, throwing a crumpled $100 on the bar. 'I thought "stuff it" and drove with him to his house. A huge lab, all professional looking. He strapped me in, injected me. At first, nothing happened, and I was ready to leave, but it wasn't to be. That's when I met Aoki. Part of the deal was I had to do some work for him. And they'd pay me.'

We clink beers; a strip of sticky froth coated my hand. I drink, mind whirring. 'You just let some guy you didn't know inject you with some random substance?'

Elvis shrugs. 'He showed me a few test subjects in the lab. Literal guinea pigs. They seemed fine. So, I drove with him, Aoki and a few goons to Glitters.'

'He owns that?'

'Owns damn near every joint in the Valley.' Elvis scans the room like a cold war spy, but there's no point. The bartender is deep in his phone, the guys playing pool are focused on their game. The only sound is the twang of the pool cue and clunk of the balls ramming into each other. Elvis keeps his voice low.

'I was getting a lap dance in a private room from a short, bleached blonde with gigantic tits and fish lips. She collapsed halfway through *Cherry Pie,* writhing around on the ground with foam bursting from her mouth. She'd OD'd.'

I pull out my pouch and go to roll a cigarette, but my fingers are trembling. 'So, what happened next?'

'I can't explain it,' says Elvis, 'but I knew what to do. I reached down and put my hands on her head. I could feel something inside me like electricity and it went into her. It was like I could see into her and withdraw the poison. I brought her back.'

His eyes are wide, like he still can't believe it. I knew the feeling.

'Thing is,' he says, reaching for the pouch, 'I don't think it was an accident. I think someone injected that girl on purpose. They were testing me.'

I stare at Elvis, momentarily numb. I brush the loose tobacco strands off the bar into my pouch and we head to the smoking area. I hand my little pink lighter to Elvis and he lights up, breathing deep, puffing blue smoke from the corner of his mouth.

'That was only the start,' he says. He looks like Popeye, one eye narrowed, talking out one side of his mouth, the cigarette dangling from the other. 'Then it was always the same. A couple of gangster-looking guys would beat the hell out of some poor sod. Then I'd have to fix them.'

A pang of jealousy flares. Healing was my thing. My defining achievement. Why him? But this is swiftly replaced with fear. This is bad for both of us. 'You've seen them do this?'

His rollie extinguishes. I relight it.

'Mostly the aftermath. Grizzly, lots of broken bones. I felt good because I could help them, but...'

I light my own cigarette. 'You're an accessory, Elvis.'

'I know.'

'How much did you say they pay you?'

'The five grand, then five hundred bucks a pop. Easy money.'

I take a huge glug of beer. I can't hide the anger. 'Why didn't you say no?'

His face contorts. 'I couldn't. I mean, I did, but by then, I was too far in. With friends like these...'

I feel his eyes burn into me. 'Who needs enemas,' I finish.

We sit and smoke in silence. When we go back in, he stares at the green felt of the pool table for a moment and watches one of the guys sink his last biggie before setting up for a shot at the eight ball. He misses.

Elvis picks up a pool cue and spins it around in his hand. 'You want to know why me, right?' He bites his lip. 'They said if it wasn't, then it'd be you. I figured you'd been through enough.'

I stay silent.

'It all made sense when you told me about what happened to your goldfish and training your ability. That's why I asked you about E.'

An ugly mix of negative emotions swirls in my chest and I force a deep breath to push them down, for his sake. Elvis is a goner if I don't say something. The problem is, I've got nothing constructive to say. Instead, I grab a couple of beers. We clink bottles and wordlessly agree to leave it for now.

The two guys on the pool table finish up their game.

'You boys are up. Wanna play us for $50?' one of them asks.

We look at each other.

'Make it a hundred,' Elvis says as he withdraws another $100 note and slams it on the table. Thanks to the magical number of beers, we win. We don't bask in victory for long. Moments after Elvis sinks the winning shot his phone rings and he ducks off to the bathrooms. I take the $100 note from the guys and get the bartender to split it.

Elvis is a healer, a liar, and he's in deep trouble.

He hurries back and snatches the note from my hand. Sweat covers his face, his voice tremors. 'Can you book me an Uber? My phone's dead. Get it to drop me at Heartbreakers.'

I type in the address, tick an option and request it as we walk outside.

'Manny,' Elvis says. 'There's something else you should probably know.'

I sigh. Of course, there is.

'There are others.'

'How many others?'

'I don't know, just that there are more.'

I take a series of deep drags to stop from hyperventilating.

The Uber arrives by the time we finish our cigarettes.

Now I don't need to find Jam to get to E. I can follow Elvis.

As soon as his car turns around the corner, I race over to the taxi rank and tell the driver the destination. We take the bridge; Elvis's car takes the long way because I ticked no tolls. I get the driver to stop a few doors down from Heartbreakers, on the other side of the road, then wait at a bus stop and check the app. He's still two minutes away.

The Uber pulls up at the front of Heartbreakers. Elvis emerges, looks left and right like a good boy, then walks straight past Heartbreakers' glass doors and marches towards the end of the street.

I didn't expect this, so I stay across the street, follow him at an angle outside his peripheral vision. But I'm no private eye. I lose sight of him as a huge Woolworths delivery truck passes, and then see he's transitioned into a jog.

I weave between the traffic and run across, following Elvis until he hangs a left down an alley. By the time I poke my head around the bricks, he's gone. The red-brick alley reeks of garbage water and neglect. There's silence apart from the squeak of my shoes and the occasional puddle splash. A thin layer of grime covers every surface; the only sign of life is a small, tailless rat scurrying between the large, green bins and graffiti-covered, brick walls.

The alley finishes in a dead end. I spin around to face the street. On my way back, a soft, muffled scream emanates from the wall. Peeking from behind one of the bins, there's the top of a black door. I wheel the bin back slightly and put my ear to the metal door. Another muted howl. Pleasure or pain, I can't tell. This is the only alternate exit from the alley.

Elvis must be in there.

I inch the door open and look inside but it's too dark. Bleach burns my nostrils. The noise is coming from another room. Despite various internal organs telling me to walk away, I press forward.

I move in and shut the door behind me. There's a small rectangular window with cross-hatching in the corner of the room. It's the only source of light.

My eyes adjust. An industrial kitchen, metal cabinets and benches, and concrete lined with those black rubber mats with holes in them. I duck across to the corner, flinching when I hear another larynx-shredding scream. I check to make sure the bench is sturdy, then hop onto it to take a better look. I squint through fluorescent lights in the next room. Good thing: means no way anyone in there will be able to see me. It takes a few moments for my eyes to adapt. Whoever was screaming has already been dragged away.

An empty chair sits in the middle of the room. Attached to it are several straps snaking along the floor, and either side of it, what looks like a couple of wooden gymnastic pommel horses. Several CCTV cameras line the wall, all pointed at the chair in the middle of the room. A crimson pool is the source of a bloody trail leading to a few offices on the far side of the room. I duck as a group of men emerge from one, hitting my head on a metal hinge. I clench my teeth until the pain recedes. After a few moments, I risk another glance into the room. They're all facing away from me. One of the men raises his arm and waves some unseen individual in.

I recognise two of the men.

Elvis, flanked by E, who looks even older than he did the other day. There's also a dark-haired man with a tuxedo-wearing skeleton tattoo on one forearm, a huge snake wrapped around a dagger on the other. It has to be the man Elvis mentioned: Aoki.

Big Serpent.

They wait a few moments. An important looking boss man in an expensive looking suit walks into the room and shakes Aoki's hand. Boss Man is followed by two meatheads, dragging a skinny, sweaty guy with them. They expertly tie the man's legs to the chair, straighten his arms and attach his hands to the pommel horses. Not their first rodeo.

The man screams, but the sound is muffled by the dirty rag shoved in his mouth. Large veins throb on his purple face.

They finish fastening the man. Aoki nods to the meatheads, who then each wheel over a metal table. The tables hold an assortment of bats, chains, metal rods and other blunt instruments. The bound and gagged man's eyes widen so far, they look ready to pop right out of his head. It's like the scene in *Total Recall* where Schwarzenegger's faceplate smashes on Mars and there's no oxygen. I bet Elvis is thinking the same thing.

The fastened man struggles in vain to release his binds.

Boss Man's eyes are still lit up from the weapons stockpile. He settles on a wooden baseball bat. He grins maniacally as he twists his hands around the bat's handle and gets into a traditional baseball stance. He brings the bat behind his head, then pauses for a few moments.

Boss Man says something inaudible. Everyone except for the bound man laughs. He drops the baseball bat onto the table and switches it for a cricket bat.

Gray-Nicholls. Classic. Must think it's more Australian.

On the other side of the glass, Boss Man's knuckles whiten as he brandishes the cricket bat and points it between the petrified man's eyes. He nods to one of the thugs, who rips the gag from the bound man's mouth.

The man in the chair shakes his head like a laughing clown sideshow game on amphetamines.

Boss Man slowly circles the guy.

I can't turn away.

Boss Man draws the bat high over his head and brings it down with absolute force across the man's body. He explodes with a frenzy of blows, the thumping so hard I can hear it through the walls. It sounds like a butcher pounding raw steak with a mallet and looks worse.

I can't hear what the man yells. His jaw's too busted to talk but he's obviously bargaining for them to let him go. Boss Man does not comply.

The pounding recommences, harder and more furious than before.

My eyes move to Elvis, standing silent, wincing as the guy's limbs bend in ways they're not meant to. Blood pours down the guy's face and he spits globs of blood and broken teeth onto the floor.

Boss Man only stops when his shaking arms can't raise the bat anymore. He drops the bloodied bat to the ground. Aoki nods to him and Boss Man exits, drenched in sweat.

Aoki looks to Elvis, now a whiter shade of pale, looking like he's trying his best not to vomit all over the floor. Elvis shuffles forward and pauses a moment in front of the bloody pulp in the chair. He raises his hand to touch the man and begins. One by one, the bound man's injuries undo. Elvis's hair sticks to his forehead.

It takes him a few minutes, longer than it used to take me, but he succeeds.

Elvis undoes the straps.

The beaten-up man is back to normal physically, but a beaten dog expression paints his face. He's shaking, crying, arms clutching himself. He still has blood on his face and will need a trip to the dentist, but as far as any medical professional could determine, he's okay.

As Elvis walks to the corner closest to me, I risk tapping the glass softly to get his attention, but he looks too exhausted to notice. He rinses the blood off his hands in a stainless-steel industrial sink and dries them with an old dishtowel.

I lean further over and wave through the glass.

I don't notice the metal bowls on the shelf next to me until my elbow connects with them, sending them clattering to the floor.

Everyone in the room turns to the window.

Elvis looks in my direction for a second, his eyes go wide, and he collapses to his knees.

I hop off the metal bench and sprint for the door. I push it open, but the bin must have rolled back, allowing a much smaller space to squeeze through. The foul stench of the alley now smells like freedom. Lucky Elvis bought me some time by falling to the floor. I can only hope they didn't see me or he's in deeper.

The adrenaline feels enough to push me through a needle's eye and I make it through to the outside to the alley. My back and ribs are cut up and grazed, but I'm alive. I shove the bin against the door and put another there as a safety, then sprint down the alley, feeling fast enough to win a regional title of some description. I look back, nothing.

My thoughts are racing so fast as I round the corner that I don't see the man in the trench-coat with the gun until it's too late.

Life flashing, all that.

I'm about to overdose on adrenaline. Then trench-coat lowers the weapon.

'Sorry for scaring you, Emmanuel,' he says. 'Can't be too careful.'

'How the fuck do you know my name?'

His head flicks to the white van parked outside the alley. 'Come on, before they see you.'

He holsters the gun, and the van door opens from the inside. I hop in, and as the door closes, I see men burst through the door into the alley. The van speeds off.

'What's going on? Who are you?'

He removes the trench-coat and hands it to another man in the van.

'Call me Agent Johnson. Everything else is classified.'

I scoff. 'Classic. Okay, "Agent Johnson" it is. What's a government agent doing abducting an Australian citizen for the purpose of experimentation? I thought the Nuremberg trials sorted this out.'

'Emmanuel, look…'

'It's Manny. How'd you find me?'

He takes a deep breath. 'Fine, Manny. We had a flag on E's daughter's file. We received the alert after someone accessed it. We assumed this was you.'

He must've noticed my eyes widen. 'You found her?' he asks.

'Jam? No. Dead end.' I tug at my hair. 'How did you find me tonight?'

'Tracking your rideshare apps.'

'Is that legal?'

He brushes something invisible from his pants. 'It was necessary to follow Elvis.'

It's like he reads my thoughts.

'Yes, we know all about your housemate *and* E. The experiments…'

'Elvis, he's in trouble.'

Agent Johnson nods. 'We know. Have you noticed any major changes in his behaviour?'

The van stops at a set of lights.

'Aside from him being able to heal people who've been beaten to a pulp?'

Agent Johnson smiles tightly. 'So, you know about that. Good. Which segues nicely into my next question. Your friend is healing people. You used to be able to, but now you can't.'

I look between the agents. 'If you know who I am, why aren't you bringing me to a secret facility or whatever and interrogating me?'

Agent Johnson chuckles. 'Real life doesn't quite work like that, Manny. Besides, we know you don't have the ability anymore, otherwise you would've healed that little girl in the hospital corridor, right?' he sighs.

My fists are tight balls. 'What did you do?'

He shut his eyes for a moment. 'She wasn't long for this world, Manny. She had days. We merely accelerated her decline.'

I think of the poison running through her body. 'You killed her.'

'The ends justified it. Manny, certain people wanted answers. An ability like yours is…' He corrects himself. 'Was worth billions. We had to confirm.'

I dig the heels of my palms into my eye sockets.

Agent Johnson taps my leg. 'Look, Manny, your friend Elvis is in big trouble.'

'Why don't you just stop E?'

'This is all relatively new for us too,' he says. 'We don't have jurisdiction, so we don't have the proof. Technically, he's helping heal people, not hurting them himself, and without concrete evidence, we can't prosecute for anything.'

'What about the others like Elvis?'

His eye twitches. 'You know about those then.'

I nod. 'He told me.'

Agent Johnson stares at the van's roof, searching for the words. 'Unfortunately, most of the other firsthand witnesses are in psychiatric wards, so you could imagine what a judge would say about that. The defence would tear it apart in seconds.'

My forehead scrunches. 'Psychiatric wards?'

Agent Johnson pulls out an iPad and shows me a bunch of images of dirty, unkempt young men with sunken eyes. 'Elvis is the latest in a long line of people we suspect E has been experimenting on. The city's psychiatric wards were filling up with dozens of similar cases. All young men, all with the same story about being paid the same sum of money to engage in drug trials and hired to heal people. At first, the story seemed impossible, classic delusional storytelling. But then there were more, then…' He shrugs. 'The only thing more impossible than the stories told by these young men was that it was happening to so many. Collusion on that level is close to impossible.'

'What do I have to do with it?'

'CT scans on all of them showed they all presented with the same abnormality near their cerebrum. Very unusual.'

I know what's next. I wait for it.

'But this abnormality has been observed before, and always deadly. In fact, there's only one person who's ever survived this specific abnormality. Want to hazard a guess?'

I lower my eyes. The van pulls up outside my house and Agent Johnson opens the door.

'What now?' I ask.

'Go about your life, normally, but stay away from the place where we found you today. Don't talk to Elvis about anything you saw, or try to contact E or his daughter. We accessed some of E's communications from the cloud. He's merely a small cog in a global machine that wants you, bad. Fortunately for you, all they have is a code name. We didn't connect the dots until we began following Elvis.'

I step out of the van. Agent Johnson is already closing the door.

I grab it. 'What if Elvis gets hurt, or worse?'

'It's a chance we're willing to take to bring down the organisation behind this.'

I hit the side of the van with my fist, to the obvious disapproval of the agents.

'So, I just eat, go to work, ignore a potentially psychotic roommate, and pretend I'm not tied up in an international conspiracy?'

'Correct,' he says, then slams the door and the van disappears into the night.

FOURTEEN

I pull Mila's hand away from the candle flame several seconds after removing my own, admit defeat and give her the $10. She hides her hand under the tablecloth as the familiar and unwelcome smell of burning flesh fills the air.

We're in a vegan junk-food bar. Its name doesn't matter. It's merely one of the rotating list of local vegan hotspots springing up and shutting down every few months. Gluten-free toast of the town, darling of plant-based blogs and flexitarian restaurant reviewers. Then, gone. People's attention spans aren't long enough to foster long-term restaurants. Blame social media.

'They call it congenital insensitivity to pain,' she says, while I melt an ice cube in my hot hand. 'Except I wasn't born with it. But yeah, I can't feel anything.' Mila holds her blistering hand up in my face. 'Basically means my pain receptors don't work properly.'

The raw flesh on my hand turns to its regular shade of pink. 'What happened?'

She stirs the ice around in the glass with a carboard straw. 'There was an incident when I was a kid, so traumatic it caused a massive endorphin dump. Then bam, no more feeling.'

She'd mentioned something about the pain thing at putt-putt, but I thought she was mucking around.

'That's crazy. So, what's it like? Day to day.'

Mila forks more mac and not-cheese into her mouth. 'Well, I only know I have to pee because there's a pressure inside me. I've got to be careful around knives, as you saw.' She nods to the candles. 'Of course, I burn myself a lot. One time I fell asleep in a hammock in the sunshine and my glasses acted like a magnifying glass and set my dress on fire. I thought I'd spontaneously combusted. Ended up in the burns unit for a few days.'

We take bites of our surprisingly delicious faux cheeseburgers. She continues.

'I'd pretend to hurt myself at school sometimes, so the other kids would think I was normal. One time, I stuck a compass into my arm and accidently nicked an artery; blood spurted everywhere. The teacher probably thought I wasn't screaming because I was in shock but no, it was because I didn't feel a thing.'

I shove a wad of truffle oil-soaked shoestring fries into my mouth. 'At least you went to school.'

Her cheek twitches. 'I missed a lot. I was sick, in and out of hospital and home. Once the school became aware of my condition, I wasn't allowed to play sports or muck around at lunch in case I got hurt. They figured I could end up with internal bleeding or something and not even know it, then sue them.'

Mila finishes her organic hemp beer and signals for another and more gluten-free bread. 'One night I went into the Valley, and a Neanderthal-looking steroid freak was eyeing me off in Ric's Bar. I was uncomfortable, so I left. He followed me.'

The bread arrives alongside two more organic beers.

'Then what?' I ask.

'I walked faster, but he was a big dude, his long strides kept up with my smaller ones.' She pauses to take a large swig of her beer. 'I turned down the next alley. He grabbed me by my arm and spun me toward him. I was sure he was going to rape me. I froze.'

Unsure of how to respond, I eat a few cruelty-free mixed nuts from the wooden bowl.

'He slammed me into a brick wall, then slapped me as hard as he could, probably hoping to subdue me.'

She's calm, like she's talking about a bartender spilling her glass of Coke on the bar.

'And then?'

'I screamed and doubled over. He lurched towards me, and I exploded, punched him in the balls as hard as possible.'

I smile at the thought of her incapacitating a huge Hulk-like figure.

'Then it was *him* doubling over. I brought my elbow down on the back of his head, as hard as I could. Then I swung a punch at his bloated face so hard he dropped like a sack of flour. Out cold. Some lady from the street was running towards me shouting, 'What did he do to you?''

'And?'

'I said, 'Nothing, I'm fine,' but then I followed her open-mouthed gaze to my dangling right arm. I'd whacked this jerk so hard I'd snapped my arm in two. It didn't look right. I passed out right there in the alley. So, again, to the hospital.'

We clink glasses.

'To the hospital.'

I drain my beer and signal the waiter for two more. He brings them back. They have pictures of The Phantom on them. 'Anything else folks?' he asks.

Mila picks up the bottle and scans the label. 'Yeah, if The Phantom had to get his arm amputated, reckon he'd experience phantom limb syndrome?'

The waiter seems unsure, more focused on freeing up the table. We order some spongy rubber dessert-like ball. He walks away with a confused and disapproving frown.

The beer tastes of the jungle.

'So, where do you work?' I ask.

'The vet on Stanley Street, few doors down from Brewhouse.'

Lightbulb.

'It's the vet next to The Fish Café, right?'

She nods.

'That's where Scraps is,' I say. 'Sue's corgi. A paramedic dropped him off.'

Mila laughs so hard she begins to cough. She wipes the tears from the corner of her eyes. 'His name is Scraps? The woman who dropped him off never told me. I've been calling him Odie.'

'Odie? Because he overdosed?'

'No, because he didn't have a name tag and mainly because I love Garfield.'

I drink my Phantom beer and consider the coincidence. 'You right to look after him for a while?'

'Of course,' she beams.

I cut a slice off the weird dessert ball. 'Always thought it was a weird combination of establishments. Fish and chip shop and a veterinary clinic.'

'If I had a dollar for every time someone asked if we supply them with our dead fish, I'd be able to buy the joint.'

A comfortable pause surrounds us.

Mila clears her throat. 'Are you afraid of intimacy?'

I don't know how to respond.

She laughs it off. 'Well, that answers that one. Don't worry, the entire human race is.'

She bites a chunk of the purple sponge. 'You ever hurt yourself at school?' she asks.

I think for a few moments and a memory floods back.

'I borrowed a kid's wheelchair after one of the bigger kids dared me to go down The Big Hill – a steep concrete slope, lined by those chains connected to poles. I didn't realise the wheelchair's brakes were shot. I achieved so much speed down the hill, I had to bail before I ended up in the huge duck pond at the bottom. I jumped out and slid

166

a few metres on my hands and knees. Raw bloody mess but healed myself before class…' I catch myself.

I sip my beer and my words hang.

'Have you been holding out on me, Manny?'

'It's kind of unbelievable.'

'More than my condition?' she scoffs. 'Tell me, tell me something unbelievable.'

'I, uh… used to have a healing ability, I guess.'

I still can't admit my situation without stumbling. But she hasn't left yet. A good sign.

'Like a superhero,' she says.

I shake my head. 'Not quite.'

'Go on,' she says.

'Whenever I touch someone with my hand, I can see inside them, well I can see their sickness or damaged organs or whatever. But then there was a car accident, and then…'

'Do me. Tell me what you see.'

I reach my hand out and grab hers, instantly feeling the energy running between us.

It's electric. It's everything. I have to let go.

'You've got extensive nerve damage,' I say.

'I could tell you that.'

'I would've been able to heal it, once.'

'But not anymore?'

I lower my head.

Mila drains the rest of her beer. 'But you were a superhero.'

'More a reverse superhero,' I mumble. 'Had powers, lost them.'

Her face lights up. 'You're not in rare company. Ask Spiderman, Superman, Captain America, The Thing, Wonder Woman and pretty much every mutant ever.'

I finish my beer. 'Sure, but their powers returned. Plus, they're comic book characters.'

The waiter drops the cheque on the table, we each throw down a couple of $20 notes and walk into the night.

'It could be worse,' she says.

I take a deep breath. I know she means well. 'The only thing worse than not having superpowers is having them, then having them stripped from you. My deficiency is permanent; I'm destined to live the rest of my life as a worker ant.'

She punches me in the arm. 'Geez, way to bring the mood down.'

'Sorry. Want to go watch a band?'

'Sure.'

I grab her hand and we walk down the street. We're about to cross the road when I notice her eyes brimming with tears. 'What is it?'

'I can feel your energy.' Mila kisses me then pulls back. 'I've got to go. Sorry.' She disappears into the night.

FIFTEEN

THE dog is on the side on the footpath, outside our house. It's a somethingadoodle, a female puppy. She's dripping wet, shivering under the mailbox. Tiny, needle teeth slobbering, her name tag says, "Chew Barka."

Despite her current situation, she looks well looked after. She's a chestnut colour that lightens when I dry her off at home. I don't have any dog food, so I pour her a bowl of Corn Flakes, heat up some leftover roast chicken, and fill a bowl with water. She laps it up, tail wagging manically. Elvis enters the kitchen. He looks like a walking corpse.

'What's that?' he asks.

'A dog.'

'Why though?'

'Her parents were dogs.'

He chucks a couple of pieces of bread into the toaster, looks at me like he's waiting for me to continue.

'I found her this morning, all wet and shaking. Figure I'll take her to Mila's vet and see if she's microchipped or whatever.'

He eyes me. 'So, you abducted a dog from a kid at the park.'

'Serious, man, found her, no collar or anything.'

I can't think of how to ask, so I rip the band aid off.

'Elvis?'

He braces against the kitchen sink, stares at the backyard. 'What?'

'I need you to take me to E.'

'No fucking way,' he says, then starts heaving like he's hyperventilating. When he spins to me, a thick vein stands out on his forehead. He snatches the toast as it pops up from the toaster. 'Don't follow me again, Manny, or I'll have to hurt you, if only to save you.'

He storms out.

Once Chew Barka finishes eating, I wrap her in a towel and take her to the car. I keep her in my lap for the drive. She burrows herself and eventually settles while I stroke her soft fur. I park right outside the vet.

Mila processes the patient while I read glossy pamphlets about pet behavioural issues, worming, flea treatments and hip dysplasia until she comes back. When Mila does, she's smiling. 'She'll be fine, she's actually having a sleep. Big morning.' She checks her watch. 'I'm on break now, want to join me for lunch?'

I nod, then tuck the pamphlets back into the clear acrylic holders.

We sit at the Fish Café next to the Vet, picking chips like a couple of seagulls, people watching. A guy across the street is walking his dog, a huge Alsatian. When it stops to do what dogs do, the guy pretends he doesn't notice and continues with his day like his giant dog hasn't just left a knee-high pyramid of shit behind.

'People,' I say.

'Aren't they just the worst,' goes Mila.

Seconds later a police officer marches the guy back to the pile of dog doo and watches cross-armed while the guy cleans up the evidence. The guy looks angry and humiliated; the dog doesn't seem too fussed.

'What's the one behaviour you'd ban people from doing?' Mila asks.

I don't have to think.

'Clapping on the downbeat in songs.'

She sips her milkshake and nods approvingly. 'I like that one.'

Mila squeezes lemon on some of the chips, I cringe.

'Lemon no good?' she asks.

'Never got it.'

She shrugs, tucks a few strands of hair behind her ear. 'What's it like working at the hospital?'

'Oscillates between unbelievably interesting and mind-numbingly boring.'

'I wish it was like that here,' she says. She pulls out her vape and blows a blueberry cloud over me. 'I love animals. It's the owners that are hard work.'

I grab a handful of non-lemon chips, dip them in the blob of tombo sauce. 'Did you always want to work in a vet?'

Her shoulders do a little jig. 'When I was real young, I wanted to be a doctor and work in a hospital, seeing as though I spent such a huge chunk of my childhood there. Wanted to help people. Ended up helping animals.'

'Not a bad thing.'

She finishes her milkshake. 'But to answer your question. Fell into it by default. The family business. There are worse things than growing up with thousands of animals, even if they are transient.' Concern crosses her face. 'What's the weirdest stuff *you* see?'

I think for a tick. 'Dead bodies are pretty standard. Lots of messed up stuff from accidents. It's been a weird couple of weeks.'

I tell her about the Viagra coma guy, the hostage situation, the whisky enema, the ice addict falling through the roof, the plastic surgery addict hoarder, the fattest man in Brisbane.

'Wow,' she says, taking a huge draw of her vape and exhaling the cloud. I grab it off her and take a drag. It's like candy. No wonder the kids like it.

'Guaranteed weirdest day every year is Valentine's Day,' I say. 'Most hospitals put on extra staff to deal with it.'

Her eyes widen. 'What happens on Valentine's Day?'

'Sex accidents galore. Lots of solo stuff. Various items in orifices that don't belong there. Candles, bottles, Matchbox cars, frozen hotdogs.'

'What else?'

I scratch my beard, think how to put it less crudely. I fail.

'One dude tied a rubber band to keep his erection, and it was so tight he ruptured a bunch of blood vessels. Another guy covered himself in peanut butter, and his dog bit half his knob off and buried it in the backyard. Standard penis-getting-stuck-in-things like vacuum cleaners, bottles, even saw an orthodontic incident with braces once. The couple were in the ambulance together. Took the doctors an hour to separate them.'

'Fascinating,' Mila says, genuinely captivated, before turning solemn. 'All my experiences at hospital were terrible. Agony. Cancer's a bitch.'

Something twigs, but I can't clutch it. I shake my head.

'I thought you have that pain insensitivity thing?'

She nods, grimaces. 'Yeah, but before. I've had it all. Got the issues, told you already.'

My brain was running a couple of clicks slow. 'Shit!' I stand so quickly I feel lightheaded as I rifle through my pockets.

'What is it?' Mila asks, eyes white and wide.

'I've been getting these notes lately.'

Mila grabs my arm.

I pull out my wallet, but it's gone.

'I burnt it. I burnt the note. It said some 'power is inside you' crap, but I'm pretty sure the last line was 'cancer's a bitch.' And when you said it just now, it took a second, but I remembered.'

Mila shifts in her chair. 'Coincidence.'

Her watch alarm beeps.

'I have to go back. You're a fascinating specimen, Manny,' she says, holding my hand. Her dazzling eyes stare into mine. 'You've been through a lot, and you're amazing. I wanted to tell you.'

'Thanks,' I shrug.

'And thank you for bringing Chew Barka in. Her family will be so happy when they pick her up this arvo.'

'Glad to hear it.'

'Want to do something tomorrow before work?'

I think for a moment. 'I've got two free tickets for the Kookaburra Queen, that old-timey, river boat, and they expire soon. A patient gave them to me. Could be fun, in an ironic way.'

'Sure,' she says, kisses me on the cheek and goes back to work.

No note when I get home. No Elvis either.

SIXTEEN

MILA and I walk through hordes of tourists along the cobblestones and wooden slat pathways of Riverside. The tour operator rips our tickets as we board the Kookaburra Queen. The old-fashioned paddle steamer leaves the dock, rolls smoothly along the big, brown snake that is the Brisbane River.

We have a couple of beers, then join a large group of geriatrics in line for the buffet which consists of an array of slow-cooked meats and softer foods that won't hassle dentures. A big Kiwi guy, pulling double duty as the tour guide *and* the onboard entertainment, sings an uninspired version of *Brown Eyed Girl* on a cheap, portable karaoke machine. The accident flashes in my mind.

The boat ride lasts two hours, feels longer. I mention how worried I am about Elvis, but Mila barely acknowledges my concern. Says there's nothing I can do. She's right.

Back on land, we sit on a bench and stare out at the river.

Mila kicks my foot, knocking me from my trance.

I blink a couple of times. 'Huh?'

'I'll come visit tomorrow, if you're home.'

'It's a date.'

We hug, Mila heads to work and I drop by the hospital to visit Sue. Her skin is grey and her forehead is sweaty and matted with hair. She must be detoxing badly. She has a book of Aesop's Fables clutched to her chest.

She opens one eye. 'You read any of these?'

I shake my head. 'They any good?'

'Yeah, wasn't much choice when the library girl came around. Aesop wrote these in jail.'

'Right. He probably should've written a fable about staying out of jail and followed his own advice.'

Sue places the book on the side table. 'You cut down drinking yet?'

'Been thinking about it,' I say, shuffling my feet on the floor. Never thought I'd see the day where Sue was concerned about anyone else besides herself.

'Thinking?' she says. 'You need to find a balance between your mind and body.'

'Where's this coming from?'

'Our circle of trust sessions.'

She shuts her eyes. I remain silent while checking her chart. She's on a bunch of meds I've never heard of. The ones I have, though, are detox meds. She'll be loopy for a while. Her single eye opens again. 'It's only fear preventing you from seeing the light.'

'Okay, enough for today.'

'Sure, run away,' she says.

'We'll continue this tomorrow.'

'Yes, why do today what you can put off until tomorrow? What if there is no tomorrow?' she whispers, before falling asleep.

Outside into the oppressive heat. It's the kind of muggy, humid summer day Queensland is renowned for. And of course, there's no hot, clear blue day without an afternoon storm. The kind that rolls in when the heat forces the heavens to open and blow the guts out of everything. Sure enough, by afternoon, the thick, dark clouds move over the city and unleash sheets of torrential rain. Water floods the streets. Garbage rushes the gutters and blocks the drains. Billboards and unsecured backyard trampolines fly into already damaged cars.

~

175

The next day, still no sign of Elvis, but I don't know what I could say to the police without them shipping me straight to the mental health ward.

I stick a pre-made, tofu turkey roast in the oven for late lunch and choose an old episode of *The Simpsons*. Within five minutes there's a knock on the door: Mila.

'What's going on?' she asks.

'Waiting for the tofurkey to cook.'

'Did you know the first meal eaten on the moon was a roast turkey?'

She walks in and I close the door. 'I did not. How's your day?'

'I walked Poe and then watched a lecture on neural plasticity.'

'That's still weird, the cat walking.'

We sit around the kitchen table, all domestic like.

'Do you think they should be teaching kids about how the aliens built the pyramids in history class?' she asks.

'Huh?'

'Do you think they should be teaching kids about how the aliens built the pyramids in history class?' she repeats, elbowing me from my daze. 'What's up with you?'

'Elvis still hasn't come home.'

'If he's going to mess around with the type of people you said he was, there aren't many options. You lay down with dogs, you get up with fleas.'

'The police could do something, maybe.'

'They're a little too preoccupied with proper police work to take on conspiracy theories.'

Instead of listening to the niggling inner voice telling me something's seriously wrong, I retrieve a couple of beers from the fridge and pop the tops with a knife.

'Sorry. History class, aliens and pyramids, sure. Give the kids the information.'

We finish eating and wash the dishes together. She stops drying a coffee cup and stares at it. It has a hand painted dolphin on it.

'What?' I ask as she hands me the cup.

'Let's go to Sea World. Take your mind off things. Then we could go to the beach. Stay down there, sleep on the sand if we want.'

'Sea World. Now? There's probably only a few hours until they close.'

'Perfect. You have any sleeping bags?'

I put the tea towel on the rack. 'I do somewhere, from when I camped at Woodford Folk Festival.'

I search through the linen cupboard and find two red sleeping bags stuffed in the bottom. Good to go. We listen to '90s Aussie rock on the trip, arriving at Sea World two hours before closing time.

The ticket attendant sells us a couple of heavily discounted tickets. Only a few straggling families remain, so we have the park mostly to ourselves. We see the penguins, manta rays, polar bears, sea jellies, sharks (not the cool ones), creatures of the deep and do a few rides. It's almost closing time by the time we make it to the dolphin enclosure.

We watch the dolphins dart in and out with each other.

I grab Mila's hand. 'Beautiful huh.'

'One of the most magical animals I've ever seen.'

The dolphins' slick movements as they carve the water is hypnotic. I realise this is the first time I've seen them in real life. Five minutes later, the park sound system activates with the pre-recorded closing message. I check the time. 'Wish we came here first. I could watch them for ages.'

Mila smirks. 'Follow me.'

Despite every inclination not to, I do. I follow her around the dolphin enclosure to the trainers' entrance. The heat rises to my face.

'Boost me,' she says.

'What? We're not going in there.'

'Heck yeah, we are. Boost me.'

I grab Mila's wrist, probably too hard but she can't feel it, so it doesn't matter. 'This is crazy.'

I shut my eyes tight for a moment. Breathe, wait for the heat to die down. I'm almost ashamed how quickly I flip flop.

'Alright, let's go.'

I can't see any cameras and the park looks deserted bar a few exhausted parents dragging their sugar-crashing children towards the exits. We climb the fence with ease. The dolphins aren't paying much attention to the fact we've entered their domain.

'Give me one of those,' Mila says, pointing to the toy container next to my feet. I choose a blue, rubber baton with an oval ball attached to its end. The dolphins' curiosity piqued, they circle the end of the enclosure closest to us.

'Play it cool,' she says.

So I do.

'Pick up that bucket of fish,' she says.

So I do.

'You watch that doco about the orca at SeaWorld in the States who killed four people?'

'Serial Killer Whale?' I offer, trying to lighten the mood and settle the flooding anxiety.

'*Blackfish.*'

'What about it?'

She lets out a huge whoosh of air. 'We've got to free these dolphins.'

Next moment, I'm pulling the metal pegs from the main gate while Mila holds the dolphins' attention with the toys and a few juicy fish. She strokes their snouts and they seem completely at ease with her. I hit the green button to raise the gate, setting off an alarm, but the dolphins know what to do.

We all bolt.

The dolphins swim into the causeway towards the big blue ocean. Mila and I run towards the trainer room. We exit through the staff entrance. We've made it to the car when I hear yelling and see the security guard sprinting towards us. I jump behind the wheel and fire up the ignition. The engine splutters.

'Come on!'

Again. It coughs, dies. What a time for it not to turn over.

Now I'm going to jail for dolphin liberation. Great.

The security guard, red-faced and puffing, knocks on the window. He's holding something in his other hand. I wind my window halfway down.

'Emmanuel Ellison?' he asks.

'Yes.'

'Sorry to startle you, folks. You must have dropped this earlier.'

My wallet. I take it from his hand, my fingers shaking.

'Thanks a lot, man.'

'No worries. Have a pleasant evening and Merry Christmas, hey.'

'You too.'

My heartrate settles as I try the ignition again and it turns over. We head south, towards Burleigh Heads.

'Close,' Mila says, as she takes my hand. She wraps her arms around me and kisses me. The car swerves, I breathe the salty air.

'You don't want the window halfway down,' she says. 'All the way up or all the way down. Reduces the risk of decapitation.'

I crank the handle and wind it all the way down.

She grabs my hand on the gearstick. 'Didn't that feel good? Saving those poor dolphins.'

'It was risky.'

'But worth it, right? You saved lives today, Manny, without your ability. Maybe you don't need it back after all. Maybe you can be normal and be okay with being normal.'

I shift my hand from hers to the steering wheel. I know she means well but it's irritating to hear, like being told it's okay to be impotent and insignificant. I'm sick of being normal – normal sucks. I speed around a moving truck and take the Smith Street exit.

'I'm going to get it back, even if it kills me.'

We find a good park right on the esplanade and soon enough we're sitting on a bench in the sand, staring at the water. Dozens of seagulls hang around doing whatever seagulls do. Mila eats chips while I drink a too-hot almond latte in a small bucket.

'Coffee is for chumps,' she says. 'Actually, let me rephrase. Paying for coffee is for chumps. Do you know how much it costs to make a cup of coffee?'

'No idea,' I say.

'It's like eleven cents. Same as popcorn, except with popcorn it's marked up 2000%.'

'Oh well, what are you going to do,' I say.

'Nothing,' goes Mila. 'I don't drink coffee or eat popcorn.'

'Right, you're one of those people coffee drinkers hate. And what's wrong with popcorn?'

'The kernels get stuck in my teeth.'

I throw a lame seagull a chip.

'Can't you read?' teases Mila, pointing to the sign. 'It says, don't feed the seagulls.'

'Yeah, but this one is missing a leg and he looks hungry. I'm helping him.'

'What about natural selection? Now the other seagulls are going to peck the tar out of him because he got food, and they didn't.'

Some points are hard to rebuke.

'Is that thing about birds exploding when you give them paracetamol true?' I ask.

'It's not good for them. Rice at weddings is not good for them either.'

'Seagulls have no business being at weddings.'

'What about beach weddings?'

'Oh, right.' I pull out my Marlboros, but the wind seems to pick up every time I flick the wheel of my lighter to spark one up. Fires always seem to go out when you don't want them to, and when you do want them to, they burn your house down.

I throw the coffee in the bin and go to lay out the open sleeping bag so we can lie down, but Mila goes straight for the sand. She pinches some sand and rubs it between her fingers.

'It's exactly what anyone could want from a beach. There's the sound of water lapping against the shore, the organic salty smell in the air you can also taste. And look,' she says sweeping her hand across the horizon, 'thousands of shards of light glistening off the ocean surface. But the touch, oh god, I wish I could feel the sand and the breeze. Then this would be perfect.' Her smile looks faint. 'Describe what the sand feels like. I can't remember.'

My brain struggles. I think for a moment.

'It's soft. It moulds to the shape of my body like a memory foam pillow. It's still warm on top but cooler when I burrow my feet in it. Feels comforting, safe.'

Mila picks up a handful of sand and lets it drain like an hourglass across my legs.

'That tickles but it's not only that. When the breeze picks up, the sand feels more like hundreds of tiny needles.'

Night falls – the moonlight and stars reflect across the dark expanse of the ocean. Mila grabs my hand. 'It's a perfect night to sleep on the beach.'

We lie down on the sleeping bags and burrow into the sand. Mila falls asleep with her head on my chest. I listen to the ocean and her soft breathing. For a moment, everything feels right. I sleep dreamlessly until the sun peeks over the horizon.

When I wake, Mila is gone.

Her clothes are in a heap next to me.

I sit up and rub the sleep and sand from my eyes and hold my breath as I scan the beach. I exhale when I see her skinny dipping in the ocean. She waves, paddles around for a while before running back. The water droplets on her naked body glisten in the morning sun. The light forms a halo behind her and her perfect silhouette. I pull her towards me, she's covered in goose bumps.

'Can you feel cold?' I ask.

'No. I still shiver, my lips still turn purple and my teeth chatter, but that's it.'

There will be tourists and families on the beach soon, so we don't have much time alone.

We spend the day together. It's nice. It's normal.

I don't drink.

I don't smoke.

I don't need anything besides her.

SEVENTEEN

I'M reading in my room when I hear the thud.

Elvis is back. On his back, writhing on the floor, screaming and trying to pull his hair out. One eye is fused shut in an ugly purple and black mess. I try holding him down, but he's too strong and keeps bucking me off.

'They're in my brain,' he screams.

He's thrashing around and drenched in sweat, slipping through my fingers. It reminds me of trying to hold onto my suicidal goldfish.

'I can feel them in me, Manny.'

I finally sit on his chest and pin his arms with my knees, holding his head between my hands. 'What are you talking about?'

'They're screaming in my head.'

I slap him, hard, both eyes open wide, filled with fear. I remember the shivering dog, stroke his hair. Miraculously, he begins to settle.

'Breathe, dude,' I tell him.

His face scrunches as he bursts into tears and takes great, big, honking breaths trying to calm down. 'He never told me.'

'Try to relax,' I say, and soon feel him soften beneath me. I hop off and help him sit against the wall.

'Get me a beer, Manny.'

'I don't know if that's a good idea.'

He searches my eyes. My heart cracks for him.

'It's the only thing that quietens the sounds,' he says. He's regressed into a little kid.

I move to the fridge, grab two beers and pop the tops off with a lighter. When I return, he's curled into a foetal position, so I cradle his head in my arm and pour the beer into his mouth. I feel like I'm feeding an abandoned kangaroo joey. He gulps it, shaking, but settles after a minute. Now I'm shaking. I drink the other beer.

He sits up, running his hands through his sweat-soaked hair.

'Get me outta the house.'

I pick Elvis up and half drag, half carry him into the backyard. I plop him on a camping chair in front of a table made from wooden pallets. I head inside, pull my phone out to call the police, but chicken out. I grab his leather jacket in case he's cold. When I get back, there's a cigarette dangling from his lips. He's statuesque, except for his hands, which shake so much he can't light his cigarette, so I do it for him.

'Elvis.'

He's got the thousand-yard stare going on.

'Elvis.'

I grab his shoulders and shake him.

'You've gotta cut the cord, man. You need to get out.'

He twitches but continues staring through me. He takes a long drag of his cigarette and holds it in for a long time before finally releasing the plume from the side of his mouth.

'Can't. They'll kill me.'

'Then leave town for a while, I'll vouch for you at work.'

Elvis drops his head. 'They'll hurt you. E told me they would. Told me more too.'

'What else?'

'You're special to him, Manny. You healed his daughter when no one else could.'

'I told you. Then the accident happened. He injected me so I could be normal again.'

184

'No, Manny,' Elvis shudders. 'You're not normal. He hid it from you is all. That stuff E injected you with after the accident. You said he did it after the car crash.'

'Yeah?'

'It's only a suppressant to mask your ability. He wants to awaken it.'

'Awaken it?'

Elvis takes another drag and looks me dead in the eye. He coughs a glob of blood into his hand. I grab a tea towel that's fallen off the clothesline and hand it to him.

'I'm dying here, man,' he says, his teeth are pink with blood.

'Oh fuck.'

'Yeah, oh fuck, all right. I'm in way over my head.'

I grab us another couple of beers. We sit and deliberate, searching for an escape.

Contact the cops. Rejected.

Contact the fair work ombudsmen. Redundant.

Contact Batman. Ridiculous.

There's no clear exit. No light at the end of any tunnel.

Elvis sits frozen, staring into the distance.

He slams his half-empty beer bottle on the table. 'You're right, I've got to cut the cord.'

'You're going, right now?'

'No time like the present.'

'You sure this is a good idea?'

'No, it's an atrocious idea, but it's the best of a bad bunch.'

'I'm coming with you,' I say, and toss the empty bottles into the bin.

'No.' Elvis cauterises the conversation.

He puts on his leather jacket and lights another cigarette.

'I'll be back in two hours. It's safer if you stay.'

'What happens after two hours? Call the cops?'

'Don't bother.'

185

He necks the rest of his beer and stands before I have a chance to respond.

We engage in a standard man hug; two pats on the back. He's lost a lot of weight; I can feel his ribcage through his jacket. Elvis hacks another glob of blood into his hand and wipes it off on his jeans. 'I'm sorry, man.'

I just nod.

'And one more thing,' he says. 'Your girlfriend isn't who you think she is.'

He's crazy, but my mind whirs as he exits.

~

The night noise creeps in. Ceiling fan, delivery trucks, passing planes, alien signals.

I start to drift off, but right before sleep comes, there's a tap on my window.

A bird or a possum.

The tapping persists, so I pull myself from bed, slip on a pair of boxers and shuffle to the window and open it. Nothing.

Mila pops into view like a jack-in-the-box, breathes a cloud of blueberry vape steam into my room. I step back and trip on the clothes basket. I help pull her inside and we tumble to the floor.

Her arm flies and hits me in the face. 'Sorry!'

'This house has a front door.' A thought scratches the edges of my brain. 'How did you know where I lived – the first time when you left the note?'

'Followed you after I saw you at the river. To make sure you weren't a maniac.'

'You stalked me?'

'Right.' Mila stands and holds out her arms and helps me to my feet.

'You hungry?' I ask.

She walks into the hallway. 'Sure, I could eat. What've you got?'

I lead the way to the kitchen.

186

'Wedges or chips or something.'

'Perfect.'

I dump the bag of wedges in the air fryer and stare out the window. I shouldn't have let Elvis go alone.

Mila sidles up to me. 'What's up?'

'Nothing. Give me a minute.'

She looks hurt, moves to the lounge room. I disappear into a thought vortex.

What if he gets hurt? What if he dies? What if he ends up in the mental health ward? Is this all my fault? Maybe I can call someone? I need to find E.

My mind spins, scenarios play out. None of them good.

The air fryer beeps. I bring three different-sized, wooden bowls on a matching wooden tray into the lounge room. Mila picks up one of the crunchy ones, blows on it and dips it in both sauce bowls.

'The first person to put sour cream and sweet chilli together with wedges was a freaking genius.'

'Uh huh,' I say, through a mouth full of wedges.

We eat in silence.

She stares at me as I absentmindedly take the last wedge.

'What's going on, Manny. You're somewhere else.'

My ringing phone mercifully interrupts.

'Hello?'

'Manny, Agent Johnson here. Just checking in.'

'Oh, hey,' I say, moving into the kitchen.

'I'll get straight to it,' he says. 'Have you seen Elvis recently?'

'He came back tonight for a while but disappeared a few hours ago.' I check the time on my phone. 'He should've been back by now. Why?'

'Two young men who were experiencing psychotic episodes were arrested today. One attacked an old lady in the botanical gardens and now she's in ICU. Another got into a fistfight at the Plough Inn with a bunch of guys watching the footy.'

'Jesus.'

'Also, I'm sorry to say a young man jumped off the Story Bridge this evening.'

My knees buckle and coldness rushes over me. Oh no.

'Elvis, I'm sorry,' I say, in a small voice.

The silence on the other end, I soon realise, is from Agent Johnson's confusion.

'Huh? No, geez, sorry Manny, I didn't mean to give you that impression. I just finished interviewing the young man's family. They gave a similar story about him having a new job and his personality changing. Goddamned tragedy.'

Realising I've been holding my breath, I let out a huge whoosh of air. 'So he's okay?'

'If okay means not dead, then probably. But I need you to go through Elvis's room, find anything you can that may help provide information to this wider syndicate. We need to get on top of this. He's our only active lead.'

'What about the building?'

'There's been no further activity in there since we first met. No one in or out. We've stopped surveillance, we need all the resources we can get.'

'Right.'

'Call or text if you find anything. Be safe. And stay away from that building.'

Don't push the big red button.

'Yeah, no worries,' I say.

I hang up and head back to the lounge room. Mila's looking concerned. 'What's wrong?'

I grab my stuff off the table. 'I need to find Elvis. I'm going to the building where he healed those people. See if I can find some clues or something.'

'I'm coming with you,' she says, like I'd said to Elvis earlier.

She gets the same response.

'Why not?' Mila grabs my wrists, but I shake her off.

'Too dangerous.'

And I'm not sure I fully trust you.

Elvis's warning about Mila rings in my ears. She looks hurt but doesn't push it. She walks off as I hop in the car and drive towards the alley near Heartbreakers.

I park a few blocks away. No one's following. Even though it's late, people walk up and down the footpaths, going about their lives, carrying shopping bags, takeout or dogs in prams, an escalating trend of concern.

One more scan of the neighbourhood before entering the alley. Nothing, but I'm not very observant, so it's not overly comforting. Aside from it being shrouded in darkness, the alley looks and smells the same as when I was here last. I squeeze in between the bins to the door, careful to leave enough space between them this time for an unobstructed escape.

The next phase depends on whether the purple key I copied is actually for this door. Otherwise, I've wasted a couple of bucks and I'm shit outta luck. I withdraw it from the tiny square watchpocket of my jeans. Before I can stick it in the lock, a figure moves at the end of the alley.

I duck, listen for footsteps, look under the bin to the end of the alley. No human silhouette, just the street streetlights. Maybe a drunk person accidently stumbling into the alley for a moment. I wait another minute to be safe, stand and shove the purple key into the keyhole. It turns first go.

I carefully open the door and stick my head in. It's pitch black. No light from the bigger room. I slide into the kitchen, reaching blindly for the light switch. Should've brought a torch – phone flashlight will have to do.

I move from the kitchen into the huge room where I'd watched Elvis heal that poor, tortured guy tied to a chair.

The coppery scent of blood cuts through the stink of cleaning chemicals. The smell reminds me of a school trip to the Murarrie

189

Meatworks. I'm still unsure why someone thought it was a good idea to take a bunch of primary school kids to a slaughterhouse; maybe Australia Zoo and the Daisy Hill Koala Sanctuary were already booked out that day.

In the torture room, there's still no obvious light switch. The main light panel must be on the far side of the room near the offices, but I'm going to need to risk it. I creep over and find the main switch. The fluorescent lights stutter for a few moments before exploding to life.

The chair's gone, the blood's gone.

The floors have been scrubbed. Nothing left behind but mop streaks of white residue, but I'm sure if I had a black light the whole room would look like a sea of luminous jellyfish.

The main office is the next stop. It has a wooden door with a glass window. I pull out the key in hope it will fit this lock too, but I'm not that lucky. I stuff the key in my pocket, search for something to smash the window. For a torture room, it's ironically lacking tools for an office break-in, so I'm going to try kicking the door in. Movies have taught me to kick near the lock, but this isn't a prop door. I raise my knee and kick the sole of my shoes against the door to test it. There's a little give, needs more power. I retreat a few metres, take a running start and a flying kick with all my force. The door frame splits and the door smashes against the wall and I crash to the ground, winded. I'm too busy rolling on the ground gasping for air to enjoy my first experience as a human battering ram.

After catching my breath, I use the busted door frame to stand, then limp into the office and search for anything helpful. Unfortunately, I don't know what that is. My conversation with the girl from the mental health ward and what she said about finding a needle in the ocean comes to mind. I sift through the papers on the desk and the drawers: invoices, financial statements, shipping orders. I've almost given up when, in the rear of the bottom drawer, I find a yellow envelope in a tin box. I dump its contents onto the desk. Dozens of USB sticks with random letters and dates.

'Holy shit.' It could be nothing, it could be everything.

Fingers crossed as I turn on a random laptop, my excitement is extinguished when the password request comes up. I hadn't noticed usernames or passwords in my search, and I'm not playing that game. I close the laptop lid, slide the USB sticks into the yellow envelope and shove it into my pocket. I shut the desk drawers and try to neaten things, but with my lack of attention to detail issue, it's probably obvious someone's messed around in there. The door hanging off its hinges for instance.

'What the fuck are you doing?'

I spin around to the doorway, where there stands what looks like a shaved gorilla in a security uniform. His shoulders touch the sides of the doorframe, his blockhead crew-cut grazes the top of it. His face is red and his steroid-inflamed muscles are swollen enough to burst through his skin like an unforked BBQ sausage. He doesn't move – there's nowhere else for me to go but straight through the man mountain, an impossible task. He smiles as he beckons me towards him with a bratwurst finger. Hopeless, I move forward.

His fist is as big as a car battery. He grabs my arm, which he could probably snap in two like a chopstick. 'Give me the envelope,' he grunts.

I reach for the envelope, but he drags me outside the office and throws me to the floor.

The shaved gorilla pulls out his phone and dials. A few seconds later someone answers.

'I've got him.'

He watches me for a moment, spits on the ground.

'Nah, he's alone.'

I think about making a move, but he must have read my thoughts because next moment there's a gun pointed at the middle of my face.

'Hang on a sec,' he says into the phone, then to me, 'You think about moving, I'll shoot ya. Got it?'

I nod.

'Close your eyes until I tell you to open 'em.'

I feel like a coward as I shut my eyes tight but it's an angry, steroid gorilla with a gun. He says to the person on the other end of the call, 'I'll tie him up and bring him over. Yeah, yeah, I won't rough him up too bad. You got the cash? Good. See you in twenty.'

His phone beeps and there's silence for a moment.

'Keep your eyes shut,' he says, then walks off, returning in seconds, dashing any hopes of a getaway.

He grunts as he leans down. The heat radiates from him as he wraps the rope around my wrists. He pulls it so tight it burns my skin. It takes me back to school and the days of Chinese burns or Indian burns, or whichever culturally-insensitive-named burns.

'Okay,' he says. 'Open 'em and stand.'

I figure he means my eyes, but I pause. The slap to my face feels like a hot basketball and my head connects with the wall. Stars spin around. My hands are filled with pins and needles, arteries poking out.

'The rope's too tight.'

'Tough. Now get up.'

I've never tried standing with my hands bound and it shows. I'm rolling around on the ground; a newborn calf trying to stand for the first time.

A giant boot connects with my stomach. 'Hurry up.'

'That's not helping,' I gasp, floundering, before finding my footing. I press my back against the wall for leverage, slowly creeping up against it. When I find my feet and stand straight, there's a loud crack and the giant shaved gorilla deflates and collapses to his knees. Another crack and his eyes open wide before rolling back and he falls to the floor.

Standing over the hulking giant is Mila with a baseball bat.

It's like a re-creation of the famous photo of Muhammad Ali standing over the stunned Sonny Liston laid out on the canvas. The giant between us groans, already stirring.

'Quick,' Mila says, 'let's get outta here.'

192

I snatch the envelope with the USB sticks from the steroid gorilla's gigantic paw. Blood leaks from his head, forming red pools on the floor.

We cross the floor, scramble through the kitchen and burst out into the alley.

Running with my wrists tied is bloody difficult.

'Where's your car?' Mila asks.

I awkwardly gesture down the street. She reaches into my pocket and grabs my keys.

As we pass other pedestrians, I smile and nod, doing my best not to look suspicious with my hands bound and blood running down my face. Their stares suggest it's not working.

We reach the car before Mila reveals an important obstacle.

'I can't drive.'

I think for a moment. 'Can you undo these wrist things?'

Mila tries to unpick the knots but the guy must've been a ship rigger or scout leader for a previous occupation. Her attempts to free me only make the knots tighter.

'No time,' she says. 'You steer, I'll change the gears. Let's get some space between us and that, then we'll sort you out.'

My bound hands make it hard to enter the car. Mila protects my head and helps me into the driver's side like a cop shoehorning a criminal.

She puts the keys into the ignition and starts the car and runs to the passenger side.

'Okay,' I say, 'shift the gearstick into the number as I call it out. Say 'in' when it's in.'

'This will be fun,' Mila says. I'm sure it's to lighten the tension.

It works. I grip the steering wheel. 'Let's do this.'

I spin the wheel with my bound hands, let the clutch out and pull away from the curb.

'Two.'

She shifts. 'In.'

The car shudders, nearly stalls, but we're moving. Thankfully, there are no cars behind us.

'Three.'

Shifts. 'In.'

I keep it in third, hands on top of the steering wheel. A few blocks away from the building, my hands are turning purple. There's an all-night chemist down on the right. I stomp the clutch and pull over in front of it.

'What are we doing?' Mila asks.

'I need you to grab some scissors from this chemist, quick.'

'There's no time,' she protests, then notices my eggplant-coloured hands. 'Oh my God.'

She jumps out and races into the chemist, returns with a pair of nail scissors.

'This is all they had.'

Mila frantically snips, and though the nail scissors are tiny, they cut through the ropes enough for me to unravel them. I toss the rope into the backseat and speed off, watching my hands turn back to their normal colour. We drive in silence, the adrenaline wearing off. My mind cascades. We stop at traffic lights and one thought smacks me.

I didn't tell Mila where the building was.

'How did you…'

I'm interrupted by ringing. My phone, another private number. It's like everyone's a paranoid control freak. I put the phone on speaker and place it on the dash.

'Emmanuel Ellison?' the voice on the other end of the phone enquires.

'Yeah, speaking.'

'This is Sergeant Wilburn from The Gap Police Station.'

Fear and guilt wash over me. Elvis is dead or in hospital. It's my fault. Then I glance at Mila for a second and it hits me like a whale tail. 'Sea World,' I say.

'Pardon me?' he asks.

194

A deep breath. 'Nothing.'

'Mr Ellison, there's been an incident at a residence owned by Susan Gardener. I don't want to alarm you, but "incident" might be underselling it. We cannot currently locate her, and you're listed as next of kin.'

'I'm her nephew. She's at the Wesley Hospital.'

'That's a relief. In that case, I'm going to need you to come into the station first thing tomorrow, then over to her property, what's left of it. There are a few questions that need answering.'

'What happened?'

'You'll see soon enough, son. I wouldn't believe it unless I'd seen it with my own eyes.'

'Sure, what time?'

'8AM work for you?'

'No worries. See you then.' I hang up.

We're both exhausted. I barely muster the energy to drive home, and I shower before dropping into bed and passing out. When I wake, Mila's gone.

It's only when I pull on my jeans that I feel the bulk of the USB-filled envelope in the pocket. I'd forgotten about it. Checking my phone, I've still got time before I head to the cop shop. I pick one of the USB sticks at random and shove it into my crappy laptop. A video program opens and a screen pops up. I'm expecting the video to show the same interior of the building, but the grainy preview pic shows a different torture room with an empty chair. I press play. Though the location and primary personnel are different, it's a similar sequence of events to those I saw in person. A scientist type, a creepy looking hitman type and a young dude. Then, bodyguards drag a struggling victim in, with an important looking boss man or woman trailing. They proceed to beat the hell out of the person in the chair, before the young guy comes in and heals them.

I eject the USB and stick in the next one. Same setup, different rooms, victims and healers. I shut the laptop and chuck the USB in with the rest, walk outside and shove them in the letterbox before firing off a text to Agent Johnson.

I've got something you need to see, in my letterbox. I'm leaving now.

The reply is instant.

No, stay there. Will arrive in 20 mins.

I'm already running late.

Sorry, can't. Got a date with the boys in blue. Check the letterbox.

My phone rings, private number. I ignore it and drive to the police station.

~

The interrogation room process is disappointingly different from the ones on TV.

No good cop/bad cop routine, just a series of dull questions from one sloppy, grizzled sergeant regarding last night's whereabouts. They do bring me scalding black coffee and a stale donut, so that's something. I'm saved at the thirty-minute mark when another officer enters the interrogation room, leans over and whispers into the sergeant's ear. He nods and his demeanour switches, a fake smile plastered across his face.

'Emmanuel, you're free to leave, but would you mind escorting me to the site and helping us put a few pieces together?'

A female officer wordlessly joins us as we exit the police station. It feels nice leaving, even if I haven't done anything wrong. The officer is blonde, thin-lipped, square-jawed; seems too attractive to be a police officer. She rides shotgun while I sit in the back.

She turns and leans over the divider. 'Aunt in hospital, huh?'

'Yeah.'

'Lucky.'

'She OD'd, so I wouldn't exactly call her lucky.'

'Oh, she was lucky alright. You'll see.'

There's something mildly thrilling about riding in a police car when you haven't done anything wrong. It's the type of event I

196

should've experienced as a kid, instead of opening another frozen meal in front of a busted TV set while Sue opened another bottle of gin.

As we round the corner to Sue's property, a swarm of bug-eyed busybodies swivel towards the police car. They're gathering in front of a cordoned-off area, straining their necks to catch a glimpse of the scene. An officer with a bullhorn attempts to disperse them, to no avail. Further along, police and military vehicles line the street. The air smells acrid and sweet simultaneously. Our car pulls up next to the group of stickybeaks and as the crowd parts it reveals the full extent of the damage.

A giant crater stands where Sue's house was. Any remnants of the actual house have been blown to smithereens. Nothing left but smouldering wreckage. I stand there, slack-jawed.

The explosives in the garage. Play it cool.

'How did this happen?' I ask.

'Aliens,' someone says, and several others share their crackpot theories.

After a while, a military officer with short-cropped hair approaches, shows me her ID and confirms my identity, then shoves me into a van.

Another day, another van.

'Where are we going?'

'Wesley Hospital,' she says, then nothing more for the rest of the trip.

When we pull up at the hospital entrance, she opens a small brown satchel and checks some papers inside. The satchel stinks and she notices me noticing.

'It's made from camel skin,' she says. 'Got it during a trip to Marrakesh last year.'

She opens the door and we hop out.

Sue's eating green jelly and custard when we walk into her room. Whatever happens next, she'll probably remember this meal for the rest of her life.

'Susan Gardener?'

Sue eyes the woman in uniform next to me. 'Yes,' she says warily.

'I'm Lieutenant Perry, with the Royal Australian Air Force. There's no easy way to say this, but your house is gone.'

The jelly wobbles on Sue's spoon. 'Gone?'

'Yes, gone. Blown up is probably a better way to describe it.'

Sue snatches a glance at me. 'Go on.'

'The culprit was a rogue satellite owned and operated by the RAAF. It deviated from its flight path, fell from the sky and struck your shed. It obliterated anything within a 10m radius. Fortunately, the neighbouring houses were unoccupied, and they only sustained some superficial damage.'

Sue and I must be thinking the same thing because we share another look. The stockpile of homemade explosives didn't cause the destruction, but they surely accelerated it.

'You were extremely lucky you weren't there, ma'am.'

Sue seems too shocked to say anything, just spoons more custard and jelly into her mouth. We wait until she's done. She rests the spoon in the bowl and pushes the tray away.

'What now?' she asks, dabbing her lips with a napkin. 'All my things were there.'

Lieutenant Perry nods and whips out an envelope and an A4-sized piece of paper from her camel satchel.

'The RAAF is willing to offer you an immediate two million dollars compensation package,' she says, placing the envelope and paper on the tray table.

Sue's eyes widen. 'What's the catch?'

'No catch, just sign this non-disclosure agreement and the money's yours.'

I'm about to talk when Sue hushes me with a look.

'Got a pen?' she asks, to which Lieutenant Perry pulls one out and hands it over.

Sue rips open the envelope and scans the two-million-dollar cheque, bites it, then signs the NDA without reading it and hands it back.

Lieutenant Perry places the document into her satchel. 'Thank you, Mrs Gardner.' She turns to me and nods. 'Emmanuel.'

'No worries,' I say.

She pulls out a business card from her pocket and hands it to me. 'Any issues cashing the cheque, just get me on the blower and I'll get finance to sort you out.' She spins and walks out, leaving us behind, too stunned to speak.

EIGHTEEN

THE taxi passes frantic, last-minute Christmas Eve shoppers rushing about for poorly-thought-out gifts. I arrive at the restaurant with twenty minutes to kill before Mila arrives. I sit on steps in the alleyway, smoking rollies, mind drifting from the gutter to the stars. Elvis said not to call the cops, but it's been way too long. I type in triple zero and hover my thumb over the green call symbol, imagining the conversation.

'Emergency services, do you want police, fire or ambulance?'

'Hi, yeah, I'm not sure, but a couple of shady guys have abducted my housemate who has this miraculous healing ability, the same one I had before this crazy scientist injected me with a suppressant, to protect me, supposedly. Anyway, these shady guys are paying my housemate to heal people who get beaten up in this hidden room next to an alley. I escaped the first time, but when I went back to investigate, I was caught by a shaved gorilla. Fortunately, I was saved by my possibly untrustworthy new girlfriend and a baseball bat. I gave video evidence to this government operative who first informed me of this group experimenting on young men, who then end up in the nuthouse. Then the Air Force blew up my aunt's apocalypse bunker. Oh, and my housemate's name's Elvis.'

Yeah right. I stuff the phone back in my pocket.

A shadowy movement in my peripherals sends a chill through me. 'You scared the hell out of me.'

'I'm very stealthy,' Mila says, followed by a curtsy. She's wearing a light-blue, halter dress and kitten heels. I can't help but smile.

'You look gorgeous.'

She does. I don't have to exaggerate one bit.

'This ol' thang? Gee thanks, mister.'

She performs an imperfect twirl.

I feel underdressed.

We hug. She holds on for a few beats longer.

'What is it?' I ask.

She wipes her eyes with one hand and grabs my hand with the other. 'No big deal, but…'

'What?'

'I can feel you, Manny. Your energy, I mean. It's been so long since I've been able to feel human contact or feel anything, but you,' she stammers, 'you're different.'

'A good thing, right?'

'It's wonderful, but it churns up the past.' Mila wipes her eyes. 'Gives me hope too, which I thought I'd given up on a while ago.'

I kiss her on the cheek.

She composes herself and looks around the alley. 'You hungry?'

'Starving, let's do it.'

We link arms and walk around the corner to an Asian fusion joint named San Choy Mao's. It's packed, so the server sits us in a corner. The starters and mains arrive at once in a smorgasbord. Tom yum soup, spicy salad, veggies with cashew nut, plus a pot of jasmine green tea. We talk and eat, and drink and talk some more. Mila keeps eyeing the lobster tank, down to its last two lobsters.

'We're taking them.'

'What?'

'The lobsters.'

My head swivels around the room then back to her to decide if she's joking. She isn't.

A hole opens in my chest. 'Where will we take them?' I ask, scrambling for an excuse.

'The river.'

'What if we get caught?'

'Look how busy they are. This place is packed. You get the bill. I'll liberate the lobsters.'

I wonder if all vets are eccentric, animal liberators. I pay the bill, trying to avoid looking suspicious – which probably makes me look more suspicious – and watch Mila from the corner of my eye. She plucks the two remaining lobsters from the tank. Sure enough, the wait staff are too busy to notice.

Elation replaces fear as we exit the doors and walk straight to the river's edge. Mila carefully unties the rubber bands and releases the lobsters into the Brisbane River. We walk under the full moon, shining like a big happy Buddha, then sit on a park bench. I don't know why, maybe the feeling of excitement after the fear of getting caught, but it feels like the right time to tell Mila about healing Jam, the young girl with cancer.

It takes a while.

Silence hangs heavy in the air after I'm done talking. I'm not sure if she believes me.

I take a drag of my cigarette and when I look at Mila, there's a snail trail from the tears on her face.

I shuffle uncomfortably. 'What is it?'

She lets out a whoosh of air. 'Nothing, it's a beautiful story is all. Jam was lucky to have you.'

'I hope she still is, wherever she is. With that megalomaniac as a father, I can only hope.'

Back at my place, Mila falls asleep on my chest while I stroke her hair, which smells of blueberry vape. When I open my eyes in the morning, she's gone, perhaps turned into a pumpkin and rolled away. But she left a note.

I've got another special assignment for you tonight if you don't have a prior engagement. My people, your people, etc.

Xxxooo Mila

P.S. I know this may seem fast, but I love you. Please don't say it back to me or make it awkward, just know I do.

~

Mila and I are dressed head-to-toe in black, balaclavas and everything. It's close to midnight by the time we reach the compound. We leave the car to walk the last few hundred metres on foot. The compound consists of ten humungous concrete warehouses with necklaces of fluoro lights. It's surrounded by chainlink fencing crowned in razor wire.

We walk the fence line until we're opposite the third warehouse along; our target.

The compound looks deserted. Mila says the guards make their rounds every fifteen minutes.

On cue, an overweight security guard wearing headphones walks past the front of our target. He's singing an old Edison Lighthouse song. He turns and goes down the middle of the target warehouse and its neighbour. We wait until he disappears and his out-of-tune rendition of *Love Grows (Where My Rosemary Goes)* fades into the ether.

The night air becomes still and silent again.

'How are we going to—' I say, before Mila hushes me with a finger to her lips.

She takes a puff on her vape, drops her backpack, and retrieves two sets of bolt cutters, answering my question.

The bolt cutters make short work of the fence and we have a human-sized hole in a couple of minutes. Mila steps through and I follow.

'How did you find out about this place?'

'Through the Animal Liberation Society Alliance.'

'Why you?'

'Why not?' she whispers. 'Trust me, we'll be in and out in ten minutes, fifteen max. Then we can get pancakes.'

Of all the stupid things guys have done across history to impress girls, this is one of them. Mila leads the way towards our target.

I stop abruptly at the strange, high-pitched sounds emanating from the warehouse.

'Come on.' Mila tugs me forward through the darkness.

I peek through the warehouse windows; it's cloaked in shadows but there are soft hooting and banging sounds coming from inside.

Mila pulls out a scrap of paper with a map of the facility and handwritten instructions on how to disarm the alarm and input the entry code.

I'm in over my head.

The fear is back, ten-fold. 'How did you get those?' I whisper.

'A comrade cleaner on the inside. The Alliance has infiltrated almost every animal testing facility in Australia on some level.'

Mila punches a six-digit code into the keypad and a small red bulb turns green. 'We're in,' she says, rubbing her hands together like a cartoon robber.

The guard's coming back, fortunately singing loud enough to ruin any element of surprise. I close the metal door behind us and duck when a torch beam lights up the window. We kneel against the door until the security guard's singing and footsteps dwindle. Mila hands me a torch and scans the scrap of paper. She moves down the aisles with me following close behind. I bump into her when she stops.

'Eighteen down, four across. That's where the chimps are,' she says, taking my hand.

'What's in the other ones?'

'Rabbits, cats, guinea pigs, everything.'

'So why the chimps?' I ask.

'Because they're the cutest. Everyone loves chimps.'

'Except for those ones that rip people's faces off. How are we going to bring them all with us?'

Mila stifles a laugh. 'We're not taking all of them, only one. The smallest one with the biggest and cutest eyes. We'll take photos of the others. Then we'll give them to the Alliance to distribute over social media. It'll blow this whole operation wide open. Just don't look in the other cages,' she says solemnly. 'It'll only make you sad.'

Don't push the big red button.

Our torches are the only source of illumination as we creep down the aisle. Curiosity gets the better of me and I swing my beam into one of the wire cages containing a large white rabbit. It tries to jump when it sees me, but its head hits the top of the tiny cage and it falls on its side. Patches of fur are missing from its body and sores cover its feet. Red and swollen eyes look up at me, the same sorrowful look Chew Barka had when I found her outside in the rain. I stick my fingers through to pat it but the rabbit snaps at them.

I yell as I withdraw my still-luckily-attached fingers.

Mila shushes me. 'You're going to get us caught.' She drops her backpack, unzips it and hands me a carrot. 'I knew you wouldn't be able to resist. Feed her this, then she'll let you pat her.'

I grab the carrot.

'How do you know it's a girl?'

Mila stares at me for a few moments. I turn and push the carrot through the wires; the rabbit launches at it, gnashing. I reach my fingers through and scratch the soft tufts of fur on her neck and look down the rows of cages. Mila was right.

Sadness envelopes me; a fire burns in my ribcage.

Mila tugs on my sleeve then grabs my hand. 'C'mon, let's go.'

I take photos as we walk down the aisle. My anxiety pulses with every iPhone photo flash. The chimps are at the end of the row. They must know we're approaching because they're hooting louder and drumming on the bottom of their cages like a John Bonham drum solo. We reach the end of the row. The chimps look like what they are: depressed, confused, caged animals.

Mila ducks and scans the cages. 'This one.'

The baby chimp sticks his fingers through to touch Mila's hands. His eyes are giant saucers. He's one of the saddest, most beautiful things I've ever seen.

205

Jam and the little girl who died outside Bluebell flicker in my mind.

Mila wipes her eyes with her shirt sleeves, pulls out a couple of bananas from her backpack and pushes them through the wire. The chimp grabs one of the bananas and studies it for a moment before peeling it and shoving it into its mouth. Mila and I get to work with the bolt cutters. The grate falls away with one final snap. Mila reaches her arms through to pick up the chimp right as we're lit up by the beam of a security guard's torchlight.

'Hey! What are you doing?' he yells, jogging towards us. Luckily, he's about forty kilos overweight and slow going.

Mila snatches the chimp out of the cage, gouging herself on the sharp edges of the cut wire. She brings the chimp close to her chest.

'Grease the floor,' she says. A stream of blood runs down her arm, dripping from her elbow.

'What?'

'The blue bottle in your bag, pop the cap and pour it onto the floor.'

For a second, I'm frozen.

'Now. Go,' she urges, and runs around the corner with the chimp.

I pull out the container and remove the cap. I spill the liquid in a wide arc until it covers the patch of concrete between me and the guard closing the gap.

I sling the backpack on and run around the corner, stopping when I hear the yell and sickening crack of a head on the concrete floor. I spin, careful not to slip on the slick concrete as I go back. I'm not going to allow someone to die so a monkey can live. The guard is out cold, lying on his back in a puddle of oil.

I place my hands on him, check to see if he's breathing. He is, but he needs medical attention. I breathe, concentrate, try absorbing the injury.

Nothing.

I pull out my phone as I stand, switch it to private, and type in triple zero, then follow the blood splatters on the concrete leading to Mila and the baby chimp waiting at the door.

'The guard's hurt, I've gotta call an ambulance.'

'Wait until we're off the property.'

My thumb hovers over the call button for a moment. I dial anyway.

We open the door and run towards the boundary. An operator answers while we're crossing the yard.

You have dialled emergency triple zero. Your call is being connected.

'Emergency triple zero, do you need police, fire and rescue or ambulance?' the operator asks.

'Ambulance.'

'Address?'

We duck through the hole in the fence.

'Magworth Testing Facility. The third warehouse from the Northern end.'

'How many people are injured? And what are the nature of the injuries?'

'One guy, I don't know, he hit his head, he's unconscious.'

'An ambulance is on the way. Are you able to stay with the individual until the ambulance arrives?'

'No can do, sorry. I've gotta go.'

'Sir, it would be best if…'

I end the call.

We move through the forest towards my car, which takes way too long. The sound of the ambulance siren is comforting and terrifying all at once. Stealing a primate seemed like a big enough charge without adding manslaughter to it. We finally reach the car and Mila collapses into the back with the chimp. She's lost way too much blood. I find an old t-shirt and wrap it around her arm in a makeshift tourniquet.

'You're going to need stitches.'

'I can do it myself at the surgery. First, we drop off the chimp to the Alliance.'

Mila slams the door shut and hugs the baby chimp tight to her chest.

I race around to the driver's seat, crank the ignition and jam the accelerator down. The car fishtails in the dirt before we shoot out onto the road.

The ambulance flies past, red lights flashing, siren screaming.

'The Doppler effect,' I say. Can't help it.

My breathing calms as we put distance between us and the facility.

'The guard will be fine,' Mila says. 'He'll have a sore head for a couple of days. Serves him right for working for those monsters.'

She's right, but I don't want to give her the satisfaction.

When I touched the guard, I felt his injuries. Bad concussion, but no long-lasting damage. It was the blood that got me, but the ambos will sort him. Still, we crossed the line. I stay silent for the drive; Mila and the chimp make cooing sounds at each other.

We arrive at the meeting place twenty minutes later.

I spot the multicoloured Sandman van in the corner of the Springwood Macca's carpark and pull in next to it. The side door opens and two heavily pierced and tattooed individuals step out. Vegan-thin, long, dirty hair, colourful clothes, glazed eyes. The stench of patchouli and an absence of showers clouds them. I suppress a gag to avoid a bad first impression.

Mila walks around to the van's rear with the chimp clutched to her chest. She hugs the hippies, then tenderly hands the chimp to the girl, who looks like she falls instantly in love with it. Understandable, it's pretty much the cutest thing ever. Also, the bonding process is probably helped by the fact they smell similar.

The guy pulls out a trumpet-sized spliff from his recycled material vest and sparks it up. I do the polite thing and take a few puffs. My heart settles into its normal rhythm.

'Nice work, friends,' he says. 'We're going to destroy their whole operation. We'll shoot all our content tonight at the compound. Then we'll plaster it across socials tomorrow.'

I'm half listening; my attention on Mila now. She's pale, sweating profusely, and the blood's showing through the t-shirt wrapped around her arm.

'We've gotta go and get you stitched up. Right now.'

Mila nods and stumbles slightly. We bid farewells. She gets in the front seat.

'Job done,' she says, before letting her head rest against the window.

I drive straight to the veterinary surgery. The metallic smell grows stronger as the blood continues to leak and pool on the seat.

'Hold on, Mila. Hold on.'

She's out when we arrive. I shake her awake.

'We're here, where are the keys?'

Her eyes flicker. 'The backpack,' she whispers.

I reach into the back seat and fumble around in the bottom of the backpack until my fingers clutch a set of keys. I help her out of the car, wrap her arm over my shoulders and carry her to the door. The keys jangle in my trembling fingers but eventually find their home and unlock the door. Inside, Mila motions towards the rear of the clinic. She flicks a switch in the surgery room. Blinding, fluorescent lights stutter to life. I help her to the metal table in the middle of the room. She points a shaky finger and I wheel a trolley from the corner towards the operating table.

'Where's the gauze?' I ask, untying the shirt from around her arm. It's saturated with blood. She wipes the wound with a white towel, then pours a whole tiny bottle of disinfectant into the wound. I wince.

'In that top drawer, needles and thread too. Bring the whole tray.'

I pull out the tray and drop it.

'Can you thread this needle for me?' she asks.

I fumble but manage to thread the black silk thread through the needle's eye.

'Now, wind the thread around the needle a couple of times. Hold the other end and spin it to create a knot.'

I follow the instructions, make the knot and hand the needle to Mila. She dabs the wound.

'Okay, Manny. Pinch the skin together and keep dabbing the blood.'

I tug at my hair, greased with sweat. 'This isn't going to work, it's too big. You got a staple gun?'

She nods. 'Corner cupboard.'

I find the grey, surgical stapler, load a fresh batch of staples.

She presses it to her skin.

'No anaesthetic?' I ask.

'What's the point?'

'You really can't feel anything?'

'No pain, nothing. You didn't believe me?'

'Yeah, but holy hell.'

The stapling is done in a minute. It'll hold, though will leave an aggressive scar. I tidy the surgery and put all the utensils away. It's 3AM, and the night's events collapse onto me.

Mila looks totally depleted. Pale. The adrenaline has worn off.

'Merry Christmas,' she breathes, as I carry her to the car.

'Merry Christmas.'

I drive home without falling asleep at the wheel.

No Elvis.

NINETEEN

'LOBSTERS, dolphins, chimps, what's next?' Sue asks.

We're sitting opposite each other, drinking green tea in the packed hospital cafeteria. 'And since when did you care about animals again?'

'It was my choice. Don't worry, I'm using my head.'

She scoffs. 'Yeah right. Your little head.'

I fiddle with the tea bag, trying not to react. Sue knows how to get under my skin, and she's been burrowing like a tick all morning.

'Can't we talk about something else?'

Sue rolls her eyes, then catches herself, turns serious and leans in. 'I need to show you something, Manny.'

I shrug. 'Okay, so show me.'

'Not yet,' she says, eyes downcast.

The irritation rises. I'm trying to be nice but she makes it so hard. I escape the moment by grabbing us meals from the counter. The cafeteria menu features typical mass-produced, trough-style cuisine. But it's Christmas, so there's a special turkey dinner for those who aren't wearing dentures, and a more liquidised version for those who are.

I swallow a mouthful of turkey when a moving form catches my eye, then vanishes from view. It's him.

My chair falls to the floor as I run out into the hallway. Sue calls after me. I get there in time to see Elvis disappear around the corner. By the time I round it, he's gone. I've barely slept, so can't be certain it's him, but if it isn't, it's his doppelgänger, which is even worse. A harbinger of doom.

I shake my head and return to the cafeteria. Sue and I finish our meals, then head to her room. Sitting on her bed, she grabs the crème-coloured plastic jug and slowly pours a glass of water.

We sit in silence until I'm ready to burst. 'Let's get this over with.'

Her trembling hands raise the glass towards her lips, then place it unsteadily on the table. The apprehension radiates from her so heavily I can feel it in my chest.

She sighs. 'Are you sure?'

'I'm ready. Band-Aid time, rip it off.'

Sue pauses for an infuriating eternity. My impatience and anxiety boiling, I take a deep breath and count to seven.

She reaches into her bedside drawer. 'I brought this with me,' she says, handing me a weathered piece of paper. It reminds me of the aged, convict letters we created in primary school, made to look old with spilled tea, a few rips and some dirt rubbed into them. There's something written on one of the folds in faded ink.

For Manny, when the time is right.

I immediately recognise Mum's handwriting.

I look for an explanation. Sue begins, 'I found it going through her stuff after she...'

I wave the letter around. 'You didn't think this may have been important fifteen years ago?'

Her eyes lower, 'I'm sorry, I was...'

'Drunk,' I finish for her. 'Drunk, angry and selfish.'

Sue's face twitches. I know what she's going to say, so beat her to it.

'You lost a husband, yeah, but I lost my bloody mother. You were so busy feeling sorry for yourself you never thought about me. Not once.'

Sue looks like she's been stung. I've never articulated my feelings about then to her, didn't see the point.

212

'Honestly, Manny, I forgot all about it. I've been holding it for years. It was in my carry bag.' She looks small, old.

I unfold the paper. It's filled with Mum's handwriting.

Certain words are smudged, either from tears or carelessness.

It's dated the day before the accident.

Dearest Manny,

If you're reading this, I'm no longer here (yes, it's one of those letters). I'm writing this while you're watching Roadrunner, which is kind of ironic as we're about to do a runner ourselves.

What this all means is you're probably dealing with two losses. E has instructions that if anything ever happens to me, to take your ability away from you to keep you safe. Your ability must be hidden. A travesty, I know, but I'm afraid it's too dangerous.

All I wanted to do was help people. A world without sickness and death. That's what I wanted. But I got more, I got you.

E promised he'd neutralise you to keep you safe. I trust he followed through, because if anyone finds out who and what you are, even in death, I couldn't forgive myself.

Your ability came on with a vengeance. I knew it could happen one day and thought I'd be ready when the time came, but I wasn't, and I don't think the world will be ready for a while either.

It breaks my heart to know I can't be there for you, Manny, for whatever reasons, but I need you to know how much I love you. I love you as much as one person can love another and I need you to be safe.

You are the most amazing human I've ever known and it has nothing to do with your ability.

It's more than your intelligence or creativity. It's your kindness. Please don't ever lose that.

In a world that can be so cruel, the ability to still be kind is a superpower in and of itself.

No matter what happens, what may come of all this, I want you to know I had the best intentions.

213

A large part of me is ashamed for being involved in experimenting on animals and babies the way we did. But I wouldn't change a thing because I wouldn't have you without them. You were the miracle child, Manny. You made it when the rest couldn't. By then, I'd realised we'd gone too far. There was a fire in the lab and it was the perfect opportunity to spirit you away. I know this is a lot to take in, but you'll find out more than you'll want to know.

I need you to understand, to remember me as you did, not as some heartless monster, because I'm not. You are my heart, Manny. No matter what you feel, I am your mother, and I will always be your mother, and I will always watch over you.

I'm so proud of you and I hope you become all you deserve.

I love you,

Mum xoxoxo

The letter carries so much weight I drop it to the ground.

I'm adopted.

My entire existence is a lie.

I'm not sure how much time elapses. It's like it ceases to be a linear concept.

Sue grabs my hand. 'Are you okay?'

I'm either more mature than I figured, or numb.

I take a deep breath. 'Sort of makes sense.'

She squeezes my hand until I look at her.

'Who are my real parents?'

'I don't know,' she says simply.

That's the end of that.

Sue picks up a framed photo of her and me taken at Sizzler when I was a teenager and stares at it for a moment before placing it back on her bedside table. We're smiling in the picture. You'd almost believe we were a typical happy family.

'Officially, the army adopted you. E and your mother were your guardians. Your mum fell in love with you. Then the fire and explosion destroyed all their work. It doesn't matter where your blood comes from, we're family and despite my faults, I love you.'

I leave without saying anything, walk down the familiar hospital corridors.

Everything has changed. Nothing has changed.

~

A newly painted canvas sits on the easel in the lounge room. Black and red oils. Bleak, hellish, angular landscapes filled with demons and evil looking stick figure alien creatures. Lining the bottom, what looks like hundreds of mouths screaming in pain.

Elvis was here and it appears he's lost his mind.

TWENTY

MULTICOLOURED lights wash across City Hall's facade and dance off the pop-up ice rink's surface. The bronze statues and token trees on the bland, granite pavement of the usually unpretentious public square twinkle with fairy lights, adding a little magic to the air. The beams of light act like a beacon, drawing in hordes of Christmas tragics.

Mila glides across the ice, weaving in and out of smiling children and watchful parents. The picturesque moment is only dampened by my lack of balance and coordination.

I've never been ice skating before, a fact plainly and painfully evident to anyone watching my clumsy movements and many falls.

At least Mila finds it amusing.

By the time we sit and remove our skates, King George Square is swamped with people.

A cold finger traces my spine. 'This is what it was like.'

Mila pulls off her skate, it clatters to the ground. 'What?'

'"The Santa Claus Incident",' I say, struggling to remove my left skate.

'I can't believe I forgot to ask about the famous "Santa Claus Incident",' she jokes, pulling off her sock, her foot covered in blisters. They look painful but of course, she can't feel them.

I finally remove the skates from my swollen feet, tie the laces together and place them on the ground.

'Right here. The Christmas markets, and it was packed. A drunk, store Santa commandeered a garbage truck and drove it straight through the crowd,' I say, pointing at a space between the line of columns at the front of City Hall. 'I was one of the lucky ones, Elvis wasn't. Dozens were maimed.'

'What happened to the Santa?'

'He pulled out a pistol and shot himself. He was still wearing the Santa suit.'

Mila stands and helps me to my feet. My butt is killing me, it's going to be sore tomorrow. Mila ties the laces of her skates together and hands both pairs over to the attendant.

We walk towards Queen Street mall. Hundreds of people are carrying shopping bags; the glut of Christmas consumption unable to fill the void. Seems like the sales last for more days each year.

'So, Elvis ended up in your hospital?' asks Mila.

'Yeah, it's how we became friends.'

'How did he end up working there?' she asks.

'Oh, the servers on the ward went out one day during a storm and they couldn't get a tech. Elvis overheard and sorted it out. Ward manager let a higher up know, offered him a job.'

'Just like that?'

'Just like that.'

Mila grabs my hand. As warmth flows through me, I wonder if she feels the same.

We hop on a bus towards the Valley, next stop is Netherworld, the bar/arcade/vegan junk food/pop culture wonderland.

We order burgers and play pinball while we're waiting for them.

Afterwards, we grab a couple of Pilsners the bartender says have spicy floral and strong hop flavours, while Mila picks a board game. She chooses the game responsible for more lost tempers and fractured sibling relationships than any other in history.

She moves the dog to Kings Cross Station and buys it, like she's bought everything else. Now she has all four train stations and all I have is one of the purples, one of the oranges and two of the light blues. I'm also the banker and I hate being the banker. She places the card in with the rest of her property portfolio. Monopoly always brings out the worst in everyone and she's kicking my arse. I feel like a petulant child. I slowly claw my way back but there's no way I can win.

The Imperial Death March from Star Wars reverberates through the bar, signalling last drinks. The nerds peel themselves from the flashing arcade consoles and rush to the bar, rubbing their eyes and stretching their limbs.

We put the games away, wave to the bartenders and walk out into the night. Calm washes over me the further away I move from the evil Monopoly board. We grab another bus to Main Street, getting out at the stop closest to mine. Discordant static carries through the night air. As we get closer to my house, the sound of white noise increases. My place is shrouded in darkness, aside from the TV's blue light cutting through the curtains.

Elvis is back, in the flesh.

The now-familiar combination of relief and fear floods me.

'Want to come meet him?'

Mila stops and lets go of my hand. 'Next time, sorry.'

'What is it?'

She checks her watch. The way someone does when they're lying.

'I've got to go, I forgot I've got the early delivery at the vet in the morning.'

She leans up and kisses me on the cheek, looks once at the house, turns and walks off.

Elvis is watching static on TV when I walk in.

I turn the blaring volume down. 'Welcome back.'

'Yeah.' Only his mouth moves, nothing else. He's fixated on the screen.

I step between him and the TV, a human eclipse. 'You okay, man?'

In my shadow, he looks like death. 'Leave me alone.'

'Want me to put something else on?' I ask.

Silence.

The heat rises too fast to stop it.

'Okay, fine, sit and wallow in your secrets and see where it gets you. But if you're going to keep hiding everything from me, your supposed best friend, you can get fucked.'

Nothing.

I make straight for my bed, eventually falling into a troubled sleep.

I always wake up when I'm flying through the windshield.

But this time, I'm the one driving. I swerve to miss the other vehicle but it's too late. Always too late.

As I'm launched through the glass, I see Sue in the other vehicle. Right before my body splatters all over the highway, I wake up.

It takes a few seconds to orientate myself and find my ringing phone under the massive pile of clothes. It's work. And it's 4AM.

'Hello,' I groan.

'Hi, Manny,' the nurse manager says, in a chirpy voice unsuited to this time of the morning.

'Hey, how's it going?'

'Okay thanks. Look, sorry to wake you. I know you're rostered off today, but one of the boys has food poisoning and can't come in. Can you please cover the shift? There's no one else and we're chockas here.'

He doesn't have food poisoning. No one actually gets food poisoning. They were all out wakeboarding in the Brisbane River and drinking too much. More likely he contracted some kind of bacterial infection.

The nurse manager cuts into my thoughts. 'Can you do the shift? A few hours tops, and it's double time and a half.'

'Yeah, okay.'

I stumble around the room, grab clothes from the pile of laundry on the floor. I creep into the lounge room. Elvis is motionless in his chair, still watching static on the TV. The air is sour. Acidic.

219

A newly painted canvas sits on the easel in the lounge room. It looks as though handfuls of body parts have been haphazardly smeared across it. The slashes and tears make it look as though a rabid dog has attacked and molested it. If art is, as eyes are, a window to the soul, then Elvis's is a black, tarry cesspool.

My stomach drops and I nearly call back to cancel my shift. But the part of me that wants to intervene is smothered by the other part that's terrified of whatever's going on.

'I've gotta go to work,' I say, 'We'll debrief when I get back.'

He mumbles something. Drool rolls down his chin.

~

I'm already doing the rounds by 4:30AM and most patients are sleeping.

Only a few room entries are lit up. One of them contains an old man I've wheeled back and forth from X-ray over the past few weeks. I walk in to check how he's doing.

'Graveyard shift, ay?' he says.

'Yeah. Shouldn't you be sleeping? Surgery soon, right?'

He coughs and hacks; the death rattle in his chest is getting worse. 'Knowing you're so close to dying,' he wheezes, 'tends to make sleep not come as quickly as it should.'

'That sucks. I'm sorry.'

There isn't much more to say.

'Oh well,' he says, 'life sometimes sucks. Sooner you accept that, the better off you'll be.'

'Good luck. Take care, hey?'

'Thanks for the chat, kid.'

I still have several hours of drudgery ahead. My eyes feel like acid jelly balls.

I head to the staff kitchen and pour another cup of bitter, black coffee, then walk around completing various, low-level, mundane tasks.

The old man I'd visited comes into my awareness. A picture clear as a photo.

I walk back to his room. They're already wrapping him in the body bag.

That I was probably the last person to see him alive makes me feel both better and worse.

I sneak out to the roof where the doctors all go to smoke. I sit down and stare at the awakening sky. An ashtray full of butts lays in front of me. My radio squawks.

'3B to pre-op, Manny.'

'On my way.' I close the door and walk towards 3B. At first, I attribute it to phantom vibration syndrome, but when it continues, I pull my phone out.

Private number.

I press the button to answer, say nothing. Private number at 5:30AM, no chance it's good news.

'Manny, my boy.'

I stop short, my mind reels.

E.

I say the first thing that comes.

'A guy from the government told me all these young dudes are ending up in the nut house. That's you, right?'

E huffs over the line. Good, stuff him.

'It's not that simple.'

'Sure, it is. Did you do that, yes or no?' I say, pacing the width of the hallway, which is only a couple of metres wide.

'Manny…' he begins.

'I've seen the footage, E. I *know* it's you.'

'It's for her, all for her.'

'Who?'

'My beautiful daughter.' He clears his throat. 'Her condition isn't sustainable. Those young men are all that's keeping her alive.'

221

I don't get it. 'You've been doing this since you took it away from me?'

'No, only the past year.'

I walk back and forth across the width of the hallway like a character stuck in a video game glitch. 'How did she survive the past decade or so then?'

He chuckles like I'm an idiot, which is exactly how I feel.

'You,' he says.

The heat rises in. I lean against the wall, say nothing.

'I had enough of your blood and fluids, your...' He searches for the word. '...Essence, to keep her going until now. Think of them like concentrated cordial.'

I think of raspberry cordial in those small bottles.

'You're potent, Manny,' he says, like he's reading my thoughts. 'Thousands of times stronger than any of these poor fools of late. I had to heavily dilute your essence for her to have any chance.'

'So, you're going to use me up on your daughter and dump me with some psychos who'll probably cut me up and kill me?'

'What choice do I have?' he says matter-of-factly.

'What about Elvis?'

'Won't need him for much longer.'

I picture Elvis. Zombified, going mad.

'Why did you call, E?'

'Absolution, before the fact.'

'You're joking, right?'

'Goodbye, Manny.'

'I gave those USBs to the agent. This whole thing's going to...'

The line goes dead before I can finish. I stand there until my radio beeps to remind me about the pre-op job.

~

The TV is off, and Elvis is gone, but the lounge room looks the same.

I sleep on the couch for most of the afternoon until it's dark, only waking to an invisible presence in the room. I bolt up, hit by a wave

222

of dizziness as I swing off the couch – powerful enough for me to sit back down.

Elvis is kneeling on the floor, nose to screen with the TV. It's emanating static and a high-pitched whine.

I call to him, but he's blank, frozen.

I rise shakily, sweat pouring down my body.

He rips the cord from the outlet as he explodes upward and I'm shoved backwards into a wall, smacking my head. Stars float around in the darkness. I stand with the help of the couch, navigating the lounge room garbage and into the hallway where he's moved to. In the dark I hear him breathing, like a large slumbering beast. Walking closer, my eyes adjust as Elvis's shape forms at the end of the hallway. I flick on the hallway light, bathing him in an eerie yellow glow. He's sitting cross-legged with his eyes open but like he's seeing nothing. His mouth opens and closes like a goldfish. I stand right in front of him. He's muttering under his breath, but I can't make it out.

I ask him what he's talking about. He doesn't respond.

His body is a shell – his mind a billion light years away.

Running into the backyard, I pull out my phone. I dial triple zero. Press the call button.

You have dialled emergency Triple Zero. Your call is being connected.

'Emergency response. Police, fire or ambulance?'

'Hi, I…'

My mind races, then I'm paralysed.

'Sir, are you there? Police, fire or ambulance?'

I hang up.

When I go back inside, Elvis is in the kitchen, clutching a knife.

My phone rings but I ignore it.

'You're coming undone,' Elvis says.

Light glints off the knife as he rhythmically taps it against his leg. When he looks me in the eyes, my skin goosebumps. A madman.

'Goodbye, Manny,' he says, and limps out the front door.

His latest canvas sits on the easel in the lounge room. It looks like a werewolf has dunked its fist in a bucket of blood and scraped its claws across the virgin canvas.

TWENTY-ONE

SUE moves her IV pole out of the way. Our heads swivel to the window as the 8PM fireworks paint the sky.

She pokes my leg. 'It's New Year's Eve. Shouldn't you be out doing something?'

'I'm meeting up with Mila later.'

But it's Elvis dominating my thoughts. He could hurt himself. Or maybe worse, someone else. Maybe I should've restrained him, but he looked like a wild animal.

For a few minutes it's still and silent apart from the soft repetitive beeping of machines and muffled sky explosions. Another year, almost over. She reads my mind.

'Resolutions?'

'A couple yeah. Stop Elvis from being admitted to the crazy house. Get him out of this mess. Stop E's experiments. You?'

She stares at the colourful lights bursting over the river.

'One more task on my list, then I'm done.'

'What is it?'

'That's for me to know,' she winks.

'I hate it when people say that.'

'I'll tell you next year.'

'I hate when people say that too.'

My walkie talkie squawks, signalling another job. Sue stares out the window, smiling. It's genuine. Haven't seen that in a long time.

I press the button on the walkie talkie to accept the job.

'Happy New Year, Sue.'

'Happy New Year, Manny.'

~

Moonlight reflects off the river and shards of broken beer bottles smashed across the rocks. There's a dark shape and a tiny purple glow at the end of the pontoon.

I walk towards the water's edge, taking a moment to absorb the surroundings, then sit next to her. Mila puffs the vape and stares across the river.

For a New Year's Eve, it's relatively calm. There's the distant sounds of drunken partying and the soft rumble of cars on the Story Bridge above but for all intents, we could be the last two people on Earth.

She brings out a jam jar filled with clear liquid.

'What's that?'

'Moonshine. Intense, but pure. Trust me.'

She pulls out two plastic Winnie the Pooh cups and pours a generous amount of bootleg hooch into each of them. I'm expecting the worst, but it doesn't burn my throat or taste as bad as anticipated. The warm, inner glow passes through me. Mila takes a long drag of her vape and blows perfect rings of blueberry smoke into the still night.

'Did you know the female mantis rips the male's head off straight after sex?'

'It would make it awkward if it were before I guess.'

'Imagine the conversation. "Please be gentle, this is my first time".'

We work our way through the whole bottle of homemade liquor. My opinion and admiration of it increases the more I consume.

'Any New Year's resolutions?' I ask.

'I like the concept of a new year,' Mila says, then drags on her vape, 'but changing habitual behaviours because of an arbitrary moment chalked up to another lap around the sun, that's nonsense.'

I top up our cups. 'I like that it compartmentalises time.'

'Compartmentalising time makes it easier to deal with, instead of the feeling of endless purgatory.'

'That's a depressing way to think about it,' I say.

'Just be glad Pluto is uninhabitable. A year there equates to 135 earth years. No new year, no reprieve.'

An Elvis Presley song croons across the water. My brief reprieve from thinking about my Elvis ceases.

I still have to find him. Stop him. Help him.

Then I'm distracted again as kaleidoscopic bursts of multicolour explode across the sky as the clock passes midnight. It's more impressive than the earlier display. Colourful sparks illuminate the heavens in one last spurt of light before the birth of a new year.

Drunken singing carries across the river.

Mila says, 'I think it's a three-way tie between *Auld Lang Sine, For He's a Jolly Good Fellow,* and the birthday song for the most annoying song of all time.'

I bring her close; warmth fills me.

~

It's 2AM. Mila gets cagey when we get closer to my place and she refuses to come in. She walks off into the new year, leaving both of us alone.

Another note is stuck under the mat. I take a deep breath, exhale, then bend down to pick it up and read its contents.

Nice chat.
You wouldn't recognise me now.
You still look the same.
Happy New Year.

227

A newly painted canvas sits on the easel in the lounge room. The base is blood and it's covered in teeth and hair. That's all.

I slide down the hallway as I pull my skinny, black jeans off. I stop at Elvis's room, the door ajar. I flick the light switch; the house inspector must have missed this. The walls of his room are covered with red and black paint with one word repeated over and over.

DIE

I try to sleep, but it's almost impossible. I'll search for him when it's light. I need the old Elvis back. I only hope it's not too late.

My mattress emanates so much heat, sweat covers my body and my head itches. I wriggle around trying to get into a comfortable position. I've barely closed my eyes when a sharp prick in my arm startles me awake. I try to stand but am unable to keep my eyelids open. The silhouetted figure holding a syringe disappears out of my room.

It sounds like a swarm of bees racing around my head. The noise intensifies until they suddenly cut off. I try to move towards Elvis's room but my knees buckle and I collapse to the cold tiles. I wait for what seems like infinity. The sound detonates, a sudden crescendo that makes me want to smash my head into anything. It stops almost immediately, and a surge of adrenaline threatens to make my brain explode. I'm electric, plugged into everything. I knock on Elvis's door to abate the frantic feelings coursing through me. I bang three times, nothing.

I pry open the door, only darkness.

My eyes adjust to see nothing bar stacks of papers.

The room is empty, his window open.

I shuffle through the mess to look outside.

My hand brushes against a sticky substance and I withdraw from the windowsill.

Blood.

It's everywhere.

Not only that.

There's something else in the corner that shouldn't be here.

It should be in Sue's hospital room.

I can't call the police.

I can't do anything but wait.

~

The front door slams, jarring me awake. It's still dark.

It takes a few minutes for the fog to clear and the film to focus but then it floods back like a brain tsunami. I rush towards Elvis's room moments before the figure appears from the hallway.

'Mila?'

'I had to come back. When I told you I loved you, I meant it,' she says. 'But I haven't been totally honest with you.'

The blood.

'Wait. Right. Here.'

I run into Elvis's room.

The window is down. Everything looks normal. Maybe I was dreaming.

Then I check my hands, they're tinged with crusty flecks of blood. I lather them with soap in the bathroom and throw cold water over my face. My reflection looks different. It's tiredness, surely. I flinch when an icy claw wraps around my arm. It's only Mila.

She spins me around. 'Hey, what's wrong? You're freaking me out.'

'I don't know. Last night. Elvis…'

'Elvis what?'

I'm too tired, she leads me to bed.

~

Mila leaves early. I drink juiced vegetables and try to pretend nothing's wrong. But my stomach churns, something flutters in my chest. My phone rings.

'Hello?'

'She's missing,' Mila says.

'Who?'

229

'Poe. You've got to help me find her.'

Elvis shuffles into the kitchen.

My relief at his return is poisoned by his inhuman appearance. His skin looks like it's melting over his skeleton.

I can't focus. The spilled tobacco on my jeans looks like tiny spiders. Everything starts to look like tiny spiders.

'Where can I meet you?' I ask, but the phone's dead.

Seconds later, my phone rings again but it's not Mila. It's the nurse manager and she delivers the next set of bad news with three words.

'Your aunt's missing.'

Elvis starts repetitively banging his head against the fridge.

I try to grab him but he's greasy. He spins, blood dribbling from his forehead, psychotic eyes staring into hell. He bares his teeth and laughs like a drunk clown.

He points at the ground. I can't bear it.

They're already popping under my feet before I see them: an army of maggots leading from under the sink to my bedroom. I take the vacuum cleaner out of the cupboard and suck them all up, then spray a whole can of fly spray inside and light the inner tube on fire with a cigarette lighter for good measure. I put the vacuum back and the rancid smell overpowers as I re-enter the kitchen. Closer to the sink cupboard, the stench gets worse.

There's something in there. Something dead.

I pull the cupboard open and see black fur. It takes a moment to realise it's a dead, black cat. Its insides are hollow, but its eyeballs are still rolling around in its sockets.

They're not the cat's eyes.

Maggots writhe about in the hollow eye sockets. I slam the cupboard shut and puke in the sink, grab two large garbage bags from the drawer and put on some washing up gloves.

Elvis recommences banging his head against the fridge.

'Elvis, for fuck's sake, stop!'

He continues.

I hold my breath as I open the cupboard, shut my eyes while grasping the cat and dropping it into the bag. The bag is still pulsating as I throw it in the outside bin.

Out there, it hits me.

Black cat.

Oh no. Poe.

I rush inside. Elvis is slumped against the fridge, face soaked with blood, eyes floating.

'What did you do?'

I shake him, but he doesn't respond.

I need to think.

I grab the water jug from the fridge and drink a huge glass at the kitchen table, watch Elvis in the corner.

There's rope in the shed. I could tie him up.

Think. Think. Drink.

The aftertaste of the water is bitter, wrong. The blood rushes to my head and pulses. Elvis turns, grinning, his face an evil mask. I look from my water. He nods. I can't move. No. It's like I'm looking through a fish-eye lens, then the floor moves up and meets my face.

~

A muffled noise emanates from inky nothingness.

It takes some time to realise it's my own voice.

I'm moving, I think.

My head's pounding, I know that.

The darkness recedes, replaced by rows of blurry lights whizzing by.

They're too much to take in. I can't form words, only groan as white bolts of pain shoot through my brain. It's like I've just been born or something.

I try touching my head, but my wrists are tied. I bring my hands up together and feel the blood caked on my face, pulling some flakes off to examine them, because this isn't real, right?

Wrong.

231

I turn to the driver's seat and mumble something; I still can't think properly, let alone talk. All my senses attempt to focus. Suddenly, music that sounded like it was sent through a low pass filter shoots into high-fidelity. The number one driving song of all time, *Radar Love*, bursts from the car radio.

Through the windscreen of Sue's car, colours and lights swim in dizzying sparks.

Elvis has his eyes straight forward; white knuckles grip the steering wheel. 'Hi, sleeping beauty.'

I sit up straighter. Every part of me hurts. 'What's happening?'

'We're going for a little Sunday drive.'

'It's not Sunday,' I whisper.

Memories drip, then the dike bursts and they flood back.

Mila.

'Where is she?'

He stares at me in the rear-view. 'It's just you and me, buddy. And soon there'll be nothing.'

'What are you talking about?'

He taps his fingers against his skull. 'The noise in my head, it's too much.'

'This isn't you, Elvis.'

'No, I see the light, but I have to take you with me.'

My eyes move to my mobile phone on the dashboard.

Elvis laughs. 'You want your phone? Want to call the police? You're all tied up. Forget about Mila. She's a liar.'

He shoves the phone into his pocket.

I shake my head to clear the fog.

'Honestly, I was hoping you stayed asleep,' he says sadly. 'I didn't want you to feel anything.'

White light of the oncoming cars sharpens into focus, but my brain is a large ball of cotton wool. Eyes dead ahead, Elvis takes his hands off the wheel, lights a cigarette and takes a long, slow draw before holding it up to my mouth. I take a large drag. A thick plume of smoke fills the car's interior as Elvis exhales and takes another drag. Through the smoke I can make out the dots of light crowning the distant bridge.

He turns to me and nods. 'We're about a minute away from hitting the water. We can't continue to exist. If we're alive, we're dead.'

I say nothing. No point.

'You've had your time,' he says. 'I'm doing you a favour.'

A muffled bang comes from the boot, like something or someone is rolling around back there. I struggle against the ropes binding me.

My mouth feels like it's covered in sawdust.

'Let her go,' I whisper.

If Elvis hears me, he doesn't acknowledge it.

'We're abominations, and she's collateral damage. He tricked me, Manny. He said I could be like you.' He punches the steering wheel. 'It's the screaming. I can't stand it anymore. They're all in my head buzzing like millions and millions of cicadas. I can't sleep.'

My mind races. The bridge is coming up fast and the steely look in Elvis's eyes suggest he isn't kidding about driving into the river.

Elvis tosses the cigarette out the window and orange sparks dance in the air.

It's strange the kinds of details you notice when death is imminent.

'I'm sorry it has to be like this, but it's the only way.'

'Elvis, don't...'

'Everyone could do with a near-death experience.'

He accelerates and rips the wheel to the side. I snatch across with my bound hands and try to counteract the steering, but it isn't enough. The car hits the skirting, flips over the barrier, and descends towards the murky water below.

Gravity takes hold.

Time grinds to a halt.

I'm in the familiar but unwelcome feeling of a car crash.

Cue Elton John's *Circle of Life* please, Mr DJ.

I'm about to enter a watery grave. My brain struggles to comprehend the situation but instinct kicks in. My life doesn't flash before my eyes; the only feeling as we shoot over the abyss is regret.

The car freefalls into a sickening spin. At one point in the chaos, Elvis and I lock eyes – an insane, determined expression etched on his face.

Then there's a temporary absence of sound, itself a beautiful sound.

The water's surface looks like a black velvet mirror as it moves towards us in slow motion. My head collides with the windscreen when the car spears the water. Blood sprays my vision.

The moment of impact is different from what I anticipated – Elvis too, no doubt.

The spot where we land is more of a mudbank than a river. He mustn't have compensated for low tide. Psychosis will do that.

The rushing water flips the car over onto its roof and we're floating slowly down river. Running water calmly enters through the air conditioning ducts and sounds like a trickling garden feature as it drips onto the upside-down car's ceiling.

It's peaceful.

The car catches on another segment of the mudbank and the current's power builds in intensity until it flips the car right way up, eventually catching on the jagged rocks jutting out from the mudbank.

The need to escape becomes secondary – the need to close my eyes and sleep overpowers me. Blood pours from my forehead and down my face. The warmth feels nice against the surrounding cold water.

Outside, a fist bangs on the window.

Attached to the fist, a body silhouetted against a magnificent moon.

The wish to rest is all-encompassing.

Blackness takes over.

TWENTY-TWO

THE warm embrace of the white light. Heaven. The atheists had it wrong.

I'm lying on a comfy cloud, surrounded by bright, reflective surfaces.

It's bliss, though the tubes in my arms and nose are an unwelcome addition.

I don't remember tales of tubes in Heaven's waiting room. They'll need to update the Bible. A desperate wave of thirst overcomes me. It feels like I've been eating desert sand, washed down with powdered camel bones.

'Water,' I rasp.

A glass fills next to me.

'Here,' a weathered voice whispers.

The glass touches my hand but I lack the strength to clasp tight enough to bring it towards my mouth. The thirst is all consuming. An angel brings the glass to my lips and some god-like liquid spills in my mouth. It's probably only tap water, but it's the best thing I've ever put in my mouth. And my saviour is not some divine creature of retribution.

It's an old man. An ancient man. I'm guessing, Methuselah.

Deep crevices forge patterns across his weathered face, straggly pure white hair spouts from his scalp, paper-thin skin covers gnarled, bony fingers. He's not an angel, but I couldn't be more willing to sing his praises. The magic water withdraws.

'More.'

'No, you'll be sick.'

On cue, my stomach lurches and turns over on itself, but I hold its contents down.

'Where am I?'

'You're safe.'

'Heaven?'

'No.'

'The hospital?'

The ancient man sighs. 'No.'

I try to sit up, a futile gesture. 'What happened?'

'You drove off into the river. It's some miracle you survived. The car jumped the barricade and hurtled into the mudbank. We pulled you out.'

This man looks too decrepit and frail to lift a mouse from its cage, but his eyes tell the truth. His eyes... there's something familiar. I shoot up in the bed when I remember the pounding in the boot, but my thoughts aren't working, they're slippery.

'What about Mila? She was in the boot.'

He shakes his head. 'No, you're mistaken.'

He rests his bony hand on my shoulder.

'Lay down, you've been out for twelve hours now.'

I force my eyes open. 'Mila?'

He lowers his head, turns and walks to the window, pulls open the white sheer curtains. The large windows showcase an ornate garden with manicured hedges and topiary. It's not the hospital but vaguely familiar all the same.

The cotton wool starts to leave my brain as I gain a better bearing of my surroundings.

The floors and equipment look like a standard hospital room. The only real difference is the walls; they're decorated with cartoon character princesses and butterflies.

It's a homemade hospital room for a little girl.

The ancient man turns to face me. 'My daughter's.' He looks over two centuries old. 'They diagnosed her with cancer at a very young age. I constructed this room so she wouldn't have to spend so much time in the hospital.'

I rip the IV out and attempt to get out of the bed. My strength is returning but I still struggle to stand – my legs rubbery. The ancient man helps me out of bed. The floor feels cool. Now we're face to face, I take him in properly.

Behind the ancient man's withered face are the hypnotic blue eyes and the same twinkle I encountered all those years ago.

'E?'

'That's right.'

'You can't be.'

He's aged horribly, unbelievably since I saw him at Aunty Sue's.

'I know,' he says. 'I look terrible. But I'll get to that.'

He motions towards the photo on the side-table. I pick it up, looking from the photo to his face, but don't need to. It's the polaroid he took the day I fixed his daughter, Jam. Something twigs. I clutch the IV drip pole for support, stare at him, waiting.

'I'll explain,' he says, as he ushers me out of the door.

I bloody hope so. Last time we spoke he basically said he wanted to drain my liquids and dump me with psychos. I stop. 'What were you doing there? Where we crashed.'

'GPS tracker in the car.'

My brain kicks in again. 'Mila. She was in the boot.'

He turns and flicks another light switch. A warm orange glow replaces fluorescent madness. 'No, she wasn't. There was nothing in there apart from a baseball bat, some rope and a fire extinguisher. That must've been what you heard.'

He's lying.

E leads me into a huge library, wall to wall with leather bound books. There's a sliding ladder, a huge globe in antique housing, solid oak desk, various taxidermy creatures in glass casings.

He motions towards one of two studded leather chairs.

He coughs into his fist and makes old man sounds, groaning as he sits across from me. We stare at each other for what feels like too long. I hold my glass and take a sip of water.

'Scotch?' he asks, gesturing to the large bar next to him.

I nod. He stands, pours the amber liquid from a decanter and places the glass in front of me. A waft of smoky peat fills my nostrils; it's like a campfire. E's joints crackle and pop as he sits opposite.

'Where's Mila?' I ask.

He ignores me. 'What do you know about mine and your mother's work?'

I repeat my question.

'Our work before you came along, I mean.'

Fine, I'll play along.

The room tilts. My face itches, I don't know whether that's a good thing. 'Enough,' I wince as I rub my fingers over my forehead stitches. 'I read the letter about abducting me after the lab fire, explosion, whatever.'

He nods. 'Both of us mastered in chemical science at the University of Queensland. We were the top two students in the class. Your mother was always just slightly ahead of me. One day, during our last semester, a recruiter for the Australian military approached both of us. He offered us an opportunity to work together in a newly formed experimental procedures division. We both leapt at it. We were there for nearly four years when your mother made the discovery. I'll never forget the day she first unlocked the healing formula.'

'It was her?' I ask, incredulous. Mild-mannered Mum.

E scratches his arm, breaking papery skin. Blood flows down his wrist. 'Yes. The main component was based on the tissue repairing

238

gene MG53. Like a version of that on super steroids, so to speak. She named it "Immuluble". It was the scientific breakthrough we'd been waiting for since the dawn of medicine.'

I place my glass on a coaster, knowing where this is heading.

'A super healer.'

E uses a handkerchief to dab the blood on his arm, then clears his throat. 'An immune supercharger. Allowing rapid and substantial healing, yes. About 10,000 times more effective than the MG53 gene. We tested the formula on juvenile mice, then progressively increased various factors. The results were incredible.'

My brain kicks into high gear for a second, but it tires me immediately.

'"Progressively increased various factors' sounds like damage control speak,' I say.

He smiles sadly. 'There are billions of dollars of resources available to the army. Hundreds of top minds searching for a common solution to the major problem with battle: dead and dying soldiers. We'd discovered that solution.'

I feel like I'm outside my body, looking at myself, mute and numb.

E closes his eyes. I think he's fallen asleep, before he kicks back to life. 'We began small. Injecting minute amounts of the formula into mice, then administering local anaesthetic, inflicting varying degrees of damage from tiny cuts to severing tails and limbs. Brought several back to life after electric shocks.'

He must notice the horror painting my face.

'All in the name of science,' he coughs. 'Besides, we didn't waste a single rodent. They all survived, even the "dead" ones flourished, in fact. And thus, Project Lazarus was born.'

'Blasphemously apt,' I snap. I feel like I've got sea legs. There's a noticeable void in my stomach. 'Have you got anything to eat?'

E slaps his knee. 'I'm sorry, my boy, I got carried away. You must be famished and I could do with some nourishment myself.'

He struggles to push himself out of his chair. He leaves for the kitchen, hunched over. E's more arthritic looking than a few minutes ago – if that's possible.

I reach for my phone, intending to drop a pin on my location and fire off a text to Sue to call the police, but of course, the phone's gone. It's probably smashed and submerged at the bottom of the Brisbane River.

Damn.

My mind's whirling but I'm trying to act casual.

I study the photos on the shelves and look around at the room's various curios and artefacts.

A giant tarantula rears up in an oval glass case.

A ram's skull stares eyeless at a giant marble globe.

Glass domes encasing pinned butterflies weigh down ancient maps.

A taxidermy deer sits above geodes and other volcanic looking rocks.

Exotic-looking, stringed instruments hang from the wall below a line of voodoo dolls.

Egyptian artefacts pepper the room.

Eventually, E returns with a wooden board, holding several sandwiches cut into triangles.

We sit in silence as we devour them. He wipes the cracked corners of his lips with a napkin, pours us each another scotch and returns to his story. I don't feel up to escaping, so have no choice but to sit and listen.

'The institution higher-ups were ecstatic, practically frothing at the mouth. Project Lazarus, the search for the ultimate soldiers, was over. Soldiers who could self-heal. It was the greatest medical accomplishment of all time, a boon to humanity. Can you imagine the possibilities? Serious disease and medical maladies a thing of the past. Cancer, heart disease, Alzheimer's, all fixable with a single injection. It would've won a Nobel Prize. We'd stumbled on a goldmine.'

I let the information sink in as best I can. 'So, what happened?'

'The army refused to release the discovery to the outside. Your mum saw the bigger picture, wanted everyone to have access to the healing tech. But it didn't matter, we got the go ahead.'

'Volunteer soldiers,' I say, in between sips.

'Yes, handsomely compensated of course, but we almost got shut down immediately. Despite the success with the mice, the human experiments vastly differed. Most of the test subjects ended up getting worse. They were exhibiting degenerative physical and mental symptoms. We tested dozens of men with the same results. You've seen it in Elvis.'

Elvis.

I jump to my feet and a rush of blood to the head nearly tips me over. 'Where is he?'

E waves me off. 'All in due time.'

'No, I want to know what's going on.'

His face darkens. 'I'm telling you what's going on, and how you came to be sitting here, boy. If you want to know, or see your friend again, sit down and shut up. If you don't want to know, then what was the point in me saving your life this time?'

My fists clench, but they're still weak.

'Sit, Manny.'

I don't move.

'Now,' he growls, I drop into the chair. His chest rapidly rises and falls and he closes his eyes for a moment. When he opens them, he's calm.

'We figured out it was because the subjects were adults. All the mice we'd tested on were juveniles whose cells were still developing and were able to adapt to the formula. We needed younger test subjects.'

The penny drops. 'The babies.'

241

He nods solemnly. 'At first, the experiments appeared successful. Then the deaths…' E shakes his head. 'Very unfortunate. The army had no choice but to shut Project Lazarus down.'

My stomach drops. 'How many deaths?'

'All the subjects exhibited temporary self-healing abilities, but it didn't last.'

'How many?'

'For most of them, their immunity was compromised. They used up their healing energy on themselves, you see. It increased at an exponential rate, like a perpetual motion machine. They cooked themselves from the inside. Out of the group of 100 orphans in the facility, you were the only survivor. You were stronger, a marvel of genetic engineering, a miracle child. But we couldn't let anyone else know. Your life was in danger.'

'One hundred,' I say, down the scotch and collapse onto the studded leather sofa.

'It was all over,' he says. 'Years of work down the drain with one strike of the pen. They weren't only closing us down, they wanted to destroy the evidence. We knew we had to get you out and fate intervened when there was a huge electrical fire in the lab. Your mother got you out just in time but officially, you'd been lost to the fire. It covered up everything, but we lost years of projects and research. Your mother and I needed a plan to keep you safe. The best way was for you to stay with her. The only issue was, of course, your latent abilities and what would happen if they came back, or anyone found out about them.'

He picks up a small round stone off the table next to him and rolls it around on his palm.

'Your abilities took around seven years to manifest again. And it was more than I could have dreamed of. Not only self-healing abilities but an ability to heal others. Fantastic. Your mother was so protective of you as a child. It's why I spent all those months with you to help you control and master it. She and I had big plans for you.'

He leans forward and places his hand on my shoulder as some form of comfort. I can't bring myself to shrug it off.

'Protecting you was the most important thing in her life. That year, while you and I were in the shed, she worked on a way to make it easier for you to harness your abilities. She knew that with them you were the most important human on the planet. When I came to see you after the accident, I knew I had to continue our work.'

'It was a failure,' I say, gritting my teeth.

'On the contrary, Manny. We lost all the research in the lab explosion. I had to start again. Then, after she died, it was my turn to take over and recreate the healing formula. And I did.' He pours more liquid into his glass. 'What do you remember about the accident?'

I sit for a moment. I don't know. I've thought about it so many times now it's like a bad photocopy. I'm not even sure what's real.

'Aunty Sue and Mum fighting,' I say. 'Mum wanting to leave. She was angry, scared. We'd made it out of the city towards the coast and some huge black car, like a 4WD, came across in front of us, and that's it. We came off the road and she died.'

He holds my gaze, like he's urging me to go on.

'Sue already told me she was in the other vehicle,' I say. 'Said some kind of *Men in Black* dudes brought her with them.'

E sits for a while, not saying anything, before taking another sip. 'Close. The vehicle that caused the accident that killed your mother was military. The army found out about you.'

He stares at his trembling hands. When his eyes met mine, they're wet and dull. 'The army had been monitoring me ever since my discharge. They suspected something was amiss.' He rubs the back of his neck. 'Their surveillance teams discovered Jam's recovery. There was no other way to explain her extraordinary return to health.'

His face is so tight I can see his bared teeth. 'They came knocking. I had no choice. I had to tell them the truth. That's why your mother left that day.'

My mind flickers to the accident and the transport truck. I jolt in the chair.

'It wasn't a normal ambulance.'

E shakes his head. 'No, it wasn't. You were brought over to the hospital in an army medical transport unit. They analysed you and had me come in to test you. When I confirmed you lost your ability in the accident and were just a normal kid, they let me go too. Do you remember me coming to visit?'

'No,' I say, biting my lip, 'I don't.'

I don't know why I lie to him. 'Why didn't the army abduct me then?'

When he throws his hands up, I notice how ill-fitting his clothes are, like they were made for a broom handle scarecrow. He coughs into his hand. We both notice the spots of blood. He plucks a tissue from a box on the large desk and wipes his fist.

'Your abilities had vanished. As far as they knew, you couldn't heal people anymore.'

'You injected me,' I whisper.

'I had to Manny, but your abilities aren't gone, only hiding.'

He leans forward and grabs both sides of my face with his craggy palms.

His blue eyes twinkle. 'I can bring them back for you, Manny. You aren't merely the first human with the ability to heal yourself and others. You are the first human to achieve possible immortality. Can you imagine how valuable that made you? Makes you?' he says.

I push E away and he doubles over and goes into a coughing fit. It's so bad it takes a full minute for him to have enough breath to continue. I wait. With each word his voice becomes raspier, like a tiny work crew is sandpapering his vocal folds.

'Every single rich man on the planet will be baying for your blood, working out the best way to leech you and bottle your fluids to synthesise their own formula. Billionaire ticks, cutting you up, vivisecting you like the bloody Nazis did in World War II.'

I've heard enough but can't bring myself to leave before I hear it all.

He pours another scotch, sits down, rubs his loose-skinned, bony arm across his face.

'These young guys in the loony bin,' I say, 'they're all your guinea pigs?'

He scoffs and waves me off. 'I made a mistake with Elvis and the others. I had to perfect the formula first. And it wasn't just them who were the guinea pigs. Look at me, Manny. I have the body of a 150-year-old, and it's only been a few weeks. I don't have much time left.'

It's like he's aging before me. Another hour and he'll be dust and bones.

'Do you remember,' he says, 'the very last experiment we did?'

I nod. 'Jam. You were just speaking about her.'

'I was?' he asks. Confusion washes over his face and his eyes are cloudy now. He shakes his head, then looks at me like I've appeared from nowhere. 'Elvis has tied her up in a room. It's up to you to save her.'

'The only person I care about finding is Mila.'

'Exactly.'

Either his brain's deteriorating or the drugs are kicking back in.

'Am I missing something?' I ask.

'We both are,' he says. 'My daughter.'

It hits me like a cold slap. 'Mila is your daughter.'

He nods, but something's not right.

'Your daughter's name was Jam.'

'Yes,' he says. A tight smile crosses his face. 'Short for Jamila.'

There's nothing for me to say.

'The day you healed her, I synthesised a solution. Your blood, your "essence" as I told you. It was the key to keeping her alive. But of course, there was the downside.'

Of course, she'd hinted. 'Her condition,' I say.

'Yes, her insensitivity to pain is a by-product of the healing process. But it wasn't your fault, your body hadn't fully adapted to the ability yet.

Mila.

Cold sweat covers me, though my face burns.

I feel like a real dummkopf.

'It. Us. It wasn't real.'

E rubs his temples. 'It's my fault. I tried keeping you two away from each other, for your own safety. One day, Mila stumbled across some documents in my study. She discovered the work I'd done on the other subjects, and the photos of you. At first, I thought it was a disaster, then realised I could use her. Elvis too.'

I scoff at his word choice. 'She's the one who used me.'

'I understand how you could think that, but no. She's loved you ever since the day you healed her. She was protecting you. Whatever you think you have, is real.'

Another realisation smacks me across the face.

Mila's work. The veterinary surgery.

'You bought the veterinary surgery so you could test on animals.'

He doesn't meet my eyes but he nods.

Thoughts cascade and tumble like a broken jar of marbles.

'Why the notes on the front porch?' I ask.

'Drama and intrigue. But also, to prepare you for what was coming. Mila dropped the notes off for me because I couldn't risk direct communication. They're always watching,' he air quotes with his fingers. 'Even now, I'm not sure we're safe.'

His eyes dart around the room like a paranoid android, before settling on me.

'Understand, Manny? Your abilities are gone, but I'm going to give them back. I'll fix you, then we can find Mila and fix her. Look.'

E shows me a grainy photo on his phone.

A gut punch.

A white, tiled room. Bleeding and bruised. Tied to a chair.

She stares with pure rage at the photographer.

Mila.

My immediate purpose is a sharp, clear glass spire.

Revenge.

'Are you ready?' he asks.

I look at the image again. Gritted jaw, teeth grinding, I nod.

He extracts a small medical case from a drawer and pulls out a syringe.

'It's time,' he says, and moves over to me.

His wrinkled hand feels cool at first.

The prick of the needle – the warmth moves through my body into my head.

It's a rush; pure energy nearly knocks me to the ground.

E shuffles out, beckons me.

I follow as he lumbers further down the hall. He pushes the door open with what little strength he has left, revealing a metal chair with large leather straps and a body tied into it.

Elvis.

E coughs into his fist, wipes the blood on his pants. 'We need him alive if we're to save Mila.'

I have no choice. 'Okay.'

'I sedated him after the accident. I'm going to wake him up, then you can heal him. I don't have the energy for it.'

He shuffles to the corner cabinet and preps another syringe with a purplish liquid. He comes back and cleans the crook of Elvis's elbow with a cotton ball and a clear solution.

E locks eyes with me

I drift towards Elvis, reach my hand to his forehead. When E injects him with the solution, Elvis immediately springs forward and struggles against the straps that barely hold him down. The energy moves from me into him. In my mind's eye, I clearly see the grotesque black ball that has taken over his brain. The light expands from my hands, the energy moves, he calms. He bucks less and less until he stops altogether. The madness spills into the ether and disappears. Elvis opens his eyes.

'I'm Hank Marvin.'

~

He mustn't have eaten in days. Elvis wolfs down a whole barbecue chicken like a starved dingo, picking the carcass clean in minutes.

He wipes his face with his shirt sleeve, looks at me sheepishly.

'I never meant for her to get hurt, man, and I sure as hell didn't mean to hurt you.'

The old Elvis is back.

'It wasn't your fault. If anything, it's his,' I say, pointing at E.

E takes the barb in stride.

'Where is she, Elvis?' I ask. 'What'd you do with Mila?'

He looks genuinely shocked. 'What are you talking about?'

I nod to E. 'Show him the photo.'

E grimaces as he shows the photo on his phone to Elvis.

'I don't know where that came from,' Elvis says, pushing away from the table. I snatch the phone from E and push Elvis back into his chair, shove the phone in his face.

'Tell me where she is! Where'd you send this from?'

Elvis shakes his head frantically. 'Manny, it's not a message. It's on the phone's camera roll.'

We both turn to E, who shrugs and smiles sadly.

'Well done you two. It may be time to open that detective agency.'

I rush towards him, stopping when the gun appears.

The gun barrel alternates between Elvis and me.

'Lead the way,' E says, motioning us towards a long corridor. We stop at a large, steel door. E presses his thumb against the small blue screen bordered by a large silver plate.

While E is distracted, I lock my grip around his arm. His pure white life force depletes as it passes from his body into mine. Instead of healing, I harm him. That little nugget I'd kept to myself. As well as giving life, I could take it away.

Eyes widening, E collapses forward. The gunshot echoes down the cavernous hallway and Elvis thumps to the floor, like a sack of flour. Blood pulses from his gut like a toddler squeezing a jam donut.

'Leave him!' E barks, firing off another shot that hits the wall, plaster exploding. The white dust settles on us like snow. Flecks of plaster mix with Elvis's blood, looking eerily like some of his latest artworks in the depths of full-blown insanity.

I hold Elvis's arm long enough to repair some of the damage in his guts before I feel the warm metal barrel poke my right kidney.

'Help me up but only touch my clothes,' E hisses.

I hesitate, then comply when I think about Mila. I leave Elvis to bleed out on the dusty floor.

'Don't even think about doing that again, Manny,' says E. 'Or I'll put a bullet through your skull.'

He struggles with the door, gives up and leans against the wall, gasping for air, musting enough energy to weakly wave the gun. I open the door out of pity, not fear. I walk in and E follows, unable to close the large steel door to silence the sounds of Elvis dying in the hallway.

~

The cavernous room is divided into two parts. The back half is a large laboratory, benches filled with a large array of standard lab equipment and various instrumentation, plus what looks like analytical or measuring equipment.

The front half is a white-tiled room, the sides lined with small wire cages filled with a variety of animals. They screech and squawk at our arrival. Worse still, two larger cages closer to the lab area each hold a small, grubby child. A little boy and a little girl.

E notices me staring at them.

'My little human guinea pigs,' he says deadpan, and shuffles further in.

As horrifying as the sight of the caged children is, Mila's worse. Beaten bloody, she's slumped on a wooden chair in the middle of the floor, arms and legs tied to the chair with cable ties, a dirty rag jams her mouth. Messy splotches of blood coat the tiles around her. The room smells of rancid meat and bleach.

Worst of all is Aoki standing next to her.

He's holding a wad of Mila's hair in his fist, grinning like the tuxedo-wearing skeleton on his forearm. I struggle to comprehend how Mila's own father is letting this happen.

The heat rises, I spin around to E. He's holding the gun between my eyes and shakes his head.

My jaw tightens.

'What's he doing here?' I ask.

'You didn't think I could do all of this to my baby girl, did you?' E says. Something like sadness touches his eyes. 'I'm just a small fry out of my depth now. It's you and your ability they want. Look what they've made me do to get it.'

'What, the government?'

'Oh no, Manny, far beyond that. The government is one of their play toys, and they know you're here. They won't be long.'

I turn back to Mila.

Her flickering eyelids are the only sign of life. Aoki takes a few steps back and picks up a blue bucket. E shuffles backwards, still pointing the gun at me, then removes the gag from Mila's mouth before Aoki throws the bucket of cold water over her.

Mila screams between gasps for air. 'You bastard! How could you?'

E flinches. 'Show me your stuff,' he says to me, holding the pistol against his only daughter's head.

Aoki pulls a gun from his waistband and follows me as I walk over to Mila.

Her bleeding broken smile breaks my heart in two. I reach out but Aoki knocks my hand away.

E shakes his head. 'Fix me first, Manny, or I put a bullet in her head too.'

'You couldn't...' But the look in his eyes says otherwise.

250

'Hurry up,' he says. His shaking hands holding the gun to Mila's temple. Up close, E's condition is more pronounced. His papery skin is folded and sagging, veins and liver spots surrounding deep wrinkles; his eyes look jaundiced above thin purple lips. I slowly reach forward to touch the side of his head and the familiar feelings flood me. The aging process immediately begins reversing.

In less than a minute, E transforms from a decrepit old man with a death rattle to a robust man in his fifties. As I remove my hand from his head, he walks over to a mirror to inspect himself.

E doesn't react as I place my hand on Mila's forehead, sticky with blood and sweat, and begin. She has several broken bones and she's bleeding internally.

I can only thank whoever's in charge that she can't feel pain.

Mila's so depleted that she convulses as the first wave of energy passes into her. The healing light fills her. Her broken bones slide back into place and her organs heal. More than that, her nerves are regenerating and responding.

Minutes later, we're done. I open my eyes; she's already staring deep into them. Mila grabs my hand and brings my palm to her cheek.

'I feel you, for real,' she smiles, as dual tears roll down her face. 'You saved me, again.'

I embrace her for a moment before E rips me away.

'How do you feel, Manny?' he asks.

'I feel like killing you,' I spit.

E claps his hands together the best he can while holding the gun. 'Glad to see the fire. But you understand you were wasting your life, Manny. Now you've returned to your true purpose.'

'What now?' I ask.

'You're my greatest accomplishment, but I must hand you over.' He sighs, looks at me with tired, sad eyes. Then they widen into ping pong balls.

Movement in my peripherals causes a double take. A person walks in wearing a huge vest, black and blue wires sticking out of a couple of grey putty bricks.

Sue is strapped with enough explosives to blow up a beached Humpback whale and spread its disintegrated guts across Surfers Paradise.

'You didn't think I kept all my explosives at home, did you?' Sue grins. 'Kept some in a storage locker.'

E and Aoki stand statuesque, guns held high. I can almost see the thoughts spinning through their heads like pokie machine reels.

'What are you doing, Sue?' E says, 'Take that off now, you crazy bitch.'

She stares E dead in the eyes. 'Let the kids go, while the oldies have a little talk.'

Sue touches my shoulder and whispers. 'Behind me. Now.'

I move behind her. 'How did you find me?'

'Family tracking app. It works both ways, you know.' She winks.

E stands his ground, but then Sue reaches under her shirt and pulls out a small remote. She makes a show of pressing her thumb to the red button.

'I'm loaded with enough explosives to disintegrate this entire house of horrors. If my thumb releases, due to you or that cockroach shooting me,' she says, pointing at Aoki, 'then we're all dead. No mucking about, I'm going to count down from three. Three. Two.'

E realises Sue isn't bluffing.

He lowers his gun and nods for Aoki to do the same.

Sue withdraws a pocketknife from her pants and hands it to me. I move over to Mila and cut through the zip ties. Though she's covered in blood, she still smells of blueberries. I pull her to her feet and we move behind Sue.

Sue's running this whole situation like a pro – her apocalypse preparedness training paid off. 'Where are the keys for the cages, E?' she asks.

His eyes flick to them. 'They're pin codes. Mila's birthday,' he adds, avoiding eye contact with his daughter.

'You two,' Sue says to Mila and me, 'grab those kids out of the cages, then all of you get out of here as fast as you can. Go up on to the hill at the back and watch the fireworks.'

We hesitate.

E's eyes open wide.

'Do it,' Sue yells, and we move as one. We open the cages and Mila and I each pick up a shivering child and back away towards the main door.

'Wait a minute,' Mila says. 'Grab that trolley in the corner and load up as many of the animal cages as you can. Take them outside and we'll call animal control. We can't leave them here.'

I load the cages onto the trolley, while Mila soothes the kids.

The animals loaded, Sue beckons me.

'Give me a hug.'

I embrace her in a huge bear hug.

'I'm so sorry,' she says.

'It's okay,' I say, meaning it.

'Will you find Scraps a new home?' she asks Mila, who nods.

Sue and I lock eyes.

'You know what to do,' she says.

I squeeze her shoulder, then walk over and open the metal door.

'And Manny?' Sue calls after me. 'Take care of her, she seems like a keeper.' She winks at Mila.

Guilt engulfs me as I shut the door and step into the hallway and see a bloody Elvis.

~

Elvis is deathly pale. His unseeing eyes stare at the ceiling, blood flecks either side of his mouth. But he's alive, just, enough for me to work with.

'Take the kids outside, I won't be long.'

Mila bites her lip like she's about to protest. 'Don't be long, okay?' she says.

I pull up Elvis's shirt and press my hand over his stomach wound. Closing my eyes, I feel the bullet move towards my hand as ripped organs and severed nerves regenerate. Soon enough, the only evidence of his gunshot is the hole in his shirt and the lake of blood surrounding him.

Elvis comes to but he's still weak and we need to escape. I latch his hands on the trolley for balance. We push together towards the front door, where Mila and the kids are waiting, then step through into the cool night air. We push the animal trolley to the other side of the street.

'We should call animal control now,' Mila says.

Elvis is leaning on the trolley like he's about to collapse. 'Phone in my jeans.'

I reach into his pocket for the phone, surprised to find two of them.

Then I remember how Elvis pocketed mine before the crash, which explains how Sue tracked me.

Both phones have cracked screens but have miraculously survived the plunge into the Brisbane River. I hand the phone to Mila and she calls animal control while I support Elvis, wrapping his arm around my neck. Together, we walk the path along the side of the house, making our way towards the stairs. We ascend in single file towards the top of the hill. It's slow going with Elvis's limited mobility, and the kids soon complain, so we carry them for the last leg. They're not much more than fragile bones.

My heart nearly bursts when the little girl rests her head on my shoulder.

No one follows us.

The little girl snuggles into me further. I wrap my arm around her and whisper that she's safe now. Her shivering slows, then stops. The five of us sit on the edge of a small stone wall, far above the mansion of horrors at the bottom of the hill.

Time stops as the city breathes in.

Moonlight bathes the electric landscape.

Elvis lights a cigarette with a shaky hand.

We wait.

We see the light first. The mansion's windows waver before exploding into billions of tiny shards. A massive fireball bursts through the back of the property, upwards towards the sky. The warmth of the fireball caresses my face. The thunderous explosion knocks the little boy onto his back, but he's laughing. The boom is incredible, rocking organs, trembling rib cages.

Elvis takes another drag on the cigarette perched between his grinning lips.

I turn to Mila. I see the world.

Firelight dances in her eyes. The most beautiful thing I've ever seen. It's everything.

Car alarms and distant sirens fill the post explosive silence.

They'll be here soon.

Fire in the sky.

TWENTY-THREE

IN the immediate aftermath of the explosion, we head down the other side of the hill away from the madness, then catch a taxi home. The rising sun is an unwelcome presence. We're in the kitchen eating bowls of colourful cereal when someone pounds on the door so hard that the windows rattle. The kids crawl under the kitchen table.

I open the door to a group of suited, booted, serious-looking individuals with earpieces and mirrored sunglasses. Standing at the front of them is Agent Johnson but he seems content to let the other agents take over.

The *Men in Black* wannabes invite themselves into the kitchen. 'You're all coming with us.'

It's not a question, but I still say no. A chiselled agent steps up to me. I can smell Juicy Fruit on her breath. 'I'm afraid you have no choice, Emmanuel. It's for your own safety.'

Agent Johnson steps in. 'You've been involved in an extraordinary occurrence and twisted up in something bigger than you could imagine. We want to unravel you but we need some answers.'

As Mila shoots up, her chair hits the kitchen cabinet and crashes to the floor.

'Haven't these kids been through enough? Haven't we all been through enough?'

'It's for your own protection,' Agent Johnson calmly says.

'Oh, that is such a bullshit government line,' Mila says, fingers frantically rubbing her temples. 'I know how this goes. First you strip us of our rights, then you silence us, ostracise us, make us fearful of each other, all for our own protection.'

He takes a breath. 'Be that as it may. Like I said, you've stumbled on something a bit bigger than this situation. We've been engaged in this operation for the past twelve months and you blew it right open. No pun intended. We need you.'

We look to each other. The kids are wide-eyed, shivering.

'Please,' he finishes.

Mila sits. 'Can we at least finish eating our cereal?'

Agent Johnson nods and ushers the others outside.

The five of us sit. It could be the last time we're all together without electronic ears listening in.

'It's going to be okay. No one is going to hurt you,' I say to the kids, but also Mila and Elvis. No one responds. We spoon the cereal in silence.

After we're done, the five of us walk outside, holding hands. The invisible branch of the government hauls us to a small hotel, then to Archerfield airport, where we board a plane that probably isn't on any manifest to fly to a facility that most likely doesn't officially exist.

I can't tell where it is, but I've never had a good sense of direction. All I know is it is away from the ocean, so somewhere west. We land on a large strip of deforested land, then board a helicopter.

'Where are we going now?' I ask an agent.

'A facility,' she says curtly.

That's the only information we get.

The kids are clingy for the whole trip, their eyes wide with amazement as we fly over endless, green canopy of undisturbed forest. None of us have ever been in a helicopter, so we're all feeling the same way. After an hour or so, we see it.

It's a giant, grey monolith, as big as fifty football stadiums. When we land and disembark from the chopper, I look around. We're surrounded by forest as far as I can see.

My heart lurches when a tiny, older woman in spectacles walks over and pries the kids from us. She gives us a reassuring smile when she says she will look after them while we answer some questions.

The little girl breaks free and wraps herself around Mila's leg like a boa constrictor, so she goes with the kids to settle them. When she returns, they usher us into the bowels of the facility.

~

They probably don't call this room the interrogation room, but it has all the hallmarks of one. A box with three plain walls and one-way glass on the remainder. The room's empty aside from a single table in the centre of the room holding a bottle of water and a stack of polystyrene cups. Three chairs are positioned on one side of the table. Elvis, Mila and I sit down.

Agent Johnson stares at his folder of notes, either considering how to proceed or stalling for time. There's a dull thud as he drops the folder on the table.

'It's been agreed the best possible outcome is for you all to stay here for a few months until this blows over.'

All three of us explode from our chairs and lean over the table.

'A few months?'

'What about work?'

'What about our lives?'

He looks each of us in the eye. 'Sit down. Please.'

We lower into our chairs.

'Look, you're in danger,' he says sombrely. 'I'm afraid going back to your old lives isn't a viable option. They have the means to find you, and they *will* find you.'

'Who's they?' Mila asks.

'They call themselves, The Nexus of Dominion.'

We burst out laughing.

He shrugs. 'Comic-booky, I know, but it fits their modus operandi. And trust me, it's better if they believe you're gone.'

'Better off dead,' I mutter.

He grabs his folder of notes and holds it to his chest like it's a security blanket.

'It's not all bad news. We've made some progress over the past year, leaps and bounds the past few days, thanks to you, Manny, but it'll take time to bring them down. As much as we don't know about The Nexus, we do know their network stretches across the globe, with almost unlimited funds.'

Agent Johnson makes a 'what can you do?' gesture.

'Those USB videos Manny found helped more than any other intel over the past year. We analysed the time stamps, the meta data. It's almost like someone wanted him to find them.'

E really did want it all to end.

'We're working with several international agencies, but we need time to ensure not only your safety but the safety of any other guinea pigs in their facilities.'

'By guinea pigs, you mean people, right? Human people,' Mila sneers.

The agent clears his throat. 'Correct.'

'And this all started because of Manny?' Elvis asks, then glances at me. 'Sorry, man.'

I shrug.

Agent Johnson drops the folder. 'Manny's ability was the greatest unpublished scientific discovery of the century.'

'Yeah, but how did all this happen?' Mila waves her arms wildly. 'How did my father, one person, turn Manny's ability into this international torture syndicate?'

Agent Johnson stares at Mila's fists until they unclench, then takes a deep breath.

'Your father sought some investors, exhibited showreels of Manny's abilities, including healing you. There were some interested parties, and then it was a snowball effect.'

'More like Mickey Mouse and the magic brooms in *The Sorcerer's Apprentice*.'

Agent Johnson nods thoughtfully. 'I'll agree with that. Now, back to the matter at hand. In all the recorded documents and data obtained, Manny, as I've already mentioned, you're referred to by a code name. Mila, simply as the letter J, for Jamila, obviously.'

The interrogation room door opens and a person walks in pushing a trolley filled with assorted confectionary. 'Coffee?' they ask.

We all nod. White polystyrene cups fill with scalding black water. They leave behind a bunch of those tiny UHT milk portions and various sugars.

Agent Johnson tips several pink packets of sweetener into his coffee.

'That'll give you cancer, ya know,' I say.

'Lucky I've got you then.'

When none of us laughs, he apologises.

Mila's hands tremble as she pours a cup of water. 'I still don't get it. Why would Dad do this? Hand Manny over for money to this Nexus of Domination?'

'Dominion,' Johnson corrects and clears his throat. 'I've wondered that too. From what we've gathered, your father wasn't interested in money for money's sake. He did it for you.'

'I was their bargaining chip?' Mila asks.

Agent Johnson nods. 'We've been monitoring all E's communications. They threatened to abduct you and keep you until he resurrected his original test subject's abilities…' He nods to me. 'And hands them over.'

Mila says nothing.

'So, he was willing to sacrifice me,' I say, deflating in the chair.

Johnson shakes his head. 'He was between a rock and a hard place, Manny. The only reason he experimented on so many people was to avoid handing you over to them in the first place. Unfortunately for you both, depending on how you look at it, you're unique. Look what happened to Elvis. And then there's the mental health wards filled with dozens of young men who may never be the same again. When his plan didn't work, they put the squeeze on him and used his daughter as leverage to get to you.'

'They kept Manny on ice until E perfected these experiments?' Elvis asks.

'We think so.'

'And they couldn't find Manny because of a code name,' Elvis asks.

'Uh huh.'

'What was it?'

The agent spins the folder around and points. 'Kid A.'

'Great album,' Elvis and I say in stereo.

Agent Johnson stares at us a few beats before pulling out sheets of paper held together with a paper clip. 'With this in mind, are we all agreed that staying here for the next few months is the best course of action?'

The three of us nod.

He slides over three pieces of paper and a pen.

'Good. Read through these and sign, please. Standard liability forms for staying onsite.'

We flick through, sign and slide them back across the table.

'Thank you. Now, when it comes to notifying next of kin, Mila and Manny, is there anyone else for either of you besides Sue and E?'

We both shake our heads. 'No.'

'What about you, Elvis?'

'Mum's gone. No siblings. Dad's either lurking around Graceland or performing in a bistro in downtown Las Vegas. He's dead to me.'

The agent writes something on his notepad. 'Okay, that makes everything easier.'

Mila crushes her polystyrene coffee cup.

'Sorry,' Johnson says. 'I'm not great with people sometimes.'

'You think?' Mila says.

~

It took several weeks, but the responders eventually discover DNA scraps of E, Aoki and Sue amongst the piles of concrete and steel. They were vaporised in the explosion. The mansion was reduced to jagged tiles, loose sections of brick and molten metal.

Local roadworks crews were diverted from their ordinary roles of standing around watching one guy dig a hole. Instead, they were paid exorbitant amounts to stand around and watch one guy operate a bulldozer.

Meanwhile, Agent Johnson's people discovered a cache of documentation and videos of experiments on a backup server – not that it helped too much in bringing E to justice. It's hard to prosecute a body that's been blown to smithereens.

The most disturbing revelation was just how large The Nexus of Dominion's network of scientists is. Hundreds of them were performing similar experiments in purpose-built facilities across the globe. By the time Interpol discovered them and sprang into action, many of the facilities had been stripped and abandoned. God knows what happened to the test subjects. I try not to think about it.

An upside of the facility closures means the experiments have ceased, temporarily at least. Though there's no trace of them, it doesn't make me sleep any easier, and Agent Johnson believes The Nexus may be hibernating for now until they can build new secure facilities.

But we're safe for now. A small victory.

Of course, when several of the documents were leaked, the conspiracy theorists got in on the whole deal, comparing the experiments, not unfairly, to those of the Holocaust. They demanded action from their relevant governments to bring the monsters to justice, but the monsters were already ghosts. Any organisation with the means to operate as they did are rarely brought to justice. They're too well funded by soulless billionaires who care nothing for anyone without at least seven figures in offshore bank accounts.

It's nothing new. Horrible people get away with doing horrible things to people who don't deserve it, every day. Hopefully, international attention will prevent too many more innocents from being exploited. If there's nothing else, there's hope.

Thankfully, they still sent us home.

~

A group bus filled with Aunty Sue's end of the world prepper friends takes us to the funeral. Her death has only heightened their paranoia. And like a new vegan, sober person or standing desk user, it dominates the conversation.

My wish for them to stop talking granted, they instead begin to sing. They change the words to sunny '60s pop songs, the lyrics now about salvation from above, cleansing of the earth, the decimation of man.

My thoughts drift away, but back again each time Mila squeezes my hand.

She's taken E's death hard. No matter the transgressions and behaviour, he was still her father. Despite his actions towards the end, they were each other's world for so long that his grizzly death couldn't be anything but hugely damaging to her psyche.

For a while in the facility, Mila was so overwhelmed at the accusations and atrocities. She became hardened, withdrawing into herself, barely eating or talking, mostly sleeping. But now she's beginning to bounce back.

The bus pulls up – the singing mercifully stops.

The church is filled will lilies. It looks like the Nirvana *Unplugged in New York* set with the same morose vibe. It's a nice service, as nice as a funeral service can be, I guess.

I don't drink at the wake. Don't drink at all anymore. Now, I'm one of those happy sober people I always hated, or maybe just never understood. With a clearer mind, I'm attempting to conquer the feeling I've tried to bury my whole life.

That extraordinary fear of being ordinary.

Ironic, since it's no longer the case, really.

But it's not all alcohol-free beer and Skittles. I've discovered the main downside of my ability to heal anyone is the inability to heal everyone.

We spend the next few months working our way through Brisbane's other hospitals, healing as we go, but not enough to arouse suspicion. Mila helps with logistics, obtaining cleaning uniforms or medical scrubs and access passes, while Elvis combs the hospital records to find the patients most in need. We work through the hospitals together, one person at a time.

It's a huge task, like painting the Sydney Harbour Bridge with a cotton bud, but we persist. We heal enough people that the *Courier Mail* begins reporting on the lowering death rates and unprecedented number of empty hospital rooms.

It's time to move on. There are plenty more sick people out there.

~

Elvis requests a Tequila Sunrise from the flight attendant, who playfully slaps his shoulder and tells him to wait until take-off.

I trace the scar on Mila's arm and she intertwines her hand in mine as the plane lurches and leaves the runway. The setting sun washes purple and orange across the sky and the fluffy white clouds make the shrinking city look like a child's diorama.

We rise above them towards the great expanse of the Pacific Ocean, leaving behind the great southern land. Empty luggage bags sit at home on our beds. With the clothes on our backs and a bank account filled with what seems like an endless supply of cash, it's as close to freedom as anyone could want.

By the time the sun disappears, Mila, Elvis and most of the other passengers are asleep.

I stare out the cabin window, unable to discern where the sky stops and sea begins. The plastic cool against my face, I observe the hypnotic flashes of the navigation lights until my eyelids are too heavy to keep open.

The world is a lot calmer at night.

ACKNOWLEDGEMENTS

Thank you to Carolyn Martinez and the Hawkeye team, without whom, this would still just be a story with potential, sitting on my computer.

Thanks Lori-Jay Ellis and the Queensland Writers Centre team past and present, including Craig Cauchi, Christopher Grace and Sandra Makaresz.

For guidance, advice, and/or editing assistance, Josh Donellan, Lauren Daniels, Seanna Burnett and Rory Hawkins.

Novel writing is a solitary pursuit, but I've shared this novel's journey and my own with many individuals since its inception, and I'm grateful. So wherever and whenever this was, thanks a lot.

Special thanks to my darling wife, Katie, for always believing in me, and to Debra, the ever-supportive mum who liked the first draft and every other one.

As I started to thank my family, I realised there's too many of you to name individually, but I love you all.

I also started a list of friends but it's also too big, so I'll thank Liam Waldie, Ben Hayes, Brett Henderson, Lee Henderson, and be done with it. Anyone who's been friends with me that I've neglected to thank, sorry, but get in touch. We'll hang out, and I'll thank you in the next one.

To anyone who's crossed paths with me and shared a moment, no matter how swift, I'm glad to have run into you. Let's do it again.

Thanks to every person who's shown a modicum of interest in my writing over the years. There has been nothing but interest and support, so thank you, and I hope I've made you proud.

To the publishers who rejected *Head Grenade* over the past years. You're right, it wasn't ready, but now it is.

To whoever is reading this right now, thank you so much! You're getting me one step closer to being able to write full-time, and for that, I'm forever grateful.

ABOUT THE AUTHOR

Troy Henderson is a fiction writer from Brisbane, Australia, where he has lived his whole life aside from a two-year stint in London.

Troy's twenties and early thirties were spent avoiding adult responsibilities, playing in bands and immersing himself in music. He turned to novel writing seriously in his mid-thirties.

His first book, *Head Grenade*, was shortlisted in the Hawkeye Publishing Manuscript Development Prize and the Queensland Writers Centre's Adaptable and Publishable Programs, respectively.

His short stories have longlisted in the Australian Writers' Centre Furious Fiction competition, and placed in the Genrecon Short Story competition, and FLEUR Flash Fiction Contest.

Troy continues his writing journey, with his second and third novels coming soon.

Book reviews can make or break a book. If you liked what you read today, please do consider posting a review on Goodreads or your favourite forum.

Head Grenade is available at hawkeyebooks.com.au and all good bookstores and libraries.